新制多益
聽力高分攻略

多益聽力名師

洪欣Olivia 著

EZ TALK

真誠推薦

本書提供清楚易懂的題型分析及解題技巧、大量且含多國口音的練習題，是挑戰新制 TOEIC 聽力高分的利器！

───── 黃玟君／國立臺灣科技大學應用外語系副教授

聽力是台灣考生較難在短時間駕馭的科目，而新制多益聽力難度又提升。洪欣老師在字神帝國教授多益聽力十年來的課程精華，都彙集在這本《新制多益聽力滿分攻略》。書中破解陷阱設計，分析多益出題套路，精準定位各題型出題點，並清楚羅列出常見答案句型，再加上大量擬真的實戰練習和解說，幫助考生練出：這裡是陷阱、這裡就是答案的直覺式反應。絕對是一本最了解多益聽力、可以幫助你奪得高分的解題書！

───── 康老師／字神帝國英語學院創辦人

了解多益出題邏輯 避開常見聽力陷阱

為反映真實生活中社交及職場的英語使用，2018 年 3 月，台灣地區全面實施新制多益，整體而言，新制多益更為靈活，更能測出考生真正的英文實力。

就聽力部分來說，Part 1 & 2 易拿分題減少，Part 3 & 4 新增三人對話、隱含文意題及圖表題。也代表對話篇幅加長，考生須在龐大資訊中，正確定位答案的位置，並同時對文章和圖表具統整與解析能力。

綜觀市面上的多益聽力解題書，皆僅止於題型分析，很少一針見血的告訴考生：這種題型，聽某個「關鍵字」答案就出現了，或答案就在某些「常用句型」後面。在我的多益聽力課堂中，我用分類歸納的方式，清楚的分析 Part 1- Part 4 各種題型的「關鍵字秒殺解題法」及陷阱，幫助學生在最短的時間內，理解多益慣用的出題邏輯及模式，避開陷阱，利用「關鍵字」和「常用句型」定位答案。因此考生不一定要聽懂整句話或整篇的意思，就可以直擊出題點、輕鬆答題。

本書就是我課堂內容的重點精華，是一本前所未見，幫助台灣考生快速拿到高分的技巧攻略書。重要攻略如下：

攻略一：避開陷阱

以 Part 2 為例，常見陷阱如：「重複字」，95% 不能選。

Who will lead the budget review committee?

(A) Mr. Benson will be in charge.

(B) I don't think we have enough in the budget.

(C) I hope they approve the budget.

選項 (B) 和 (C) 重複了題目 budget 這個字，為陷阱選項，立即刪除，正確答案為 (A)。

攻略二：關鍵字秒殺解題法

以 Part 3 為例，動作題：What does the man say he will do? 考對話中的男子即將要做什麼，此高頻題型佔 Part 3 大約 15% 的出題率。正解一定在對話「最後面」，當男子說到「關鍵字」：I'll... 或 I'm going to... 這類常用來表達「即將要去做」的句型，答案就出現了！

原文：I'll talk to a supervisor to make sure they get a technician over here today.

題目：What does the man say he will do?

答案：聽到 I'll，答案即在後面，選項 Speak to a supervisor 為正解。

我在本書歸納 Part 2：12 大句型，Part 3：七大題型，Part 4：五大題型，並整理出每種題型的「關鍵字」及「常用答案句型」，幫助考生精準定位答案、完美破解多益聽力、迅速提高分數。

攻略三：圖表題秒殺 3 步驟

圖表題是新制多益 Part 3 及 Part 4 的新增題型，是考生較陌生害怕的題型。但只要掌握以下我獨創的三步驟，便可以五秒內正確作答，不需浪費時間看多餘資訊。請看影片示範：

圖表題
秒殺 3 步驟

1. 預覽題目，找出關鍵字
2. 找到選項和圖表內容的關聯性
3. 聽到關鍵字，搭配圖表答題

藉由變革後，更能反映英文實力的新制多益，做為學習英文的目標，從中累積單字、聽力、文法、閱讀能力，再搭配我獨創的解題技巧，不斷模擬練習，一定可以戰勝新制多益，成為可以帶著走的英文即戰力，為職場、為未來加分！

字神帝國英語學院 資深多益名師 洪欣 Olivia ♡

使用說明

STEP 1 掃這裡，全書音檔與教學影片帶著走。

QR code 內容：

❶ 全書音檔隨點隨聽

❷ 教學影片解說清楚

❸ 內建勘誤表，若書中有任何問題，編輯可於線上勘誤

也可直接輸入以下網址連結：

http://bit.ly/2KtFSES

STEP 2 題型介紹與示範，快速了解該部分題型出題方式。

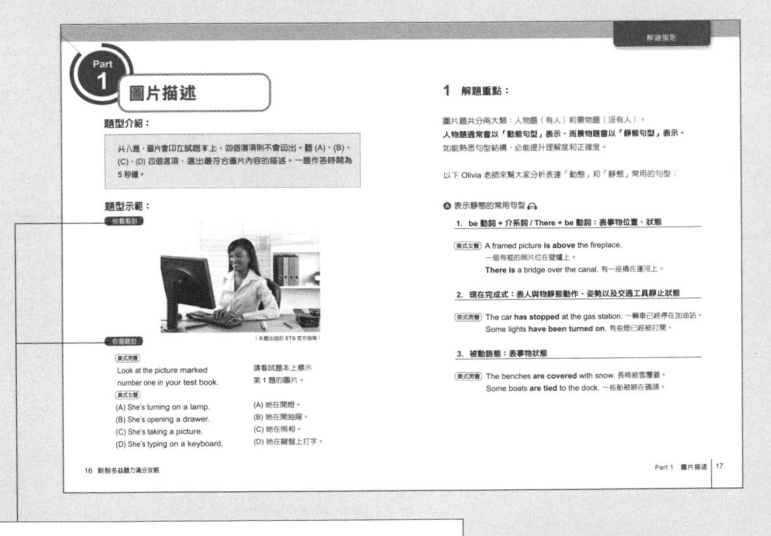

針對題目樣貌，會看到與聽到的內容，
皆清楚列出。

STEP 3 解題重點，告訴考生本部分的解題要訣。

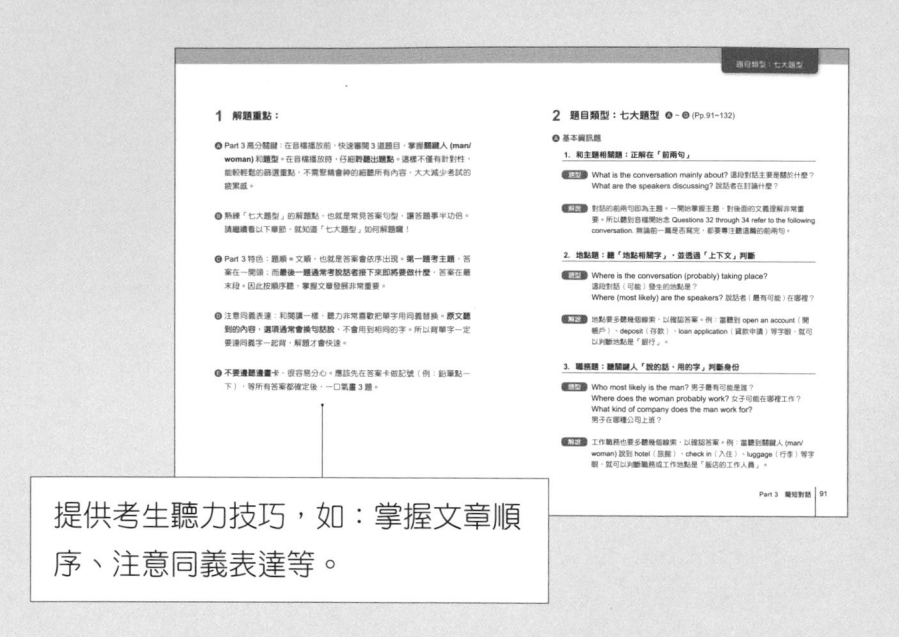

提供考生聽力技巧，如：掌握文章順
序、注意同義表達等。

STEP 4 了解常見陷阱，點出各部分常出現的陷阱，幫助考生主動避
開。

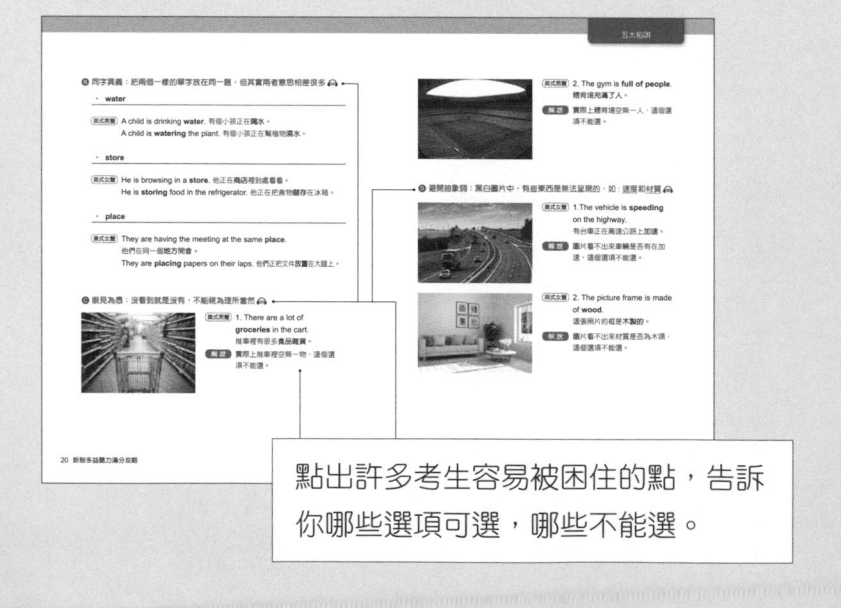

點出許多考生容易被困住的點，告訴
你哪些選項可選，哪些不能選。

STEP 5 認識題目類型，每個部分的題型多樣，要注意的地方，也略有差異。

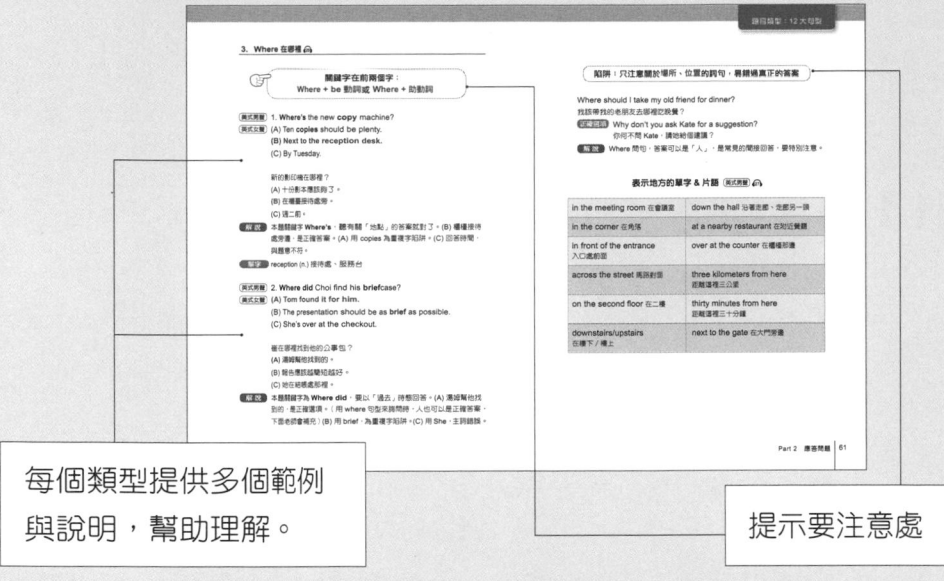

每個類型提供多個範例與說明，幫助理解。

提示要注意處

STEP 6 實戰模擬測驗 驗收實力，並提供詳細解題說明。

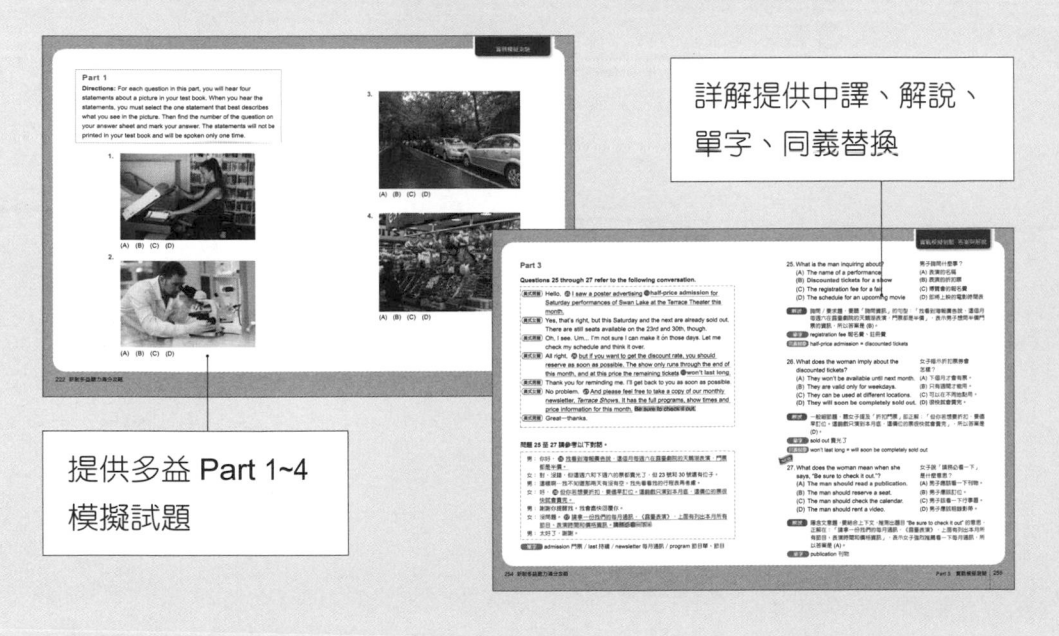

詳解提供中譯、解說、單字、同義替換

提供多益 Part 1~4 模擬試題

CONTENTS

Part 2 應答問題

Part 3 簡短對話

Part 4 簡短獨白

Part **1**

圖片描述

圖片描述

題型介紹：

共六題，圖片會印在試題本上，四個選項則不會印出。聽 (A)、(B)、(C)、(D) 四個選項，選出最符合圖片內容的描述。一題作答時間為 5 秒鐘。

題型示範：

你會看到

（本題出自於 ETS 官方指南）

你會聽到

美式男聲

Look at the picture marked number one in your test book.

請看試題本上標示第 1 題的圖片。

美式女聲

(A) She's turning on a lamp.

(B) She's opening a drawer.

(C) She's taking a picture.

(D) She's typing on a keyboard.

(A) 她在開燈。

(B) 她在開抽屜。

(C) 她在照相。

(D) 她在鍵盤上打字。

1 解題重點：

圖片題共分兩大類：人物題（有人）和景物題（沒有人）。

人物題通常會以「動態句型」表示，而景物題會以「靜態句型」表示。

如能熟悉句型結構，必能提升理解度和正確度。

以下 Olivia 老師來幫大家分析表達「動態」和「靜態」常用的句型：

Ⓐ 表示靜態的常用句型 🎧01

1. be 動詞 + 介系詞 / There + be 動詞：表事物位置、狀態

（美式女聲） A framed picture **is above** the fireplace.
一個有框的照片位在壁爐上。
There is a bridge over the canal. 有一座橋在運河上。

2. 現在完成式：表人與物靜止狀態

（英式男聲） The car **has stopped** at the gas station. 一輛車已經停在加油站。
Some lights **have been turned on**. 有些燈已經被打開。

3. 被動語態：表事物位置狀態

（美式男聲） The benches **are covered** with snow. 長椅被雪覆蓋。
Some boats **are tied** to the dock. 一些船被綁在碼頭。

4 （特殊）現在進行式：東西擬人化，描述靜態

英式女聲 Chairs **are leaning** against the table. 椅子倚靠著桌子。

Some merchandise **is hanging** on a wall. 一些商品懸掛在牆上。

❸ 表示動態的常用句型 (02)

1. 現在進行式：表人物動態動作、正在做

英式女聲 The passengers **are boarding** the train. 乘客們正在上火車。

The woman **is watering** the flowers. 女子正在澆花。

2. 被動進行式：表正在進行的動作，選項中主詞是事物，但實際上做動作的是人

美式女聲 The suitcases **are being unpacked**. 行李正被打開。

A bucket **is being carried**. 一個水桶正被提著。

3. There + be 動詞 + Ving：表人物動態動作、正在做

英式男聲 **There are** many people **waiting** in line. 有很多人在排隊。

There is a man **climbing** up the ladder. 有位男子正在爬梯子。

4 （特殊）現在進行式：東西擬人化，描述動態

美式女聲 Some trucks **are crossing** a bridge. 一些卡車正在穿越一座橋。

The fountain **is spraying** water into the air.

一座噴水池正在空中灑水。

2 五大陷阱 Ⓐ ~ Ⓔ (Pp.19~22)

圖片題有很多陷阱，Olivia 老師幫你歸類成五大類，這樣就可以輕鬆聽出陷阱，排除錯誤選項：

Ⓐ 相似音：把和題目單字發音很像的單字，放在選項中以混淆作答 🔊03

〔英式女聲〕 1. There is a **ramp** / **lamp**
　　　　　　　　　　斜坡　　燈
next to the house.
有一個斜坡 / 一盞燈在房子旁。

〔解說〕 圖片中是一個斜坡，選項中卻出現 lamp 這個相似音，這個選項不能選。

〔美式男聲〕 2. A woman is **filing** / **piling**
　　　　　　　　　　　歸檔　　堆放
the papers.
女子正在把文件歸檔 / 堆放文件。

〔解說〕 圖片中女子正在整理檔案，選項中卻出現 piling 這個相似音，這個選項不能選。

〔英式女聲〕 3. A man is changing the **tire**
　　　　　　　　　　　　　　　　　　輪胎
/ **tile**.
　磁磚
男子正在更換輪胎 / 磁磚。

〔解說〕 圖片中男子正在更換輪胎，選項中卻出現 tile 這個相似音，這個選項不能選。

B 同字異義：把兩個一樣的單字放在同一題，但其實兩者意思相差很多 🎧04

· water

(英式男聲) A child is drinking **water**. 有個小孩正在**喝水**。
A child is **watering** the plant. 有個小孩正在幫植物**澆水**。

· store

(英式女聲) He is browsing in a **store**. 他正在**商店**裡到處看看。
He is **storing** food in the refrigerator. 他正在把食物**儲存**在冰箱。

· place

(美式女聲) They are having the meeting at the same **place**.
他們在同一個**地方**開會。
They are **placing** papers on their laps. 他們正把文件**放置**在大腿上。

C 眼見為憑：沒看到就是沒有，不能視為理所當然 🎧05

(美式男聲) 1. There are a lot of
groceries in the cart.
推車裡有很多**食品雜貨**。

(解說) 實際上推車裡空無一物，這個選
項不能選。

英式男聲　2. The gym is **full of people**.
健身房**充滿了人**。

解說　實際上健身房空無一人，這個選項不能選。

D 避開抽象詞：黑白圖片中，有些東西是無法呈現的，如：<u>速度和材質</u> 🎧06

美式女聲　1.The vehicle is **speeding** on the highway.
有台車正在高速公路上**加速**。

解說　圖片看不出來車輛是否有在加速，這個選項不能選。

英式女聲　2. The picture frame is made of **wood**.
這張照片的框是**木製的**。

解說　圖片看不出來材質是否為木頭，這個選項不能選。

E 常遺漏的小細節 🎧07

1. 地方（注意：地方副詞通常在句尾！→要聽到最後面再選答案！）

(美式男聲) Cups are placed **on the counter**.
杯子被放置在**櫃檯**上。

(解 說) 其實是放在架子上 on the shelves，這個選項不能選。

2. 工具、配備、衣著（注意：與使用者的關係！）

(美式男聲) A man is wearing a **safety vest**.
男子穿著**安全背心**。

(解 說) 要更仔細觀察照片，人物的穿著配備也可能是出題點，這個選項可以選。

3. 專有名詞（注意：考單字！）

(美式女聲) A woman is looking through a **microscope**.
女子正在看**顯微鏡**。

(解 說) 常出現的事物單字要熟記，這個選項可以選。

3 題目類型 ⓐ ~ ⓑ (Pp.23~34)

包含人物題和景物題，人物題又分為單人圖片和兩人以上圖片。

ⓐ 人物題

1. 單人圖片

有人的圖片，一定要注意以下三個關鍵重點，全部都對才能選，只要其中一個錯，即刪除：

必考點：獨創 WWW 法則	
1. W → Who	人：是誰？
2. W → What	事：在做什麼？對誰做什麼？
3. W → Where	地：在哪裡？

以本張工地場景圖片為例：

Who man（男子）/ worker（工人）

What work（工作）/ stand（站著）/ use（使用）/ push（推）/ wheelbarrow（獨輪手推車）/ soil（土）/ sand（沙）

Where construction site（工地）

> **解題重點**
>
> 在觀察人物圖片時，先找 **WWW** 三大重點，再全面觀察周遭物品，如：一台獨輪手推車、土、沙。還有常遺漏小細節：人物的衣著，如：背心 **vest**、安全帽 **helmet**，這些都很容易忽略，所以要更仔細觀察照片，全面預測可能出現的正確答案！

1. 英式男聲 (08)

(A) He's pushing a wheelbarrow.

(B) **He's shoveling some sand.**

(C) He's planting trees in a garden.

(D) He's wearing safety gear.

(A) 他在推獨輪手推車。

(B) **他在鏟沙。**

(C) 他在花園種樹。

(D) 他穿著防護衣。

解說 (B) 的兩個重點描述皆正確：男子、鏟沙，為正確答案。
(A) 錯在動作描述：並沒有在推獨輪手推車，所以立馬刪除。(C) 也錯在
動作描述：並沒有在種樹，所以也刪除。(D) 的穿著描述：穿著防護衣，
不正確，聽到馬上刪除。

2. 英式女聲 09

(A) A woman is lying on the beach.

(B) A woman is looking at the sky.

(C) A woman is reading outdoors.

(D) A woman is typing on a laptop.

(A) 女子躺在沙灘上。

(B) 女子望著天空。

(C) 女子在戶外看書。

(D) 女子在筆記型電腦上打字。

解說 (C) 的三個重點描述皆正確：女子正在戶外閱讀，為正確答案。

(A) 錯在地點：沙灘，所以刪除。(B) 錯在動作描述：並沒有望著天空，所以也刪除。(D) 的動作與照片不符：並沒有在打字，聽到馬上刪除。

單字 laptop (n.) 筆記型電腦

單人圖片題：常用單字 & 片語 美式男聲 🎧10

be under construction 施工中	sign (n.) 路標
sawing the boards 鋸木板	kettle (n.) 燒水壺
hammering pieces of wood 在木板上釘釘子	street vendor 街頭攤販
climbing up the ladder 爬梯子	overhead compartment/bin （飛機）頭頂上置物艙
working on an assembly line 在生產線上工作	fire hydrant 消防栓
unloading the shipment 正在卸船運貨物	cargo (n.) 貨物
baggage carousel 行李轉盤	intersection (n.) 十字路口
baggage claim area 行李提領處	cashier (n.) 收銀員
pedestrian (n.) 行人	lawn mower 除草機
produce (n.) 農產品	merchandise (n.) 商品
pave (n.) 鋪路	railing (n.) 欄杆
bucket (n.) 水桶	rack (n.) 掛物架
curb (n.) 人行道路緣	

2. 兩人以上圖片

必考點 先注意共同動作，再注意個別動作。

兩人以上的圖片，喜歡考兩大重點。

1. 共同動作：大家都在做什麼。

　　例如：工作、散步、用餐、說話、握手、開會、看表演、排隊等…。

2. 個別動作：其中一人在做什麼。

　　觀察圖片時，也要注意每個人分別的動作。

美式女聲 🎧11

(A) The women are having a meal outside.

(B) The women are seated across from each other.

(C) One of the women is drinking from a cup.

(D) One of the women is setting the table.

(A) 她們在戶外用餐。

(B) 她們面對面坐著。

(C) 其中一人在喝杯子裡的飲料。

(D) 其中一人在陳設餐桌。

觀察兩人以上圖片時，注意兩大重點（共同動作、分別動作），再全面觀察周遭事物，如：衣著、手上和桌上的物品，包括 **drinking glass**（玻璃水杯）、**fork**（叉子）、**dishes**（盤子）。

共同動作 The women / Two women are having a meal / sitting on a bench.
兩位女子正在用餐 / 坐在長椅上。

個別動作 One of the women / One woman is holding a drinking glass.
其中一位女子正拿著玻璃水杯。

One of the women / One woman is eating with a fork.
其中一位女子正用叉子吃東西。

解說 (A) 描述共同動作：女子們正在戶外用餐，為正確答案。
(B) 錯在共同動作：並沒有面對面坐著，所以刪除。(C) 錯在個別動作：其中一位女子並沒有在喝飲料，所以刪除。(D) 錯在個別動作：其中一位女子並沒有在陳設餐桌，所以刪除。

美式男聲 🎧12

(A) A screen is hanging on the wall.
(B) They're all seated on the chairs.
(C) A woman is facing the participants.
(D) The seats are all unoccupied.

(A) 牆上掛著螢幕。
(B) 他們都坐在椅子上。
(C) 一名女子正面對開會者。
(D) 椅子都沒人坐。

解題重點 觀察多人圖片時，除了要注意上述兩大重點（共同動作、個別動作），還要注意周遭事物，如：桌上的物品 laptops（筆電）。以及多人圖片的常見陷阱，如：椅子是空的 (unoccupied) 還是有人坐 (occupied)。

共同動作 They're having a meeting / listening to a presentation.
他們在開會 / 聽簡報。

個別動作 The presenter is facing the participants / giving a lecture.
簡報者面對著與會者 / 進行授課。

常見陷阱 They're all facing in the same direction.
他們全部面對同個方向。→ 主講者沒有

They're all seated on the chairs. 他們全都坐著。→ 主講者沒有

The seats are all unoccupied. 椅子全部沒人坐。→ 都有人坐

解說 (C) 描述個別動作：女子正面對著與會者，為正確答案。
(A) 錯在「眼見為憑」：牆上沒有懸掛螢幕，所以刪除。(B) 錯在共同動作：
每個人都坐著，所以刪除。(D) 錯在：椅子都有人坐，所以刪除。

多人圖片題：常用單字 & 片語 英式男聲 13

auditorium (n.) 禮堂	platform (n.) 月台
exhibition (n.) 展覽	board 上 (v.)（船、車、飛機等）
seminar (n.) 研討會	captain (n.) 機長
workshop (n.) 工作坊 / 專題討論會 / 研討會	aisle seat 靠走道的座位
convention (n.) 會議	lane (n.) 車道 / 航道
attend a meeting 參加會議	pull over 開到路邊、靠邊停車
chair (n.) 主席	(shopping) cart (n.) （購物）手推車
briefing (n.) 簡報	try on 試穿
podium (n.) 講台	inventory (n.) 庫存 / 存貨
chef (n.) 廚師	counter (n.) 櫃台
diner (n.) 用餐者	grocery store 雜貨店
concourse (n.) （車站、機場）大廳	lean against/on 倚靠
terminal (n.) 航站 / 航廈	

⑬ 景物題

必考點 風景、物品的狀態和位置

1. 狀態：景物圖片中沒有人在做動作，因此正確答案通常是表靜態的
   句型，如：完成式、被動式。若出現動態的句型，如：進行式、被動
   進行式，通常是陷阱選項。
2. 位置：注意表位置的介系詞，及照片中的前（近）景、後（遠）景，
   都要仔細觀察。如：我家**門前**有小河，**後面**有山坡，山坡**上面**野花多，
   小河裡有白鵝…。

1. 美式女聲 🎧⑭

(A) There are houses along the lakeside.
(B) Some waves are splashing over the rocks.
(C) A boat is sitting on the shore.
(D) People are diving into the water.

(A) 湖邊有房子。
(B) 浪花打在石頭上。
(C) 一艘船停靠在岸邊。
(D) 人們正在跳水。

解題重點
照片中沒有人，為靜態，有人或動態句型的選項是陷阱。
另外，還要全面觀察周遭景物，前景：一艘船停靠在岸邊。
後景：湖中有樹，遠方有山。

解說 (C) 東西擬人化，描述靜態，為正確答案。
(A) 錯在「眼見為憑」：湖邊沒有房子，所以刪除。(B) 與照片不符：沒
有浪花打在石頭上，所以刪除。(D) 是動態描述：人們正在跳水，而照片
中並沒有人，一聽到有人的選項立即刪除。

2. 美式男聲 🎧15

(A) The shelves are full of folders.

(B) A whiteboard is hanging on the wall.

(C) A cabinet door is being opened.

(D) The chairs are on the same side of the desk.

(A) 架子上擺滿檔案夾。

(B) 牆上掛著一面白板。

(C) 有一扇櫥櫃門正在被打開。

(D) 椅子都放在書桌的 同一邊。

解說 (B) 為靜態描述：牆上掛著一面白板，為正確答案。

(A) 錯在：架子上沒有擺滿檔案夾，所以刪除。(C) 是動態描述：櫥櫃的一扇門正在被打開，而照片中並沒有人，一聽到即刪除。(D) 位置的描述不正確：椅子並非在書桌的同一邊，所以刪除。

單字 folder (n.) 檔案夾 / cabinet (n.) 櫥櫃

3. 英式女聲 🎧16

(A) People are eating a meal.

(B) Kitchen utensils are placed on the table.

(C) Candles are being lit on the table.

(D) A rug is laid out in front of a window.

(A) 人們在用餐。

(B) 餐桌上放著餐具。

(C) 桌上的蠟燭正在被點亮。

(D) 窗前鋪著一張地毯。

解說 (D) 為靜態描述：窗前鋪著一張地毯，為正確答案。

(A) 是動態描述：人們正在用餐，而照片中並沒有人，一聽到即刪除。

(B) 錯在「眼見為憑」：餐桌上沒有放著餐具，所以刪除。(C) 是動態描述：
桌上的蠟燭正在被點亮，但並沒有人正在點蠟燭，所以刪除。

單字 utensil (n.)（廚房）用具 / lay out 擺放

景物圖片題：常用單字 & 片語 美式女聲 17

atrium (n.) 中庭	pier (n.) 碼頭
awning (n.) （門窗等前面的）雨篷	patio (n.) 露臺
landmark (n.) 地標	porch (n.) 門廊
ramp (n.) 斜坡 /（上下飛機用的）移動式舷梯	sink (n.) 水槽
amusement park 遊樂園	in the corner 在角落
skyscraper (n.) 摩天大樓	at the counter 在櫃檯
office supplies 辦公用品	across the road 馬路對面
scenery (n.) 風景	downstairs/upstairs 樓下 / 樓上
fence (n.) 圍籬	next to the gate 大門邊
scaffolding (n.) 鷹架	along the street/shore 沿著街道 / 岸邊
brick (n.) 磚頭	by/near/at the curb 在路邊
blueprint (n.) 藍圖	on top of each other 向上堆疊
sidewalk (n.) 人行道	

多益實戰練習

(18)

1.

2.

3.

4.

5.

6.

7.

8.

9.

10.

11.

12.

1.

美式女聲

(A) He's playing an instrument outdoors.   (A) 他在戶外演奏樂器。

(B) He's operating a power tool.   **(B) 他在操作電動工具。**

(C) Grass is being cut with a lawn mower.   (C) 有人在用除草機割草。

(D) He's planting flowers in a garden.   (D) 他在花園種花。

解說 此為人物題的單人圖片，要看「人物、動作、地點」三個重點。(B) 兩個重點描述皆正確：男子、操作電動工具，為正確答案。(A) 錯在動作描述：並沒有在演奏樂器，所以刪除。(C) 錯在專有名詞：沒有出現除草機，所以刪除。(D) 錯在動作描述：並沒有在種花，不能選。

單字 instrument (n.) 樂器 / operate (v.) 操作

2.

 美式男聲

(A) She's adjusting the settings on the exercise machine.

(B) She's running on a treadmill.

(C) She's working on a computer.

(D) She's jogging around the track.

(A) 她在調整運動器材上的設定。

(B) 她在跑步機上跑步。

(C) 她在使用電腦。

(D) 她在跑道上慢跑。

解說 (A) 兩個重點描述皆正確：女子、調整運動器材的設定，為正確答案。
(B) 錯在動作描述：女子並沒有在跑步機上跑步，所以刪除。(C) 錯在動作描述：並沒有在用電腦工作，所以刪除。(D) 錯在動作描述和地點：並沒有在跑道上慢跑。

單字 adjust (v.) 調整 / treadmill (n.) 跑步機 / track (n.) 跑道

3.

英式男聲

(A) A shop assistant is checking the store displays.

(B) Some footwear is being stacked in a warehouse.

(C) Products are being put into bags.

(D) A woman is trying on a pair of shoes.

(A) 店員在檢查商店裡的展示商品。

(B) 有人在倉庫裡堆放鞋子。

(C) 有人在將產品放進袋子裡。

(D) 女子在試穿鞋子。

解說 (D) 兩個重點描述皆正確：女子、試穿鞋子，為正確答案。(A) 錯在人物和動作描述：畫面中沒有出現店員，也沒有人在檢視店內展示的商品，所以刪除。(B) 錯在動作描述：進行被動式表動態，女子沒有將鞋子堆放在倉庫。(C) 錯在動作描述：女子沒有把東西放到袋子裡，所以刪除。

單字 shop assistant (n.) 店員 / stack (v.) 堆放 / warehouse (n.) 倉庫

4.

英式女聲

(A) A man is doing some paperwork.

(B) A lamp in the corner has been turned on.

(C) A man is speaking on the phone.

(D) Reading materials are scattered on the desk.

(A) 男子在處理文書。

(B) 角落的燈開著。

(C) 男子在講電話。

(D) 資料散落在桌上。

解說 (C) 兩個重點描述皆正確：男子、講電話，為正確答案。(A) 錯在動作描述：並沒有在處理文書工作，所以刪除。(B) 眼見為憑：圖中沒有檯燈，不能選。(D) 眼見為憑：沒有資料散佈在桌上，所以刪除。

單字 paperwork (n.) 文書工作 / scatter (v.) 散佈

5.

美式女聲

(A) Food has been served by a waiter.

(B) A cashier is collecting a payment.

(C) Customers are ordering food.

(D) A table is being cleaned.

(A) 服務生端上餐點。

(B) 出納員在收錢。

(C) 顧客在點餐。

(D) 有人在整理餐桌。

解說　此為人物題的多人圖片，要「注意共同、分別動作」。(C) 描述共同動作：
顧客正在點餐，為正確答案。(A) 錯在個別動作：服務生還沒送上餐點，
所以刪除。(B) 眼見為憑：圖中沒有正在收錢的出納員，所以刪除。
(D) 錯在個別動作：服務生沒有在整理餐桌，所以刪除。

單字　cashier (n.) 出納員 / payment (n.) 支付款項，付款
　　　customer (n.) 顧客

6.

英式男聲

(A) The conference has just adjourned.

(B) They're watching a performance.

(C) They're seated in a circle.

(D) They're listening to a lecture.

(A) 會議剛剛結束。

(B) 他們在看表演。

(C) 他們圍坐成一圈。

(D) 他們在聽講座。

解說　(D) 描述共同動作：人們正在聽講座，為正確答案。(A) 錯在抽象詞：圖片看不出會議已結束，所以刪除。(B) 錯在共同動作：人們不是在看表演，不能選。(C) 錯在共同動作：大家沒有坐成一圈，所以刪除。

單字　conference (n.) 會議 / adjourn (v.) 散會 / lecture (n.) 講座、課程

7.

美式男聲

(A) The bus has stopped by the curb.　　**(A)** 公車停在路邊。

(B) Passengers are stepping down from　　(B) 乘客正在下
the bus.　　　　　　　　　　　　　　公車。

(C) Some people are loading luggage　　(C) 有些人正將行李放上
onto the carousel.　　　　　　　　　轉盤。

(D) The bus is waiting at a crossing.　　(D) 公車在十字路口等候。

解說　(A) 描述靜態動作：公車已停在路邊，為正確答案。(B) 錯在共同動作：
乘客並沒有正在下公車，不能選。(C) 眼見為憑：沒有行李轉盤，不能選。
(D) 眼見為憑：沒有十字路口，不能選。

單字　passenger (n.) 行人 / crossing (n.) 十字路口

8.

英式女聲

(A) The men are greeting each other.

(B) The men are seated at the desk.

(C) One of the men is using a computer mouse.

(D) One of the men is adjusting a monitor.

(A) 男子們在互相打招呼。

(B) 男子們坐在桌旁。

(C) 其中一名男子在用 滑鼠。

(D) 其中一名男子在調整螢幕。

解說　(C) 描述個別動作：其中一名男子正在用滑鼠，為正確答案。(A) 錯在共同動作：男子們沒有互相打招呼，不能選。(B) 錯在共同動作：男子們沒有都坐著，不能選。(D) 錯在個別動作：其中一個男子沒有在調整螢幕，所以刪除。

單字　greet (v.) 打招呼、問候 / monitor (n.) 螢幕、顯示器

9.

美式女聲

(A) The hikers are walking along a trail.　　(A) 登山客在小徑上行走。

(B) A path winds through the trees.　　**(B)** 一條小徑蜿蜒穿越在樹林間。

(C) Potted plants are arranged in rows.　　(C) 擺放成排的盆栽。

(D) Leaves have been collected in a pile.　　(D) 葉子收集成堆。

解說　此為景物題，要注意「風景物品的狀態、位置」，(B) 為靜態描述：一條小徑蜿蜒穿越在樹林間，為正確答案。(A) 錯在有人的動態描述，而圖中沒有人，所以刪除。(C) 眼見為憑：沒有盆栽，一聽到即刪除。(D) 眼見為憑：葉子沒有被收集成堆，所以刪除。

單字　trail (n.) 小徑、步道 / path (n.) 小徑、路 / wind (v.) 蜿蜒
arrange (v.) 排列、整理

10.

美式男聲

(A) The skyscrapers are all the same heights.

(B) The cars are waiting at an intersection.

(C) There're cars going in the opposite directions.

(D) Several lines are painted on the street.

(A) 摩天大樓都一樣高。

(B) 汽車都在十字路口等候。

(C) 汽車朝反方向前進。

(D) 街上畫著幾條線。

解說　(D) 為靜態描述，是正確答案。(A) 眼見為憑：看不出高樓大廈高度一樣，所以刪除。(B) 眼見為憑：圖中看不出是否為十字路口，一聽到即刪除。(C) 眼見為憑：圖中車子都是朝同一方向前進，所以刪除。

單字　skyscraper (n.) 摩天大樓 / intersection (n.) 十字路口

11.

英式女聲

(A) Goods are being taken off a shelf.

(B) The racks are empty.

(C) Various items have been arranged on shelves.

(D) Some produce is contained in boxes.

(A) 有人把產品從架上拿下。

(B) 架子是空的。

(C) 架子上擺放著各種物品。

(D) 一些農產品用箱子裝著。

解說　(C) 為靜態描述：架子上擺放著各種物品，正確答案。(A) 錯在有人的動態描述，而圖中沒有人，所以刪除。(B) 眼見為憑：架子不是空的，一聽到即刪除。(D) 錯在單字：選項中有 produce 農產品，但畫面中並沒出現，所以刪除。

單字　contain (v.) 容納

12.

英式男聲

(A) The restaurant has an awning over the entrance.

(B) The outdoor seating area is filled with diners.

(C) The brick floor is being swept.

(D) All tables are shaded by umbrellas.

(A) 餐廳入口處有遮陽篷。

(B) 戶外座位區坐滿客人。

(C) 有人在打掃地磚。

(D) 所有桌子都有遮陽傘遮蔭。

解說 (A) 為靜態描述，正確答案。(B) 眼見為憑：戶外座位區沒有坐滿人，一聽到即刪除。(C) 眼見為憑：沒有人在掃地，不能選。(D) 眼見為憑：不是所有的桌子都有傘遮蔭（all 是常見陷阱），所以刪除。

單字 shade (v.) 遮蔽

Part **2**

應答問題

▶ 題型介紹

▶ 解題重點

▶ 四大陷阱

    A. 相似音

    B. 重複字

    C. 主詞

    D. 時態

▶ 題目類別：12 大句型

    A. 七種 Wh 問句

      1. Who 誰

      2. When 何時

      3. Where 在哪裡

      4. What 什麼

      5. How 如何

      6. Why 為什麼

      7. Which 哪一個

    B. Yes / No 問句：

      8. 子句

      9. 附加問句

      10. 一般 yes/no 問句

    C. 11. 二選一

    D. 12. 陳述句

應答問題

題型介紹：

共25題，每題播放一個問句或直述句和三個答句，選出 (A)、(B)、(C) 三個答句中，最符合問題的選項。題目和選項皆不會印在試題本上。一題作答時間為 5 秒鐘。

題型示範：

你會看到

7. Mark your answer on your answer sheet.

你會聽到

(美式女聲) Number 7: What time are you planning to arrive?

(美式男聲) (A) Maybe three of them.

(B) I arrived at nine, as usual.

(C) I'll be there by seven a.m.

7. 請在答案紙上標出答案。

7. 你打算幾點到達？

(A) 也許他們三人都會。

(B) 我像往常一樣九點就到了。

(C) 我會在早上七點以前到。

1 解題重點：

A Part 2 最重要的就是：迅速理解各句型在問什麼，才能在短短 5 秒鐘，排除干擾選項，選出最符合題意的答案。尤其 Part 2 陷阱很多，若沒有**把正確「關鍵字」聽仔細**，例如：wh 疑問詞 who/when/where，很容易在聽選項時掉入陷阱。

B 聽到題目「關鍵字」後，**心中要默念關鍵字**，讓自己專注聽符合關鍵字的答案，才不至於在聽完選項後，忘記題目問的重點是什麼！另外，只要抓到「關鍵字」，聽不懂題目也能選出正確答案！

C 基本概念：wh 疑問句，99% 不能用 yes/no 回答，若聽到則直接刪除。那剩下 1% 呢？請繼續看以下章節就知道囉！

2 四大陷阱 Ⓐ ~ Ⓓ (Pp.54~56)

Olivia 老師幫你把 Part 2 最常見的陷阱歸類成 4 大類，這樣就可以輕鬆聽出陷阱，排除錯誤選項：

Ⓐ 相似音：把和題目單字發音很像的單字，放在選項中以混淆作答 🎧19

(美式男聲) Which **firm** will they hire to conduct the survey?

(美式女聲) **(A) Our usual contractor.**

(B) The new employee will start work tomorrow.

(C) He works at the **farm**.

他們會聘哪家公司進行調查？

(A) 我們常合作的承包商。

(B) 新員工明天會開始上班。

(C) 他在農場工作。

解說 題目問：哪一間公司，(C) 中卻出現 **farm** 這個相似音，故意和題目 firm 混淆，正確答案為 (A) 我們常合作的承包商。

單字 firm (n.) 公司 / conduct (v.) 進行 / survey (n.) 調查
contractor (n.) 承包商、承辦人

B 重複字：把和題目一模一樣的單字，放在選項中以混淆作答 ⟨20⟩

英式女聲　How **soon** will the order be **delivered**?

美式女聲　(A) I'll finish it **soon**.

　　　　(B) **Tomorrow morning, at the latest.**

　　　　(C) No, I haven't.

　　　　訂貨多久會送到？

　　　　(A) 我很快就可以完成。

　　　　(B) 最晚明天早上。

　　　　(C) 不，我還沒。

解說　題目問：這批訂單多快會送到，(A) 中出現 **soon** 這個重複字，文意也錯誤不能選。(C) 中出現 **no** 直接刪除，因為 wh 疑問句不能用 yes/no 回答。正確答案為 (B) 最晚明天早上。

單字　deliver (v.) 運送

C 主詞：用錯的主詞混淆作答 ⟨21⟩

美式女聲　**You** cancelled our newspaper subscription, didn't **you**?

美式男聲　(A) Yes, **he** has to do it.

　　　　(B) **No, I'm going to do it tomorrow.**

　　　　(C) You should **cancel** the meal.

　　　　你是不是取消訂報了？

　　　　(A) 對，他必須這麼做。

　　　　(B) 還沒，我明天會取消。

　　　　(C) 你該取消這一餐。

解說　題目問，你是不是取消訂報了？(A) 中出現 **he** 這個錯誤主詞，不能選。(C) 出現重複字陷阱 **cancel**，文意也不對。正確答案為 (B) 還沒，我明天會取消。

單字　cancel (v.) 取消 ／ subscription (n.) 訂閱

D 時態：用錯的時態混淆作答 🎧22

(英式男聲) What time are you planning to **arrive**?
(英式女聲) **(A) I'll be there by 8 a.m.**
(B) It's about five thirty.
(C) I **arrived** at noon, as usual.

你打算幾點到？
(A) 我會在早上八點前到那裡。
(B) 現在大約是五點三十分。
(C) 我像往常一樣中午就到了。

解說 題目問，「你打算幾點到？」是**未來時態**，(B) 回答現在是幾點幾分，不能選。(C) 中出現**過去式時態** arrived，直接刪除。正確答案為 (A) 我會在早上八點前到那裡。

3　題目類型：**12 大句型** ❶ ～ ❷ (Pp.57~76)

Ⓐ 七種 Wh 問句：分成以下七種，注意解題關鍵字

1.　Who 誰 🎧

> **關鍵字在前兩個字：**
> **Who + be 動詞、Who + 助動詞、Who + 動詞**

美式女聲　1. **Who's** in charge of Mr. Bruno's retirement party?
英式男聲　(A) We'll pay by credit card.
　　　　　(B) In the third-floor conference room.
　　　　　(C) It's being handled by his secretary.

誰負責布魯諾先生的退休派對？
(A) 我們會用信用卡付。
(B) 在三樓會議室。
(C) 他的秘書在處理。

解說　本題關鍵字為 **Who's**，聽有關「人」的答案就對了，(C) 是正確選項。
(A) 用信用卡付款，與題意不符，(B) 回答地點，不能選。

美式男聲　2. **Who left** this report on my desk?
英式女聲　**(A) Ms. Adams did, when you were out for lunch.**
　　　　　(B) No, it hasn't been confirmed yet.
　　　　　(C) He's working on revising the sales report.

誰把這份報告留在我的桌上？
(A) 是亞當女士，就在你外出吃午餐時。
(B) 不，尚未確認。
(C) 他在修改銷售報告。

解說　本題關鍵字為 **Who left**（誰留的），答題必須要注意「時態」，
本題要使用「過去」時態，(A) 是正確選項。(B) 出現 No，直接刪除。
(C) 他在修改銷售報告，與題意不符。

正解慣用開頭
人名、職位、部門、人稱代名詞、間接回答。

Who's going to present the award in the banquet? 誰會在宴會上頒獎？

→ **Mr. Sanchez** is. 桑奇斯先生。（人名）

→ Someone from the **marketing department**. 行銷部門的人。（部門）

→ **I don't know** if anyone's been assigned.
我不知道是否已經指派負責的人了。（間接回答：不確定）

→ Isn't there a name on the list? 名單上不是有名字嗎？（間接回答：反問）

2. When 何時 24

關鍵字在前兩個字：
When + be 動詞 或 When + 助動詞。

英式女聲 1. **When will** the new smartphone **launch**?

英式男聲 **(A) The last week of October.**

(B) They'll have **lunch** tomorrow.

(C) I don't think so.

新的智慧手機何時會推出？

(A) 十月最後一週。

(B) 他們明天會吃午餐。

(C) 我不這麼認為。

解說 本題關鍵字為 **When will**，要聽有關未來的「時間」，(A) 十月的最後一週，是正確答案。(B) 用 lunch，和題目 launch 為相似音陷阱。(C) 與題意不符。

單字 launch (v.) 推出

英式男聲 2. **When did** you move into your new **apartment**?
美式女聲 (A) Our **department** has moved to the 2nd floor.
(B) **Three days ago.**
(C) In about two weeks.

你何時搬進新公寓的？
(A) 我們部門已經搬到二樓。
(B) **三天前。**
(C) 大概在兩週後。

解說 本題關鍵字為 **When did**，要聽有關過去的「時間」，(B) 三天前，是正確答案。(A) department 和 apartment 為相似音陷阱。(C) 大約兩週後，時態錯誤不能選。

表示時間的單字 & 片語 英式女聲 ②25

過去時態	already 已經、a week ago 一週前、last week 上週、a little while ago 前不久
現在時態	now 現在、right now 現在、for now 目前、just now 剛才、usually 通常地、often 時常、regularly 經常地
未來時態	tomorrow 明天、next week 下週、in 30 minutes 30 分鐘後、within two days 兩天內、not for another hour 要再一個小時
不確定的時間（為常見答案）	**not until** next week 直到下週⋯ **during** the first week of May 五月的第一週期間 **by the end** of the month 月底前 **as soon as** it's ready 準備好之後馬上 **right after** the presentation is ready 報告準備好以後就會開始 **when** the construction is completed 工程完成後 **Let me check** the schedule. 我查一下行程表。

3. Where 在哪裡

> 關鍵字在前兩個字：
> **Where + be 動詞或 Where + 助動詞**

(美式男聲) 1. **Where's** the new **copy** machine?
(英式女聲) (A) Ten **copies** should be plenty.
(B) Next to the reception desk.
(C) By Tuesday.

新的影印機在哪裡？
(A) 十份影本應該夠了。
(B) 在櫃臺接待處旁。
(C) 週二前。

解說 本題關鍵字 **Where's**，聽有關「地點」的答案就對了。(B) 櫃檯接待處旁邊，是正確答案。(A) 用 copies 為重複字陷阱。(C) 回答時間，與題意不符。

單字 reception (n.) 接待處、服務台

(英式男聲) 2. **Where did** Choi find his **brief**case?
(美式女聲) **(A) Tom found it for him.**
(B) The presentation should be as **brief** as possible.
(C) She's over at the checkout.

崔在哪裡找到他的公事包？
(A) 湯姆幫他找到的。
(B) 報告應該越簡短越好。
(C) 她在結帳處那裡。

解說 本題關鍵字為 **Where did**，要以「過去」時態回答。(A) 湯姆幫他找到的，是正確選項。（用 where 句型來詢問時，人也可以是正確答案，下面老師會補充）(B) 用 brief，為重複字陷阱。(C) 用 She，主詞錯誤。題目問公事包，不是問人在哪裡。

陷阱：只注意關於場所、位置的詞句，可能會錯過真正的答案

Where should I take my old friend for dinner?

我該帶我的老朋友去哪裡吃晚餐？

正確選項 Why don't you ask Kate for a suggestion?

你何不問 Kate，請她給個建議？

解 說 Where 問句，答案可以是「人」，是常見的間接回答，要特別注意。

表示地方的單字 & 片語 英式男聲 ②7

in the meeting room 在會議室	down the hall 沿著走廊、走廊另一頭
in the corner 在角落	at a nearby restaurant 在附近餐廳
in front of the entrance 入口處前面	over at the counter 在櫃檯那邊
across the street 馬路對面	three kilometers from here 距離這裡三公里
on the second floor 在二樓	thirty minutes from here 距離這裡三十分鐘
downstairs/upstairs 在樓下 / 樓上	next to the gate 在大門旁邊

4. What 什麼

a) What + N / What kind of N...?

關鍵字在名詞

(美式女聲) 1. What kind of **company** does Ms. Lopez own?
(美式男聲) (A) 20 branches all over the world.
  (B) A travel agency.
  (C) **He** started the business on his own.

羅佩茲女士經營哪種公司？
(A) 全世界有 20 家分店。
(B) 旅行社。
(C) 他自己創業。

解 說 本題關鍵字為 **company**，(B) 旅行社，是正確答案。(A) 回答分店數量，與題意不符。(C) 主詞 he 錯誤，與題意也不符。

單字 branch (n.) 分店、分部

(美式女聲) 2. What **time** did the press conference end?
(英式男聲) (A) There are about 50 people in total.
  (B) By the end of this week.
  (C) Around 2 p.m.

新聞發表會幾點結束？
(A) 總共約有 50 人。
(B) 本週末前。
(C) 大約下午兩點。

解 說 本題關鍵字為 **time**，問「時間」，是過去時態。(C) 大約下午兩點，聽到「時間」，即正確答案。(A) 回答人數，不能選。(B) 時態錯誤，選項為**未來式**。

單字 press conference 新聞發布會

b) What...V/Ving?

 關鍵字在 What + 動詞

英式男聲 3. **What** should I **bring** to the seminar?
英式女聲 (A) In the meeting room.
(B) **Mr. Hoffman brought** this to you.
(C) Your laptop and business cards.

我要帶什麼去參加研討會？
(A) 在會議室。
(B) 霍夫曼先生帶了這個給你。
(C) 你的筆電和名片。

解說 本題關鍵字為 **what bring**，帶什麼，(C) 筆電和名片，是正確答案。
(A) 回答地點，不能選。(B) 回答人，不能選。

單字 business card 名片

c) What's wrong/What happened...? 出了什麼問題 / 發生什麼事

 此類句型，答案必是負面

美式女聲 4. **What's wrong** with the copy machine?
美式男聲 (A) There's something **wrong** with the numbers.
(B) It's out of ink.
(C) It doesn't matter to me.

影印機出了什麼問題？

(A) 數字出了點問題。

(B) 沒有墨水了。

(C) 我無所謂。

解說 本題關鍵字 **What's wrong**，要聽「負面」答案。(B) 沒有墨水了，是正確答案。(A) wrong 為重複字陷阱。(C) 回答：「我無所謂」，與題意不符。

單字 out of 缺乏

5. How 如何 (29)

a) How + adv / 限定語 ...?

多益常考副詞有：often、soon、far。會考的限定語有：many、much。

☞ 關鍵字在副詞和限定語

How often…? 問「頻率」

How much…? 問「錢」

How soon…? 問「時間」

美式男聲 1. How **many copies** should I make?

美式女聲 (A) A cup of **coffee**, please.

(B) Twice a week.

(C) Ten should be plenty.

我要影印多少份？

(A) 請給我一杯咖啡。

(B) 一星期兩次。

(C) 十份應該夠了。

解說 本題關鍵字：**many**，問數量，(C) 十份應該就夠了，聽到「數量」即是正確答案。(A) coffee 是 copy 的相似音陷阱。(B) 這是回答 How often（問頻率）的答案。

b) How...V/Ving?

 關鍵字在 **How + 動詞**

英式男聲 2. **How** can I **reserve** one of the hotel's meeting rooms?
美式女聲 **(A) Let me get the receptionist to help you with that.**
(B) They will hold our **reservation** for ten minutes.
(C) Please be in the hotel lobby at 9 a.m.

我要怎麼預訂旅館的會議室？
(A) 我請櫃台人員協助你。
(B) 他們會幫我們保留訂位十分鐘。
(C) 請在上午九點到旅館大廳。

解說 本題關鍵字：how reserve，如何預訂，(A) 我讓接待人員協助你，是正確答案。(B) reservation 是重複字陷阱。(C) 在回答時間，不正確。

單字 reserve (v.) 預訂、預約，名詞為 reservation ／ receptionist (n.) 櫃台人員

c) **How about N/Ving…?** …如何？

= **What about + N/Ving…?** …怎麼樣？

= **Why don't you +** 原 **V...?** 你何不…？

= **Would you like to...?** 你要不要…？

= **Would you care for…?** 你願不願意…？

= **Let's...** = 我們…

99% 的 **wh** 疑問句不能回答 **Yes/No**，
唯一例外（那 **1%**）為此種句型：
提出建議／邀請，答案可以有 **Yes/No**

英式男聲 3. **Would you like to** go the trade fair?

英式女聲 **(A) Yes, I would.**

(B) Admission is by ticket only.

(C) It's located in Paris.

你要去貿易博覽會嗎？

(A) 是的，我會去。

(B) 有入場券才可進入。

(C) 地點在巴黎。

解說 本題關鍵字為 **Would you like to**「你要去貿易博覽會嗎？」，提出邀請，可以用「Yes/No」答覆。(A)「是的，我會。」是正確答案。(B) 有入場券才可進入，與題意不符。(C) 回答地點，不能選。

單字 fair (n.) 商品展銷會 / admission (n.) 准許進入

美式男聲 4. **Let's** get together and discuss the problem.

英式女聲 **(A) All right, when is convenient for you?**

(B) He managed to fix the problem.

(C) No, I don't mind.

我們見個面討論這問題。

(A) 好，你何時方便？

(B) 他設法解決這個問題。

(C) 不，我不介意。

解說 本題關鍵字為 **Let's** 我們見個面討論這問題，提出邀請，可以有「yes/no」的回答。(A) All right 指的是好的 (yes)，你何時方便，是正確答案。(B) 他設法解決了這個問題，主詞、時態與題目不符。(C) 我不介意，與題意不符。

單字 manage to 設法、努力（完成某事）

6. Why 為什麼

關鍵字在 **Why +**（否定助動詞）**+ 動詞…?**

a) Why + 動詞…?

英式女聲　1. **Why** did the art museum **postpone** the Egyptian exhibit?
美式男聲　(A) It will be **postponed** till November 10th.
　　　　　(B) They're doing some repair work to the main gallery.
　　　　　(C) Yes, they traveled to Egypt.

為什麼藝術博物館把埃及展覽延後？
(A) 會延後到 11 月 10 日。
(B) 他們的主要美術館正在整修。
(C) 對，他們去了埃及。

解 說　本題關鍵字：**why postpone** 問「為什麼延後」：(B) 他們的主要美術館正在整修（because 通常會省略），是正確答案。(A) 回答時間，postpone 是重複字陷阱，不能選。
(C) 出現 **Yes**，直接刪除。

單字　postpone (v.) 延後 / exhibit (n.) 展覽 / gallery (n.) 美術館

b) Why + 否定助動詞 + 動詞…?

(美式女聲) 2. Why **didn't** Mr. Murray **attend** the orientation this morning?

(美式男聲) (A) Yes, he will arrive this morning.

(B) About ten o'clock.

(C) He had an important appointment with clients.

為什麼穆瑞先生今天早上沒有參加新進員工訓練？

(A) 對，他今天早上會到。

(B) 大約十點。

(C) 他跟客戶有重要會面。

解說 本題關鍵字：**why didn't attend** 問「為什麼沒參加」，(C) 他跟客戶
有重要會面 （because 通常會省略），是正確答案。(A) 出現 **Yes**，
直接刪除。

(B) 回答時間，不能選。

單字 orientation (n.) 新生 / 新進員工培訓、準備
appointment (n.) 預約

c)

正解慣用開頭：
Because/ Due to/ In order to/ To 因為…

Why did she call the library? 她為何打給圖書館？

→ **Because** she wanted to reserve a book. 因為她想預訂一本書。

→ **In order to** / **To** reserve a book. 為了預訂一本書。

7. Which 哪一個 (31)

a) Which + N / Which one of the + N...? 哪一個 …?

 關鍵字在名詞

美式女聲 1. Which **restaurant** should we eat **lunch** at?
英式男聲 **(A) The one that features classic French cuisine.**
(B) The buffet **restaurant** closes at 9 p.m.
(C) The **luncheon** will be held in the conference room.

我們該去哪一家餐廳吃午餐？
(A) 主打經典法國菜的那家。
(B) 自助餐廳晚上九點打烊。
(C) 午餐會將在會議室舉行。

解說 本題關鍵字：restaurant 問「哪間餐廳」，(A) 主打經典法國菜的那家，是正確答案。(B) 回答時間，又出現 restaurant（重複字陷阱），直接刪除。(C) 回答地點，另外出現 luncheon（午餐會）和題目 lunch 混淆，不能選。

單字 feature (v.) 以…為特色 / cuisine (n.) 菜餚，烹飪 / luncheon (n.) 午餐

b)
慣用答案：代名詞 one

Which hotel are you staying at? 你在哪一間旅館住宿？
→ The one by the train station. 火車站旁那間。
Which coffee table are you going to buy? 你要買哪一張茶几？
→ The one looks more useful. 看起來比較好用的那張。

B yes / no 問句：可用 yes / no 回答，分為以下三大句型

8. 子句 🎧32

常見不重要開頭：

Do you know 你知道嗎？

Did you hear 你聽說…了嗎？

Did anyone tell you 有人告訴你嗎？

Are you sure 你確定嗎？

Have you heard 你有聽說嗎？

Could you tell me + wh 疑問詞 ...? 你能告訴我…嗎？

 關鍵字在 wh 疑問詞 + 主要動詞

(美式女聲) 1. Do you know **who** was **elected** to be the new **committee** member?

(美式男聲) (A) He used to be on the finance **committee**.

(B) The **election** is in December.

(C) No one has been chosen yet.

你知道誰獲選為新委員嗎？

(A) 他曾經是財務委員。

(B) 選舉是在 12 月。

(C) 還沒有選出。

解 說 本題關鍵字：**who** 和 **elected** 問「誰獲選」，(C) 還沒有選出（間接回答），是正確答案。(A) 他曾經是財務委員，不符合題意，另外聽到 committee（重複字陷阱），直接刪除。(B) 回答時間，另外 election（重複字陷阱），不能選。

單字 elect (v.) 推選 / committee (n.) 委員會

英式男聲 2. Could you tell me **when** the payment **is due**?

美式女聲 **(A) Let me check the calendar.**

(B) The total amount is twenty-five thousand.

(C) He **is due** to finish at 5:00.

你能不能告訴我付款何時到期？

(A) 讓我看一下行事曆。

(B) 總金額是二萬五千元。

(C) 他要在五點鐘完成。

解說 本題關鍵字：**when** 問「何時」(A) 讓我看一下行事曆（間接回答／萬用回答），是正確答案。(B) 總金額是兩萬五千元，不符合題意，直接刪除。

(C) 回答時間，但是和題意不符，另外 be due to + V.（預計做某件事）和題目的 due 是重複字陷阱，不能選。

單字 due (a.) 到期的、預期的

9. 附加問句 🎧33

You've **ordered** the latest camera, **haven't you**?

你訂購了最新的相機，不是嗎？

The office complex **is under construction, isn't it?**

辦公大樓正在施工，不是嗎？

👉 關鍵字在主句動詞 + 附加問句（可知道時態和主詞）

第一句關鍵字在主句動詞 **order** + 附加問句 **haven't you**

→問：你訂了嗎？

第二句關鍵字在 be 動詞 **is** 及其後內容 **under construction**

+ 附加問句 **isn't it**

→問：它在施工嗎？

英式女聲 1. You've **signed** the joint venture **contract, haven't you?**

美式男聲 (A) You can **contact** me by e-mail.

(B) She has **signed** for the package.

(C) No, I'm still reviewing it.

你簽了合資合約，不是嗎？

(A) 你可以用電郵聯絡我。

(B) 她已經簽收了包裹。

(C) 不，我還在審閱。

解說 本題關鍵字：**signed** 和 **haven't you** 問：「你簽了嗎？」，(C) 不，我還在審閱，是正確答案。(A) 不符合題意，另外 contact 和 contract 是相似音陷阱，不能選。(B) 她已經簽收了包裹，不符合題意，另外主詞 She 錯誤（題目問 haven't you）、sign（重複字陷阱），不能選。

單字 venture (n.) 新創事業，投資事業 / contract (n.) 合約
contact (v.) 聯絡、接觸 / review (v.) 審查、評論

美式女聲 2. The supermarket **is scheduled to open** next week,
isn't it?

美式男聲 (A) A vendor is selling some produce.

(B) You should check the flyer.

(C) It's right beside our office.

超市預定下週開張，不是嗎？

(A) 小販在賣一些農產品。

(B) 你該看一下廣告傳單。

(C) 就在我們辦公室旁邊。

解說 本題關鍵字：**is scheduled to open** 問：「它預定開張嗎？」和 **isn't it**，(B) 你該看一下廣告傳單（間接回答），是正確答案。(A) 不符合題意：小販在賣一些農產品，不能選。(C) 回答地點，不能選。

單字 flyer (n.)（廣告）傳單

10. 一般 Yes / No 問句

Do you work on the budget review committee?

你任職於預算審核委員會嗎？

> 👉 沒有絕對關鍵字，以真正了解題意為重。
> 如果是否定問句，視為一般問句，如下面第 2 題。

(英式女聲) 1. Have you seen my red scarf?

(美式男聲) (A) I haven't met him before.

(B) Yes, they are.

(C) Check the closet.

你看到我的紅圍巾了嗎？

(A) 我以前沒見過他。

(B) 對，他們是。

(C) 去看一下衣櫃。

解 說 (C) 去看一下衣櫥，是正確答案。(A) 不符合題意：我以前沒見過他，不能選。(B) 也不符合題意：對，他們是。

(美式男聲) 2. Aren't you supposed to submit the proposal today?

(美式女聲) (A) Yes, send them to Marketing.

(B) I've already got an extension.

(C) Two weeks ago.

你今天不是該提交提案嗎？

(A) 對，把它們送到行銷部。

(B) 我已經獲准延期了。

(C) 兩週前。

解 說 此題 Aren't 當作 Are 即可。(B) 我已經獲准延期了，是正確答案。(A) 不符合題意：是的，把它們送到行銷部，不能選。(C) 也不符合題意：兩週前。

單字 be supposed to 應該 / submit (v.) 提交 / proposal (n.) 提案
marketing (n.) 行銷（大寫為行銷部）/ extension (n.) 延長

⑥ 11. 二選一問句 ㉟

1. 基礎：Do you speak **Japanese** or **Mandarin**? 你說日文還是中文？
   進階：**Can you help me with this project** or **are you busy right now?** 你能幫我做這個企劃嗎？或是你正在忙？

關鍵在聽懂 **A or B** 兩個選擇，答案通常會重複選項中的關鍵字，或把其中一個選項換句話說，或兩者皆不要，並提供不同的答案。

2. 常見答案（萬用答案）：
   a. 兩個都可以：Either would be nice. 兩個都好。/ Either is fine with me. 兩個我都可以。/ Whichever you want. 哪個都行。
   b. 兩個都不要：Neither, thanks. 都不要，謝謝。/ I don't like either one of them. 兩個我都不要。
   c. 反問：Which would you prefer? 你比較喜歡哪個？

（美式男聲） 1. Would you like to **pay cash** or **charge it**?
（美式女聲）**(A) Do you take travelers' checks?**
   (B) I'm sorry, I think I was **overcharged**.
   (C) Yes, I can help you open an account.

你要付現金還是賒帳？
(A) 你收旅行支票嗎？
(B) 抱歉，我想我被超收費用。
(C) 對，我可以幫你開個帳戶。

解說 本題關鍵字：**pay cash or charge it** 兩個選擇，(A) 是正確答案：你收旅行支票嗎，屬於兩者皆不要，並提供不同的答案。(B) 不符合題意：我想我被超收費用，另外 overcharged 和題目中的 charge 為重複字陷阱，不能選。
(C) 不符合題意：我可以幫你開個帳戶。

英式男聲 2. **Do you want to work the morning shift**, or **are you available later**?

英式女聲 (A) No, I wasn't **late** for the seminar.

(B) **Either one is OK with me.**

(C) Yes, it **works** well for me.

你想上早班嗎？或是你等一下可以排班？

(A) 不，我在研討會時沒有遲到。

(B) 我都可以。

(C) 對，這對我很管用。

解說 本題關鍵字：**Do you want to work the morning shift** 或 **are you available later** 兩個選擇，(B) 是正確答案：兩個我都可以。(A) 不符合題意：我在研討會時沒有遲到，另外 late 和題目中的 later 是重複字陷阱，不能選。(C) 不符合題意：這對我很管用，另外 work 為重複字陷阱，不能選。

單字 shift (n.) 輪班 / available (a.) 有空的、可利用的

D **12.** 陳述句：非問句 36

1. The paper shredder is out of order. 碎紙機故障了

> 沒有絕對關鍵字，以真正了解題意為重。
> 答案也沒有固定說法。

像 who 的句型通常是問「人」，where 的句型通常是問「地點」，但是陳述句的答案可以有很多變化，如上面這題：碎紙機壞了，可以回答：I'll get someone to fix it tomorrow.（我明天找人來修）或 Not again.（不會吧，又壞了）等不同回答，因此又更增加其難度。

2. 答案常用「問句 / 反問」表達，通常反問即是答案

(英式女聲) We'll have to change the conference **venue**.

(美式男聲) (A) Last night's performance went very well.

(B) The **menu** features all kinds of specialty beverages.

(C) Three days before the event?

我們要換會議場地。

(A) 昨晚的表演進行得很順利。

(B) 菜單主打各種特調飲料。

(C) 就在活動前三天？

解說 **(C)** 就在活動前三天？是正確答案。**(A)** 不符合題意：昨晚的表演進行得很順利，不能選。**(B)** 不符合題意：菜單主打各種特調飲料。menu 和 venue 是相似音陷阱，不能選。

單字 venue (n.) 表演、運動比賽、會議等活動的場地
specialty (n.) 招牌菜、特產

多益實戰練習 🎧 37

1. Mark your answer on your answer sheet.

2. Mark your answer on your answer sheet.

3. Mark your answer on your answer sheet.

4. Mark your answer on your answer sheet.

5. Mark your answer on your answer sheet.

6. Mark your answer on your answer sheet.

7. Mark your answer on your answer sheet.

8. Mark your answer on your answer sheet.

9. Mark your answer on your answer sheet.

10. Mark your answer on your answer sheet.

11. Mark your answer on your answer sheet.

12. Mark your answer on your answer sheet.

13. Mark your answer on your answer sheet.

14. Mark your answer on your answer sheet.

15. Mark your answer on your answer sheet.

1. (美式女聲) **Who's** going to **work out** the numbers?
   (美式男聲) **(A) Adrian is doing the calculations now.**
   (B) That would **work out** well for me.
   (C) Yes, the sales figures look good.

   誰要來算這些數字？
   (A) 安卓亞正在算。
   (B) 那對我來說進展得很順利。
   (C) 對，銷售數字看起來不錯。

   解說 本題關鍵字：**Who's**，問「是誰」。(A) 安卓亞即為正確選項。
   (B) 重複字陷阱：work out，此為「進展」的意思，與題意不符。(C)
   不可以有「Yes/No」的回答，直接刪除。

   單字 calculation (n.) 計算 / work out 計算、進展 / sales figures 銷售數字

2. (美式男聲) **Would you like** to **join** the new **fitness** club?
   (英式女聲) (A) Yes, she's the best **fit** for the job.
   (B) No, I'm not interested.
   (C) I **enjoyed** it very much, thanks.

   你要加入新的健身俱樂部嗎？
   (A) 對，她最適合這份工作。
   (B) 不，我沒興趣。
   (C) 我玩得很開心，謝謝。

   解說 本題關鍵字：**Would you like**，提出「邀請」。(B) 是正確答案。
   (A) 不符合題意，重複字陷阱：fit 和 fitness，不能選。(C) 不符合題
   意，相似音陷阱：enjoy 和 join，不能選。

   單字 fitness (n.) 健康 / fit (n.) 適合

3. (美式女聲) Don't we have a box cutter somewhere in the office?
   (英式男聲) **(A) Yes, it's on Aaron's desk.**
   (B) It only cost me ten dollars.
   (C) No, I shouldn't need it.

   我們辦公室不是有美工刀嗎?
   (A) 對,在艾倫的桌上。
   (B) 只花了我十元。
   (C) 不,我不需要。

   解 說 此題 Don't 當作 Do 即可。(A) 是正確答案。(B) 回答費用,不符合
   題意。(C) 不符合題意。

   單字 box cutter 美工刀

4. (美式男聲) Can you go to the event this evening or do you have to **work**
   late?
   (美式女聲) (A) I don't think it would **work** out well for me.
   (B) I think I'll be able to make it.
   (C) Yes, it **was** fantastic.

   今天晚上你能去這場活動嗎?還是要加班?
   (A) 我想這對我來說應該行不通。
   (B) 我想我應該可以去。
   (C) 對,太美妙了。

   解 說 本題關鍵字:能去這場活動嗎?還是要加班?問「兩個選擇」。
   (B) 選擇其一回答:我想我應該可以去,並換句話說,是正確答案。
   (A) 不符合題意,重複字陷阱:work,不能選。(C) 不符合題意,時
   態有誤,不能選。

5. （美式女聲）**Why** are they **clearing out** this area?

（英式男聲）(A) Take them to the dry cleaner around the corner.

(B) They're turning this space into a reception room.

(C) Yes, the area is being **cleared out**.

他們為何在清空這裡？

(A) 把它們拿到街角的乾洗店。

(B) 他們要把這空間改成接待室。

(C) 對，這一區要清空了。

解說 本題關鍵字：**why clearing out**，問「原因」。(B) 是正確答案，because 通常會省略。(A) 回答地點，不能選。(C) 出現 Yes，直接刪除，clear out 是重複字陷阱。

單字 clear out 清空 / dry cleaner 乾洗店 / reception (n.) 接待

6. （美式女聲）Hasn't Mr. Matthews commented on our promotional campaign yet?

（英式女聲）(A) Yes, he has submitted the proposal.

(B) Probably at the end of this month.

(C) He said he'd look at it today.

馬修斯先生評論我們的促銷活動了沒？

(A) 對，他已經提交了提案。

(B) 可能是這個月底。

(C) 他說他今天會看。

解說 此題 Hasn't 當作 Has 即可。(C) 是正確答案，省略 No。(A) 不符合題意。(B) 回答時間，不符合題意。

單字 comment on 評論 / promotional campaign 促銷活動

7. (美式女聲) **What** did Frank **talk** about during his presentation?
   (英式男聲) (A) **Sorry**, I won't be able to make it.
   　　　　(B) **Our most recent sales figures.**
   　　　　(C) Everyone in Marketing was there.

　　　　法蘭克在做口頭報告時說了什麼？
　　　　(A) 抱歉，我去不了。
　　　　(B) 我們最新的銷售數據。
　　　　(C) 行銷部的所有人都在那裡。

解說 本題關鍵字：**what talk**，問「說了什麼」。(B) 是正確答案。
　　　　(A) 不符合題意，Sorry 即為 No，直接刪除。(C) 不符合題意。

8. (美式男聲) Which one of these **ties** do you think looks best on me?
   (美式女聲) (A) **No**, I don't think that one looks suitable.
   　　　　(B) **I like the blue one with stripes.**
   　　　　(C) I'm afraid I'm **tied up** on that day.

　　　　你覺得我戴哪一條領帶最好看？
　　　　(A) 不，我不覺得那條適合。
　　　　(B) 我喜歡藍色有條紋的那條。
　　　　(C) 我擔心那天我會很忙。

解說 本題關鍵字：**ties** 領帶，(B) 我喜歡藍色有條紋的，是正確答案。
　　　　(A) 出現 **No**，直接刪除。(C) 不符合題意，另外出現 tied up（很忙
　　　　／有事）和題目 tie 是重複字陷阱，不能選。

單字 suitable (a.) 適宜的 / stripe (n.) 條紋 / tied up 忙得不可開交的

9. (英式女聲) Did you hear **who**'s going to **take over** the vice president's **position**?

(英式男聲) (A) Send in your **resume**.

(B) Yes, Mr. Fisher, from Japan.

(C) Our company will be **taken over** by a multi-national publisher.

你有聽說誰會接任副總裁一職嗎？

(A) 把你的履歷寄給我。

(B) 是的，來自日本的費雪先生。

(C) 我們公司會由一家跨國出版社接管。

解說 子句型的題目，本題關鍵字：**who take over** 問「誰接任」，(B) 來自日本的費雪先生，是正確答案。(A) 寄送你的履歷，故意用和職缺 position 有關的 resume 這個字來混淆作答，不能選。(C) 不符合題意，另外 take over（重複字陷阱），不能選。

單字 take over 接任、接管 / position (n.) 職位 / resume (n.) 履歷表

10. (美式女聲) Her presentation was based on the data in her survey results.

(美式男聲) (A) I wasn't able to attend.

(B) Was it reliable?

(C) No, I don't think there is enough time.

她的報告是根據調查結果的數據所做。

(A) 我無法參加。

(B) 這數據可靠嗎？

(C) 不，我想時間不夠。

解說 (B) 資料可靠嗎？反問通常是正確答案。(A) 不符合題意：我無法參加，不能選。(C) 也不符合題意：我想時間不夠。

單字 reliable (a.) 可靠的

11. (英式女聲) Your new **book** was **featured** in a magazine article.

(美式男聲) (A) The special **feature** is its slim design.

(B) The **book** has already been checked out.

(C) I can't wait to read it.

有一篇雜誌文章報導你的新書。

(A) 特色是超薄設計。

(B) 這本書已經被借走了。

(C) 我等不及要看了。

解說 (C) 我等不及要看了。是正確答案。(A) 不符合題意，另外選項和題目中的 feature 是重複字陷阱，不能選。(B) 也不符合題意，選項和題目中的 book 是重複字陷阱。

單字 feature (v.) 特寫 / slim (a.) 薄的 / check out 借出

12. (英式女聲) How **long** will the **renovation** take?

(美式男聲) (A) The new model is quite **innovative**.

(B) I'll have to ask our architect.

(C) A few times a month.

整修需要多久？

(A) 新機型相當創新。

(B) 我要問我們的建築師。

(C) 一個月數次。

解說 本題關鍵字：**long**，問「多久」。(B) 表示不知道，要問人。間接回答通常是正確答案。(A) 不符合題意，另外 innovative 和題目中的 renovation 是相似音陷阱，不能選。(C) 回答頻率，不符合題意。

單字 renovation (n.) 整修 / model (n.) 型號 / innovative (a.) 創新的 architect (n.) 建築師

13. (美式女聲) Do you know **where** to **fix** my flash drive?

(英式男聲) (A) He'll be here in twenty minutes.

(B) The **fax** machine is right across the hall.

(C) My brother can do it for you.

你知道哪裡可以修理隨身碟？

(A) 他二十分鐘後就會到這裡。

(B) 傳真機就在大廳對面。

(C) 我兄弟可以幫你修理。

解說 子句型的題目，本題關鍵字：**where fix**，問「哪裡可以修理」。(C) where 的題目可回答「人」，是正確答案。(A) 不符合題意。(B) 回答地點，但是傳真機的位置，不符合題意，且 fax 和題目中的 fix 是相似音陷阱。

單字 flash drive 隨身碟 / fax machine 傳真機

14. (美式女聲) Ms. Milan **updated** the orientation **file**, **didn't she**?

(美式男聲) **(A) Yes, about a week ago.**

(B) Just put it in the **file** cabinet.

(C) She is a corporate trainer.

米蘭女士是不是更新了培訓檔案？

(A) 對，大約一星期前。

(B) 就放在檔案櫃裡。

(C) 她是公司培訓師。

解說 附加問句的題目，本題關鍵字：**updated** 和 **didn't she?** 問「她有更新嗎？」。(A) 是正確答案。(B) 不符合題意，另外選項和題目中的 file 是重複字陷阱，不能選。(C) 不符合題意。

單字 update (v.) 更新 / file (n.) 檔案 / corporate (a.) 公司的

15. (英式女聲) Should I send the parcel by registered **mail** or by regular mail service?

(美式男聲) **(A) Which would you prefer?**

(B) I saw some in the **mailroom**.

(C) Very well, thanks.

　　　我該用掛號還是平信寄這個包裹？

(A) 你比較喜歡哪種？

(B) 我在收發室有看到一些。

(C) 很好，謝謝。

解說 二選一的題目，本題關鍵字：**掛號或平信**？問「兩個選擇」。(A) 反問通常是正確答案。(B) 不符合題意，另外 mailroom 和題目中的 mail 是重複字陷阱，不能選。(C) 沒有回答哪一個，不能選。

單字 parcel (n.) 包裹 / registered mail 掛號 / regular mail 平信

Part 3

簡短對話

▶ 題型介紹

▶ 題目類型：七大題型

A. 基本資訊題   E. 疑難雜症題

B. 動作題   F. 隱含文意題

C. 詢問／要求題   G. 圖表題

D. 建議題

題型介紹：

> 兩人或三人的簡短對話，共 13 篇，每篇有 3 道題目，每道題作答
> 時間為 8 秒鐘。聆聽對話，回答試題本上的題目，其中有 3 篇對
> 話要搭配圖表答題（此為新增題型）。

• 試題本上，每篇有 3 道題目：

題型示範：

你會聽到

Questions 32 through 34 refer to the following conversation.

英式男聲 Good morning. How can I help you, madam?

美式女聲 I'm afraid I'd like to request a refund for the phone I just bought. When I plugged it in, there was no dial tone.

英式男聲 I see. I'm sorry about that. Our store policy is no refunds, but as long as you have your receipt, you can exchange the phone for any model of equal or lesser value. And I'll check to make sure your new phone works properly before you leave the store.

美式女聲 Thank you very much. I'll have a look around then, and decide which one I want.

問題 32 至 34 請參考以下對話。

男： 早安，女士？有什麼我可以為你效勞的嗎？

女： 我恐怕要為我剛買的電話要求退款。我的電話有插上電話線，但沒有撥號音。

男： 我明白了，很抱歉。我們商店的規定是無法退款，但只要你有收據，你可以換同一機型或價格較低的電話。我會在你離開商店前，確保你的新電話能正常運作。

女： 感謝你。那我要先看一下，再決定要換哪一個。

你會看到

32. What problem does the woman have?
    (A) Her order is delayed.
    (B) Her phone isn't working.
    (C) A department lacks funding.
    (D) Some staff is inexperienced.

女子有什麼問題？
(A) 她訂的貨遲到了。
(B) 她的電話不能用。
(C) 有個部門缺少資金。
(D) 有些員工缺乏經驗。

等，共三題。

1 解題重點：

Ⓐ Part 3 高分關鍵：在音檔播放前，快速審閱 3 道題目，掌握**關鍵人 (man/woman)** 和題型。在音檔播放時，仔細**聆聽出題點**。這樣不僅有針對性，能較輕鬆的篩選重點，不需聚精會神的細聽所有內容，大大減少考試的疲累感。

Ⓑ 熟練「七大題型」的解題點，也就是常見答案句型，即可精準定位答案，讓答題事半功倍。請繼續看以下章節，就知道「七大題型」如何解題囉！

Ⓒ Part 3 特色：題順 = 文順，也就是答案會依序出現。**第一題考主旨**，答案在一開頭；而**最後一題通常考說話者接下來即將要做什麼**，答案在最末段。因此按順序聽，掌握文章發展非常重要。

Ⓓ 注意同義表達：和閱讀一樣，聽力非常喜歡把單字用同義替換。**原文聽到的內容，選項通常會換句話說**，不會用到相同的字。所以背單字一定要連同義字一起背，解題才會快速。

Ⓔ **不要邊聽邊畫卡**，很容易分心。應該先在答案卡做記號（例：鉛筆點一下），等所有答案都確定後，一口氣畫 3 題。

2 題目類型：七大題型 Ⓐ ~ Ⓖ (Pp.91~132)

Ⓐ 基本資訊題

1. 和主旨相關題：正解在「前兩句」

題型 What is the conversation mainly about? 這段對話主要是關於什麼？
What are the speakers discussing? 說話者在討論什麼？

解說 對話的前兩句即為主旨。一開始掌握主旨，對後面的文意理解非常重要。所以聽到音檔開始念 Questions 32 through 34 refer to the following conversation. 無論前一篇是否寫完，都要專注聽這篇的前兩句。

2. 地點題：聽「地點相關字」，並透過「上下文」判斷

題型 Where is the conversation (probably) taking place?
這段對話（可能）發生的地點是？
Where (most likely) are the speakers? 說話者（最有可能）在哪裡？

解說 地點要多聽幾個線索，以確認答案。例：當聽到 open an account（開帳戶）、deposit（存款）、loan application（貸款申請）等字眼，就可以判斷地點是「銀行」。

3. 職務題：聽關鍵人「說的話、用的字」判斷身份

題型 Who most likely is the man? 男子最有可能是誰？
Where does the woman probably work? 女子可能在哪裡工作？
What kind of company does the man work for?
男子在哪種公司上班？

解說 工作職務也要多聽幾個線索，以確認答案。例：當聽到關鍵人 (man/woman) 說到 hotel（旅館）、check in（入住）、luggage（行李）等字眼，就可以判斷職務或工作地點是「飯店的工作人員」。

Questions 1 through 3 refer to the following conversation. (38)

美式女聲　Good morning. My name is Christine Meyer. I have a job interview for the marketing position at 10:00 with Mr. John Adams, the head of Personnel.

美式男聲　Yes, Ms. Meyer. ❶ ❷ Mr. Adams is 🔊**interviewing another candidate** at the moment. You can sit in the reception area while you're waiting. ❸ Oh, and can you please fill out this form?

美式女聲　Yes, of course. May I borrow a pen?

美式男聲　Sure. Take your time. I'll call you as soon as Mr. Adams finishes the interview.

問題 **1** 至 **3** 請參考以下對話。

女：早安，我叫克莉絲汀麥爾。我在十點鐘跟人事部門主管約翰亞當先生有行銷職務的面試。

男：好的，麥爾女士。 ❶ ❷ 亞當先生正面試另一位應徵者。妳可以在接待區坐著等一會兒。❸ 噢，能請妳填一下這份表格嗎？

女：好，當然可以，我能借枝筆嗎？

男：可以，慢慢來。等亞當先生面試結束後，我會立刻叫妳。

單字　Interview (n./v.) 面試 / head (n.) 主管
candidate (n.) 應徵者、申請者、候選人 / fill out 填寫

1. Who most likely is the man? 男子最有可能是什麼身分？
   (A) A secretary (A) 秘書
   (B) A receptionist **(B) 接待人員**
   (C) A marketing manager (C) 行銷經理
   (D) A human resources manager (D) 人事經理

   解說 職務題，聽關鍵人「說的話，用的字」判斷身份，線索為：「亞當先生正面試另一位應徵者。你可以在接待區坐著等一會兒。」，表示男子的工作為接待人員，負責接待來公司面試的人，所以答案是 (B)。

   單字 human resources 人事部、人力資源部

2. Where is Mr. Adams? 亞當先生在哪裡？
   (A) He is on his way to the interview. (A) 正在來面試的路上。
   (B) He is in the Marketing Department. (B) 他在行銷部門。
   (C) He is in a meeting with someone. **(C) 在跟某人會面。**
   (D) He is at a business luncheon. (D) 在參加商務午餐會。

   解說 地點題，線索為：「亞當先生正面試另一位應徵者」，表示亞當先生正在和一位應徵者見面，所以答案是 (C)。

   同義替換 interviewing another candidate = in a meeting with someone

3. What does the man ask the woman to do? 男子請女子做什麼？
   (A) Provide some information **(A) 提供一些資料**
   (B) Speak with the Personnel head (B) 跟人事部門主管談話
   (C) Meet with the manager (C) 跟經理見面
   (D) Fill a customer's order (D) 填寫顧客訂單

   解說 詢問／要求題，要聽「詢問資訊」的句型，多為問句，男子：「能請妳填一下這份表格嗎？」，所以答案是 (A)。

   單字 order (n.) 訂單

Questions 4 through 6 refer to the following conversation. 🎧39

> 英式女聲　❹ Our 回**revenues** are down 30 percent this quarter. Anyone have ideas about how to bring them up?
>
> 美式男聲　I think we need to promote more heavily. Our new X-1 is a great product. Once more people know about it, sales will surge. This will create demand for our other products.
>
> 英式女聲　So, are you saying we should spend more money on advertising?
>
> 美式男聲　Not necessarily. ❻ But we should try 回**different advertisements** designed to get the X-1 in customers' hands. And we could hold some live events too.
>
> 英式女聲　Now that's an idea. ❺ Why don't we go over all the details so we can propose this to the marketing manager?

問題 **4** 至 **6** 請參考以下對話。

> 女：❹ 這季營收下降了三成，有人有提升營收的好辦法嗎？
>
> 男：我想我們需要更努力宣傳。我們的新 X-one 是很棒的產品。一旦有更多人知道，銷售量就會激增，這將能創造其他產品的需求。
>
> 女：所以你是說我們該花更多錢打廣告？
>
> 男：不一定。❻ 但為了能讓顧客購買 X-one，我們應該要試試不同的廣告模式，我們也可舉辦一些現場活動。
>
> 女：這倒是個辦法。❺ 我們何不討論一下所有細節，這樣就能向行銷經理提案？

單字　revenue (n.) 收入 / quarter (n.) 季度 / promote (v.) 宣傳、促銷
surge (v) 急遽上升 / demand (n.) 需求 / go over（重新）檢查、審視

4. What are the speakers mainly discussing? 說話者主要在討論什麼？
   (A) How to increase income **(A) 如何增加營收**
   (B) Why sales have declined (B) 銷售量為何下降
   (C) When to advertise a new product (C) 何時推出新產品廣告
   (D) Where to start a business (D) 在哪裡開展新事業

解說 主旨題，答案在「前兩句」：「這季營收下降了三成，有人有提升營收的好辦法嗎？」，所以答案是 (A)。

單字 decline (v./n.) 下跌，衰退

同義替換 revenue = income

5. Where is the conversation probably taking place? 對話的場合可能是哪裡？
   (A) A meeting **(A) 會議上**
   (B) A launch party (B) 發表會上
   (C) A job interview (C) 工作面試時
   (D) An office supply store (D) 辦公用品店內

解說 地點題，要透過「上下文」判斷，線索其一為：「我們何不討論一下所有細節，這樣就能向行銷經理提案？」，全文在討論提高營收的各種方法，最後要向公司提案，所以是一個腦力激盪以解決問題的會議，答案是 (A)。

6. What does the man suggest? 男子提出什麼建議？
   (A) Hiring more staff (A) 雇用更多員工
   (B) Launching new promotional campaigns **(B) 推出新的宣傳廣告**
   (C) Assembling a new project team (C) 組織新專案小組
   (D) Conducting a survey (D) 進行調查

解說 建議題，正解在「男子最後一個說話處」，表建議的常用句型：Why don't we「為了能讓顧客購買 X-one，我們應該要試試不同的廣告模式」，表示想用新的宣傳方式，所以答案是 (B)。

單字 assemble (v.) 集合、聚集

同義替換 try different advertisements = launching new promotional campaigns

B 動作題型：正解在「最後面」，表達「即將要去做」的句型

題型 What does the man say he will do (**tonight**)?
男子說他（今晚）會做什麼？

What does the woman want to do/need to do?
女子想要 / 需要做什麼？

What will the man (probably/most likely) do next?
男子接下來（大概 / 最有可能）會做什麼事？

解說 此高頻題型通常**出現在最後一題**，問「即將要去做的事情」，
所以正解一定在「此關鍵人最後一個說話處」。
當聽到以下句型，即為正解。

常見答案句型

1. **I'll** e-mail Tony now and see if he can help me.
   我會立刻寄電郵給東尼，看他能否幫我。

2. **I'm going to** write up the new budget request right away.
   我會立刻寫新的預算申請書。

3. **Let me** just put these files in the cabinet.
   讓我將這些檔案放進櫃子裡。

4. I have a lot of work to do **tonight** to prepare for tomorrow's company picnic.
   為了準備明天的公司野餐，我今晚有許多工作要做。

   （題目有<u>未來時間點</u>，本身即線索，例如：**tonight**、**next week**、**Friday evening**，聽到表時間的關鍵字，答案就出來了）

Questions 1 through 3 refer to the following conversation. (40)

(美式女聲) Mark, do you have a minute? ❶ I'm trying to (回)**book a venue** for our annual conference, and I need your input.

(英式男聲) Sure, Amelia. What are the choices?

(美式女聲) Well, we could use the convention center, which is very nice, but also quite expensive. The exhibition hall has a lower price, and it's more convenient, but its facilities aren't as nice.

(英式男聲) Hmm. ❷ I think you should call the convention center and see if they'll come down a little. If they do, go with them, and if they don't, go with the exhibition hall.

(美式女聲) Great idea. Thank you, Mark. ❸ Well, I'll get right on it. I have to decide by Friday.

問題 1 至 3 請參考以下對話。

女： 馬克，你有時間嗎？❶ 我想替我們的年度會議預訂場地，我需要你的意見。

男： 當然有，亞美莉亞。有哪些選擇？

女： 我們可以用會議中心，那裡很棒，但也相當貴。展覽廳比較便宜，也比較方便，但設施沒那麼好。

男： 嗯，❷ 你應該打電話給會議中心，看他們會不會降價？如果會，就選他們，如果不會，就選展覽廳。

女： 太好了，謝謝你，馬克。❸ 我立刻去辦，我要在週五前決定。

（單字） input (n.) 投入、意見 / facility (n.) 設施，設備（此定義用複數 facilities）
go with sth 選擇… / get right on 立刻去做

1. What are the speakers mainly discussing? 　　說話者主要在討論什麼？
   (A) Confirming travel plans 　　(A) 確認旅行計畫
   (B) Signing up for a training seminar 　　(B) 報名培訓研討會
   (C) Reserving a space 　　**(C) 預訂場地**
   (D) Attending a concert 　　(D) 參加音樂會

   解說 主旨題，答案在「前兩句」：「我想替我們的年度會議預訂場地，我需要你的意見。」，所以答案是 (C)。

   單字 confirm (v.) 確認 / sign up 報名、註冊

   同義替換 book a venue = reserve a space

2. What does the man suggest? 　　男子提出什麼建議？
   (A) Renewing a contract 　　(A) 續訂合約
   (B) Asking for a discount 　　**(B) 要求優惠**
   (C) Choosing a larger venue 　　(C) 選擇更大的場地
   (D) Revising a company policy 　　(D) 修改公司政策

   解說 建議題，要聽表示建議的常用句型，正解在 you should 後面：「你可以打電話給會議中心，看他們會不會降價。」，所以答案是 (B)。

   單字 renew (v.) 續訂，續約、更換（執照） / discount (n.) 折扣、優惠
   revise (v.) 修改

3. What does the woman most likely do next? 　　女子接下來可能會做什麼？
   (A) Make a phone call 　　**(A) 打電話**
   (B) Visit the exhibition hall 　　(B) 參觀展覽廳
   (C) Schedule an appointment 　　(C) 安排預約
   (D) Pay a deposit 　　(D) 付訂金

   解說 動作題，要聽表動作的常用句型，正解在「女子最後一個說話處」，提到 I'll：「我立刻去辦」，表示女子聽從男子的建議，所以答案是 (A)。

   單字 schedule (v./n.) 安排（計畫、時間表）；時間表 / deposit (n.) 訂金、押金

Questions 4 through 6 refer to the following conversation with three speakers. (41)

(美式男聲) Does anybody want to get some dinner at the restaurant around the corner?

(英式男聲) Yes. Count me in.

(美式女聲) Sorry. ❹ I have to stay and finish my presentation for the staff meeting tomorrow morning. I'm afraid I'm a little bit behind.

(美式男聲) What's it about?

(美式女聲) ❺ I'm going to train everyone how to use the new videoconferencing system.

(英式男聲) Do you need any help with that?

(美式女聲) I might. Do you have any ideas on how to make it easier to understand?

(英式男聲) Will you include a demonstration in your presentation? I always find that helpful.

(美式女聲) Yes, but I need a volunteer who hasn't used the system yet for the demonstration.

(美式男聲) I haven't. You can use me for the demonstration.

(美式女聲) Great. ❻ I'll walk you through the procedure at tomorrow's meeting.

問題 4 至 6 請參考以下三人對話。

男 1： 有人要一起去街角的餐廳吃晚餐嗎？

男 2： 有，算我一份。

女 ： 抱歉，❹ 我要留下來完成明天早上員工會議的簡報。我擔心我有點落後了。

男 1： 你要做什麼簡報？

女 ： ❺ 我要訓練大家使用新的視訊會議系統。

男 2： 你需要幫忙嗎？

女 ： 可能要，你知道怎樣才能讓大家更容易理解嗎？

男 2： 你會在簡報中加入示範嗎？我一直覺得這方法很有用。

女 ： 會，但我需要一個沒用過這系統的志願者幫我示範。

男 1： 我沒用過，你可以拿我當範例。

女 ： 太好了，❻ 明天在會議上我會跟你順一遍流程。

4. Where is the conversation probably taking place?　對話的場合可能是哪裡？
   (A) In a restaurant　(A) 餐廳裡
   (B) At a meeting　(B) 會議上
   (C) In an office　**(C) 辦公室內**
   (D) In a video rental shop　(D) 錄影帶出租店內

   解說 地點題，透過「上下文」判斷，線索為：「我要留下來完成明天早上員工會議的簡報」，晚上時間大家相約要去餐廳吃飯，她必須留下完成工作，所以答案是 (C)。

5. What does the woman say about the presentation?　女子所提到的簡報，何者正確？
   (A) It will be attended by the sales staff.　(A) 業務部門同仁會參加
   (B) Its goal is to train employees.　**(B) 目標是訓練員工**
   (C) It has been postponed.　(C) 已延期
   (D) It will take place over lunch.　(D) 會在午餐時舉行

   解說 一般細節題，聽到女子提到關鍵字 presentation 相關內容即正解：「我要訓練大家使用新的視訊會議系統」。所以答案是 (B)。

6. What does the woman say she will do tomorrow morning?　女子說她明天早上會做什麼？
   (A) Adopt a new procedure　(A) 採用新流程
   (B) Take a short walk　(B) 散步一下
   (C) Demonstrate a new system　**(C) 示範新系統**
   (D) Rehearse for a performance　(D) 排練表演

   解說 動作題，要聽表示動作的常用句型，正解在「女子最後一個說話處」，提到 I'll：「明天在會議上我會跟你順一遍流程」，女子會在會議上示範新系統的使用方法，所以答案是 (C)。

   單字 adopt (v.) 採用／procedure (n.) 程序、步驟
   demonstrate (v./n.) 示範、說明、展示／rehearse (v.) 排演、排練

◉ 詢問 / 要求題：

題型 What does the man ask for/about? 男子在要求 / 詢問什麼？

What does the man request?
男子在要求什麼東西？ / 詢問什麼事情？

What does the man ask the woman to do? 男子請女子做什麼？

解說 關鍵人「詢問資訊 / 要求對方給一些資訊」，答案通常在表達「問句」的句型。當聽到以下句型，即為正解。

常見答案句型

1. **Could you give me** a number where I can reach you?

    能否給我你的聯絡電話？

    → 詢問電話

2. **I was wondering**...?

    → I missed the first part of this morning's seminar, and **I was wondering if** you could fill me in.

    今天上午的研討會我錯過了第一部分，我在想你是否能告訴我內容。

    → 詢問早上研討會的內容

    單字 fill someone in 告訴某人

3. **Would it be okay** if I take a day off tomorrow?

    明天我是否能請一天假？

    → 詢問明天是否可請假

    單字 take a day off 休假

4. **I'm calling to find out** what time the library closes today.

   我打電話來是想詢問圖書館今天的閉館時間。

   → 詢問今天圖書館閉館時間

5. **Do you know** if American Bank has a branch near here?

   你知道美國銀行在這附近是否有分行？

   → 詢問附近是否有美國銀行的分行

6. **I'd like to know more about** the training session.

   我想知道更多關於訓練課程的資訊。

   → 詢問訓練課程資訊

7. **Would you mind** telling Ms. Jackson I'll need the estimate tomorrow?

   你能不能告訴傑克森女士我明天要拿到估價單？

   → 要求對方跟傑克森女士說明天要拿到估價單

8. **Please** send me an e-mail and tell me when the applicant is coming.

   請寄電郵告訴我應徵者何時會來。

   → 要求對方寄 e-mail 告知應徵者何時會來

Questions 1 through 3 refer to the following conversation. (42)

(美式女聲) Hello? ❶ Yes, I'd like to (回)**book a table** for 6 on Thursday at 7:00.

(英式男聲) I'm sorry madam, but we're reserved for a private party that evening. ❷ Can I recommend that you consider another day? We're open from 4:00 to 11:00 at night.

(美式女聲) In that case, let's make it Friday evening at 7:00.

(英式男聲) All right, ma'am. ❸ And could you give me your last name, please?

(美式女聲) Yes. My last name is Forrester.

(英式男聲) All right, Ms. Forrester. We'll be expecting you this Friday at 7:00.

問題 **1** 至 **3** 請參考以下對話。

女： 喂？❶ 是，我想訂位，週四晚上 7 點，六位。

男： 抱歉，女士，但我們那晚已經有私人派對預約，❷ 能建議你考慮其他日期嗎？我們晚上的營業時間是 4 點到 11 點。

女： 既然如此，就訂週五晚上 7 點。

男： 好的，女士，❸ 請問要用什麼名字訂位？

女： 我姓佛斯特。

男： 佛斯特女士，期待你週五 7 點光臨。

單字 expect (v.) 期待、預計

1. What are the speakers mainly discussing? 說話者主要在討論什麼？

   (A) A restaurant reservation (A) 餐廳訂位

   (B) A meeting agenda (B) 會議議程

   (C) A plan for a party (C) 派對計畫

   (D) A hotel room booking (D) 訂旅館房間

   解說 主旨題，答案在「前兩句」：「是，我想訂位，週四晚上 7 點，六位」，所以答案是 (A)。

   單字 agenda (n.) 議程、待辦事項

   同義替換 book a table = restaurant reservation

2. What does the man suggest the woman do? 男子建議女子做什麼？

   (A) Go to a different restaurant (A) 去其他餐廳

   (B) Hold a party on Friday (B) 週五辦派對

   (C) Make a reservation online (C) 上網訂位

   (D) Come to the restaurant on another day (D) 預訂其他日子

   解說 建議題，要聽表建議的常用句型，正解在 Can I recommend 後面：「能建議你考慮其他日期嗎？」，所以答案是 (D)。

3. What information does the man ask for? 男子詢問什麼資訊？

   (A) The number of people (A) 人數

   (B) A credit card number (B) 信用卡號碼

   (C) A name to put the booking under (C) 訂位的大名

   (D) The reservation date (D) 訂位的日期

   解說 詢問 / 要求題，要聽「詢問對方」的句型（多為問句）。男子：「請問要用什麼名字訂位？」，所以答案是 (C)。

Questions 4 through 6 refer to the following conversation. (43)

(美式男聲) Susan, ❹ when will the new Matrix 2.0 🔲MP3 player be on the market in Asia?

(美式女聲) ❹ Well, we were planning on releasing it across Malaysia and Japan this month, before expanding to the rest of Asia later this year. ❺ But unfortunately, we've had to delay the launch as we 🔲haven't reached a deal yet with local distributors.

(美式男聲) Oh, that's a pity. ❻ So, do you know when the launch date is now set for?

(美式女聲) We've just finished negotiations with a Korean company, so the product should be on the market there in July. Hopefully, the other countries in the region won't be far behind.

問題 4 至 6 請參考以下對話。

男：蘇珊，❹ 新款 MP3 播放器 Matrix 2.0 何時在亞洲市場上市？

女：❹ 我們計畫這個月在馬來西亞和日本各地發表，之後再拓展到亞洲其他地方。❺ 但很不幸，我們要延後推出，因為我們還沒跟當地經銷商達成協議。

男：噢，可惜了。❻ 那你知道目前的發表日期訂在什麼時候嗎？

女：我們剛跟韓國公司完成協商，所以產品應該會 7 月在那裡上市。希望亞洲其他國家不會落後太多。

單字 release (v.) 發表，發行 / expand (v.) 擴大，擴展 / reach a deal 達成協議 distributor (n.) 經銷商 / negotiation (n.) 協商

4. What kind of company does the woman work for?

　　女子在哪種公司上班？

(A) **Electronics**
(B) Consulting
(C) Publishing
(D) Advertising

(A) **電子產品**
(B) 顧問公司
(C) 出版社
(D) 廣告公司

解說 職務題，線索為：男子詢問「新款 MP3 播放器 Matrix 2.0 何時在亞洲市場上市？」，女子回答「我們計畫這個月在馬來西亞和日本各地發表」，表說話者公司的產品為 MP3 播放器，所以答案是 (A)。

同義替換 electronics = MP3 player

5. Why was the launch date postponed?

　　發表日期為何要延期？

(A) The products are in short supply.
(B) **Distribution agreements weren't reached.**
(C) The exact location is still under negotiation.
(D) The Asian market has been sluggish.

(A) 產品供應量不足
(B) **未達成經銷協議**
(C) 仍在商議確切地點
(D) 亞洲市場不景氣

解說 一般細節題，聽關鍵字 launch 相關內容即正解：「但很不幸，我們要延後推出，因為我們還沒跟當地經銷商達成協議」。所以答案是 (B)。

單字 supply (n.) 供應量 / sluggish (a.) 遲緩的

同義替換 haven't reached a deal yet with local distributors = distribution agreements weren't reached

6. What does the man inquire about?

　　男子詢問什麼？

(A) The date of an upcoming seminar
(B) **The timing of a product launch**
(C) The location of some distributors
(D) The venue of an important event

(A) 即將舉辦的研討會日期
(B) **產品的發表時間**
(C) 部分經銷商的地點
(D) 重要活動的場地

解說 詢問／要求題，要聽「詢問對方」的句型（多為問句）。男子：「那你知道目前的發表日期訂在什麼時候嗎？」，所以答案是 (B)。

D 建議題型：正解通常在「最後面」

> **題型** What does the woman suggest/recommend the man do?
> 女子建議 / 提議男子怎麼做？
>
> What does the woman offer to do/tell others do?
> 女子有什麼提議 / 告訴對方怎麼做？

> **解說** 此高頻題型通常**考在最後一題**，關鍵人「建議 / 提議對方怎麼做」。
> 正解一定在「此關鍵人最後一個說話處」。當聽到以下建議句型，
> 即為正解。

常見答案句型

A: 1) **If I were you, I'd +** 原 **V...**
　　我若是你，我會…

2) **I suggest / advise / recommend...**
　　我提議 / 勸告 / 建議…

3) **Why don't you / How about...**
　　你何不 / 怎麼樣…　　　　　　　　　+ 建議內容 / 事項

4) **You** (I) **could/can/should...**
　　你（我）可以 / 能 / 應該…

5) 命令句 **/ Let's...**
　　讓我們…

E.g. **Why don't we** go over all the details so we can propose this to the manager?

→ **建議**：仔細看所有細節，向經理提案

I can have the delivery driver drop them off at your office tomorrow morning.

→ **提議**：我可以叫貨運司機明天早上把東西送到您的辦公室。

NOTE

Questions 1 through 3 refer to the following conversation. (44)

> (美式男聲) Good morning. ❶ This is Corton Contractors, here to assist you with all your home needs. How may I help you?
>
> (英式女聲) Hi. ❶ My name's Kelly Larsen, and one of your colleagues came to my house yesterday and gave me an estimate for remodeling my basement. I'd like to accept the bid and have the job done, but I'm not sure how to proceed.
>
> (美式男聲) Let's see. Larsen... oh, here it is. ❷ Well, you should get a permit from the city planning office for the construction work, and from City Light for the electrical wiring. Then you can call us back to schedule the job for some time next month.
>
> (英式女聲) ❸ OK, but I thought you'd be able to start next week. At least, that's what your colleague told me.

問題 1 至 3 請參考以下對話。

> 男： 早安，❶ 我是柯頓承包商，可以協助滿足你的住家需求，請問有什麼能幫你的？
>
> 女： 嗨，❶ 我叫凱莉拉森，你的同事昨天來我家，幫我的地下室裝修估價，我想接受你們的報價，請你們完成裝修工作，但我不知道怎麼著手。
>
> 男： 我看看，拉森⋯噢，找到了。❷ 嗯，你要向市府規劃辦公處申請施工許可，向城市電力公司申請安裝電線，再回電給我們，安排下月動工。
>
> 女： ❸ 好，但我以為你們可以下週動工。至少那是你同事告訴我的。

單字 assist (v.) 協助、幫助 / colleague (n.) 同事，同僚 / estimate (n.) 估價、估計（數） / remodel (v.) 整修 / bid (n.) 報價 / proceed (v.) 開始進行、繼續進行 / permit (n.) 許可證、執照 / construction (n.) 建造，施工

1. What type of business does the man work for?
   (A) Plumbing
   (B) Electrical
   (C) Home improvement
   (D) Garden landscaping

   男子提供什麼服務？
   (A) 水電工程服務
   (B) 電力公司
   (C) 房屋修繕
   (D) 花園造景

   解說 職務題，線索為：男子說「我是柯頓承包商，可以協助滿足你的住家需求」，女子說「你的同事昨天來我家，幫我的地下室裝修估價」，表男子的是和房屋修繕有關，所以答案是 (C)。

2. What does the man tell the woman to do?
   (A) Obtain a new estimate
   (B) Make a bid on the property
   (C) Hire workers from the city planning office
   (D) Apply for permits

   男子要女子做什麼？
   (A) 取得新的估價
   (B) 競標房子
   (C) 雇用市府規劃辦公處的人
   (D) 申請許可證

   解說 建議題，要聽表建議的常用句型，正解在 You should 後面：「你要向市府規劃辦公處申請施工許可」，所以答案是 (D)。

3. When did the woman expect the work to start?
   (A) Right away
   (B) Next week
   (C) Next month
   (D) Later this week

   女子以為何時可以開始施工？
   (A) 立刻
   (B) 下星期
   (C) 下個月
   (D) 這星期稍晚

   解說 一般細節題，聽到女子提到關鍵字 start 相關內容即正解：「好，但我以為你們可以下週動工。」。所以答案是 (B)。

Questions 4 through 6 refer to the following conversation with three speakers. 45

(英式男聲) ❹ Hi, Roy. Hi, Angela. Would either of you be able to work this weekend? Superior Computer Company wants us to deliver their order a week early. I need at least five more people to help out on the assembly line.

(美式女聲) ❺ Oh, I'm afraid I can't. I'll be working the night shift on the weekend.

(美式男聲) I could use the extra money. I do have an appointment with a client on Saturday morning, but I'll see if I can reschedule it.

(英式男聲) OK, Roy. Let me know when you find out. I'm going to call around and see if any other staff members are available.

(美式女聲) ❻ Why don't you try calling Jeff? He was saying that he needs extra hours.

(英式男聲) Great! I'll do that right now.

問題 4 至 6 請參考以下三人對話。

男1： ❹ 嗨，羅伊、安琪拉，你們誰可以在這週末上班？優越電腦公司要我們提早一星期把訂貨送去。我還需要至少五位同仁幫忙裝配線。

女： ❺ 噢，我恐怕不行。我週末要上晚班。

男2： 我可以賺這筆加班費，我其實週六早上跟客戶有約，但我會看看能不能改期。

男1： 好，羅伊，等你確定就告訴我。同時我要打電話看看其他同仁有沒有空。

女： ❻ 你何不打給傑夫？他才剛說過他需要賺加班費。

男1： 太棒了！我立刻打給他。

單字 client (n.) 客戶

4. What is the conversation mainly about?　對話主要是關於什麼？
    (A) Scheduling a meeting　　　　　(A) 安排會議
    (B) Finding out the hours of operation　(B) 找出營業時間
    (C) Working a weekend shift　　**(C) 安排週末輪班**
    (D) Assembling auto parts　　　　(D) 組裝汽車零件

解說 主旨題，答案在「前兩句」：「嗨，羅伊、安琪拉，你們誰可以在這週末上班？」，所以答案是 (C)。

單字 hours of operation 營業時間

5. Why does the woman mention the night shift?　女子為何提到晚班？
    (A) To explain her work schedule　**(A) 為了解釋工作時間表**
    (B) To ask for assistance　　　　(B) 要求協助
    (C) To offer her service　　　　　(C) 提供服務
    (D) To switch work shifts　　　　(D) 換班

解說 一般細節題，聽到女子提到關鍵字 night shift 相關內容即正解：「噢，我恐怕不行。我週末要上晚班」。女子不能週末輪班，提出週末晚上要上班來解釋原因。所以答案是 (A)。

6. What does the woman suggest the man do?　女子建議男子怎麼做？
    (A) Consult a job placement agency　(A) 諮詢就業機構
    (B) Contact an employee　　　**(B) 聯絡員工**
    (C) Hire temporary workers　　　(C) 聘請臨時工
    (D) Arrange a meeting　　　　　(D) 安排會議

解說 建議題，要聽表建議的常用句型，正解在「女子最後一個說話處」，提到 Why don't you：「你何不打給傑夫？」，所以答案是 (B)。

單字 job placement 就業、介紹工作 / employee (n.) 員工
temporary (a.) 暫時的

E 疑難雜症題型：正解在「負面字眼」

題型　What happened to the man? 男子發生什麼事？
　　　What is the man's woman's problem? 男子／女子遇到什麼問題？
　　　What's wrong with the coffee maker? 咖啡機出了什麼問題？

解說　此題型考關鍵人「碰到什麼疑難雜症」，也就是負面的事情。只要聽
　　　到類似以下負面字眼，即為正解。

常見答案句型

The trip/service is **terrible**. 這行程／服務很糟糕。

My phone **isn't working well**. 我的電話有問題。

The bus/flight is **late/delayed**. 公車／航班遲到／延遲。

The printer **ran out of** ink. 印表機沒墨水了。

I'm **worried** that... 我擔心…

I'm **concerned about**... 我擔憂…

I'm **afraid** that... 我怕…

I'm **sorry**... 很遺憾…

I can't... 我不能…

I won't be able to... 我無法…

例句：

1. I **worry** that our research group lacks experience.
   我擔心我們的研究小組沒有經驗。

2. **I can't** log on to my computer. 我無法登入電腦。

   I can't find my budget report. 我找不到我的預算報告。

NOTE

Questions 1 through 3 refer to the following conversation. 🎧46

(美式男聲) Sophie, have we received a fax from Oliver at Maple Computers yet?

(英式女聲) ❶ Not yet. I called, and they said they were having problems with their fax machine. They're trying to fix it.

(美式男聲) ❷ Mr. O'Connor needs to review that document as soon as possible. It's the new service contract for our office equipment.

(英式女聲) ❸ I'll phone Oliver and see how it's coming along. If the machine's still down, I'll have him scan and e-mail it instead. Either way, I'll rush it to Mr. O'Connor's office as soon as it arrives.

問題 1 至 3 請參考以下對話。

男： 蘇菲，收到楓葉電腦公司奧利維的傳真了嗎？

女： ❶ 還沒，我打過電話，他們說他們的傳真機出了問題，正在想辦法修理。

男： ❷ 歐康諾先生要盡快審核文件，那是我們辦公室設備的新服務合約。

女： ❸ 我會打電話給奧利維，看他們的情況如何。如果傳真機還沒修好，我會請他掃描後用電郵傳給我。不論哪種方式，等我收到會盡快送到歐康諾先生的辦公室。

單字 document (n.) 文件 / come along 發展、進展
down (a.)（尤指電腦等機器或系統）停止運作

1. What problem do the speakers have?　　　說話者遇到什麼問題？

   (A) A document is missing.　　　(A) 文件遺失。

   (B) An invoice is incorrect.　　　(B) 帳單不正確。

   (C) They haven't received an important fax.　　**(C) 尚未收到重要傳真。**

   (D) The copy machine is not working properly.　　(D) 影印機出問題。

   > **解說**　疑難雜症題，要聽「負面字眼」：「還沒，我打過電話，他們說他們的傳真機出了問題，正在想辦法修理」，表示尚未收到傳真，所以答案是 (C)。

   > **單字**　invoice (n.) 費用清單、發票

2. What document does Mr. O'Connor want to see?　　　歐康諾先生要看什麼文件？

   (A) The new service contract　　**(A) 新服務合約**

   (B) The quarterly sales report　　　(B) 季度銷售報告

   (C) The revised magazine article　　　(C) 修改過的雜誌文章

   (D) The upcoming meeting agenda　　　(D) 即將召開的會議議程

   > **解說**　一般細節題，聽到關鍵字 Mr. O'Connor 相關內容即正解：「歐康諾先生要盡快審核文件，那是我們辦公室設備的新服務合約」。所以答案是 (A)。

3. What does the woman probably do next?　　　女子接下來可能會做什麼事？

   (A) Fix the fax machine　　　(A) 修理傳真機

   (B) Make a phone call　　**(B) 打電話**

   (C) Review a contract　　　(C) 審核合約

   (D) Visit Mr. O'Connor's office　　　(D) 去歐康諾先生的辦公室

   > **解說**　動作題，要聽表示動作的常用句型，正解在「女子最後一個說話處」，提到 I'll：「我會打電話給奧利維，看他們的情況如何」，所以答案是 (B)。

Questions 4 through 6 refer to the following conversation. (47)

(美式女聲) ❹ Thomas, did you contact technical support about my computer? I'm working on an important presentation, and all my work is on that computer.

(英式男聲) Yes, I called them. They told me they'd send someone over tomorrow afternoon.

(美式女聲) Tomorrow afternoon? That will be too late. ❺ I'm meeting with my clients at 2:00 tomorrow to discuss ways to promote their products. Could you please call tech support again, and ask them if they can come any earlier?

(英式男聲) Sure, I'll call them right away. ❻ I'll talk to a supervisor to make sure they get a technician over here today.

問題 4 至 6 請參考以下對話。

女：❹ 湯瑪斯，你聯絡過技術支援人員來修我的電腦嗎？我在做重要的報告，我的報告都在電腦裡。

男：有，我打給他們了。他們說明天下午會派人過來。

女：明天下午？那太晚了。❺ 我明天下午兩點要見客戶，討論怎麼宣傳他們的產品。能請你再打給技術支援，請他們早點來嗎？

男：好，我立刻打給他們。❻ 我會跟主管談，確保他們今天派技術人員過來。

單字　technical support（有關如何使用電腦的）技術支援
　　　supervisor (n.) 主管、上司

4. What is the woman concerned about? 女子在擔心什麼？
    (A) When computer software will be installed
    (A) 電腦軟體何時會安裝
    (B) When a shipment will arrive
    (B) 貨何時會運到
    (C) When a technician will come
    (C) 技術人員何時會來
    (D) When the payment will be made
    (D) 何時會付款

解說 疑難雜症題，要聽「負面字眼」：「湯瑪斯，你聯絡過技術支援人員來修我的電腦嗎？」，表示電腦維修人員還沒來，所以答案是 (C)。

單字 install (v.) 安裝，裝置

5. What will the woman do at 2 o'clock 女子明天下午兩點要
    tomorrow? 做什麼？
    (A) Discuss a budget proposal
    (A) 討論預算提案
    (B) Meet some clients
    (B) 見客戶
    (C) Contact a supplier
    (C) 聯絡供應商
    (D) Demonstrate the products
    (D) 展示產品

解說 一般細節題，聽到女子提到關鍵字 2 o'clock tomorrow 相關內容即正解：「我明天下午兩點要見客戶，討論怎麼宣傳他們的產品」。所以答案是 (B)。

6. What does the man plan to do next? 男子打算接下來做什麼？
    (A) Contact a building superintendent
    (A) 聯絡大樓管理員
    (B) Speak to a supervisor
    (B) 跟主管談
    (C) Schedule an inspection online
    (C) 上網預約檢查
    (D) Resolve a technical problem
    (D) 解決技術問題

解說 動作題，要聽表示動作的常用句型，正解在「男子最後一個說話處」，提到 I'll：「我會跟主管談，確保他們今天派技術人員過來」，所以答案是 (B)。

單字 superintendent (n.) 管理員，負責人 / inspection (n.) 檢查、審視

F 隱含文意題型（新制多益新增題型）

題型 What does the woman mean when she says,
"I can't believe it"?
女子說的「我不敢相信」是什麼意思？

What does the man mean when he says,
"I've been meaning to contact him"?
男子說的「我一直打算聯絡他」是什麼意思？

解說 此題型在考，考生是否了解上下文文意。一定要先預覽，且牢記題目
的「隱含文意句」，聽到**關鍵人**說出**關鍵句**時，連結前後文，統整聽
到的內容。

NOTE

Questions 1 through 3 refer to the following conversation. (48)

(英式女聲) ❶ Hello, I'm interested in your online course on marketing strategy.

(英式男聲) Great, but you'd better sign up quick. Enrollment for this seminar closes on Friday.

(英式女聲) Right, that's the thing. ❷ I have a busy schedule at work for the first few weeks of the semester. Would it be possible for me to start the course three weeks later?

(英式男聲) I'm afraid not. ❸ But the same course is offered next semester, so you can 回**sign up** then.

問題 1 至 3 請參考以下對話。

女： ❶ 你好，我對你們的行銷策略網路課程有興趣。

男： 太好了，但你最好快點註冊。這學期的註冊在週五截止。

女： 對，就是這件事，❷ 這學期頭幾個星期我有工作要忙，我可以晚三個星期上課嗎？

男： 恐怕不行，❸ 但下學期也有同樣課程，所以你可以到時再註冊。

單字　strategy (n.) 策略，計謀 / enrollment (n.) 註冊、登記 / semester (n.) 學期

1. What course does the woman want to enroll in?

   女子想註冊什麼課程？

   (A) Market research
   (B) Web page design
   (C) Accounting system
   (D) Marketing strategy

   (A) 市場調查
   (B) 網頁設計
   (C) 會計系統
   (D) 行銷策略

   解說 一般細節題，聽到女子提到關鍵字 course 和 enroll in 相關內容即正解：「你好，我對你們的行銷策略網路課程有興趣」。女子表達有興趣，意即想報名。所以答案是 (D)。

2. What does the woman mean when she says, "Right, that's the thing"?

   女子說的「對，就是這件事」是什麼意思？

   (A) She is afraid she can't finish her work on time.
   (B) She wants to raise her concern.
   (C) The course is too difficult for her.
   (D) She doesn't have regular Internet access.

   (A) 她擔心無法按時完成工作
   (B) 她想提出她的顧慮
   (C) 課程對她來說太難
   (D) 她沒有固定的網路連線

   解說 隱含文意題，要結合上下文，推論出題目 "Right, that's the thing" 的意思，正解在：女子說「這學期頭幾個星期我有工作要忙，我可以晚三個星期上課嗎？」，女子想在報名前確認：因時間上不能配合，晚點來上課是否可行？以解決她的疑慮，所以答案是 (B)。

3. What does the man suggest the woman do?

   男子建議女子怎麼做？

   (A) Sign a document
   (B) Register for next semester
   (C) Take an alternative course
   (D) Adjust her work schedule

   (A) 簽署文件
   (B) 下學期再註冊
   (C) 註冊其他課程
   (D) 調整工作時間

   解說 建議題，要聽表示建議的常用句型，正解在「男子最後一個說話處」，提到 you can：「但下學期也有同樣課程，所以你可以到時再註冊」，所以答案是 (B)。

   同義替換 sign up = register for

Questions 4 through 6 refer to the following conversation. (49)

(美式男聲) Carol, are you good with new technology? ❹ I bought this new tablet, but I can't seem to 回**get it to work**.

(美式女聲) Sorry, but I'm no expert either. ❺ Why don't you read the instruction manual? I'm sure it will explain how to set it all up.

(美式男聲) I tried, but it didn't really help. Would you mind looking over the manual to see if you can figure it out? It's in my office.

(美式女聲) ❻ Sure. I'll meet you down there after I get back from the sales meeting.

(美式男聲) I really appreciate it. See you then.

問題 4 至 6 請參考以下對話。

男： 凱洛，你會用新科技嗎？❹ 我買了新平板，但似乎不太會用。

女： 抱歉，我也不是專家。❺ 你何不看一下說明書？我相信上面會有清楚的設定說明。

男： 我試過了，但沒什麼用。你能不能幫我看一下說明書，看是不是能找出問題？它在我的辦公室。

女： ❻ 好，等我開完銷售會議，我會去那裡找你。

男： 真是太感謝你了，到時候見。

單字 tablet (n.) 平板電腦 / instruction (n.) 使用指南、操作說明

4. What problem does the man mention? 　男子提到什麼問題？
   (A) His tablet hasn't been upgraded. 　(A) 他的平板還沒升級
   (B) He doesn't know how to operate a 　**(B) 他不知道怎麼操作**
   　　new device. 　　**新裝置**
   (C) An item he purchased is defective. 　(C) 他買的物品有瑕疵
   (D) He can't decide which tablet to 　(D) 他無法決定要買哪個
   　　purchase. 　　平板

解說 疑難雜症題，要聽「負面字眼」：「我買了新平板，但似乎不太會用」，
表示他不知道如何使用，所以答案是 (B)。

單字 device (n.) 設備、裝置

同義替換 operate = get it to work

NEW
5. What does the woman mean when she says, 女子說「抱歉，我也不是
   "Sorry, but I'm no expert either"? 　專家」時是什麼意思？
   (A) She doesn't know a lot about 　**(A) 她不懂電子**
   　　electronic devices. 　　**裝置**
   (B) She can't find a professional to deal with (B) 她找不到專家
   　　the problem. 　　來解決這個問題
   (C) She doesn't know where to get the 　(C) 她不知道要將機器
   　　machine fixed. 　　送去哪裡修理
   (D) She lacks experience for a new project. (D) 她缺乏新專案的經驗

解說 隱含文意題，要結合上下文，推論出題目 "Sorry, but I'm no expert either"
的意思，正解在：女子說「你何不看一下說明書？我相信上面會有清楚的
設定說明」，女子建議男子看說明書會更清楚，表示女子也不太確定如何
操作平板，所以答案是 (A)。

6. What will the woman do next? 　女子接下來會做什麼？
   (A) Attend a meeting 　**(A) 參加會議**
   (B) Look over a menu 　(B) 查看電腦上的功能選單
   (C) Visit a client 　(C) 見客戶
   (D) Return to her office 　(D) 回她的辦公室

解說 動作題，要聽表示動作的常用句型，正解在「女子最後一個說話處」，提
到 I'll：「好，等我開完銷售會議，我會去那裡找你」，表示女子即將去開會，
結束後再去找男子，所以答案是 (A)。

G 圖表題型 （新制多益新增題型）

題型

Look at the graphic. Which of the **ingredients** does the **man** express **concern about**?

(A) Fat
(B) Protein
(C) Sugar
(D) Sodium

請看圖表，男子關心哪個成分？

(A) 脂肪
(B) 蛋白質
(C) 糖
(D) 鈉

Nutrition Information	
Serving size: 200 grams Calories:	**150**
	Amount per serving
Fat	5 grams
Protein	11 grams
Sugar	32 grams
Sodium	40 milligrams

營養標示	
份量：200 克 卡路里：	**150**
	每一份量
脂肪	5 克
蛋白質	11 克
糖	32 克
鈉	40 毫克

（此為官方指南例題）

解說 考生需同時專注圖表和聽文章，並整合內容作答。不僅閱讀速度要快，解析資訊的能力也很重要。因此，洪欣老師獨創『秒殺三步驟』，讓大家考試不手忙腳亂，迅速了解圖表解題線索。

秒殺三步驟：

→ **解題步驟一：預覽題目，找出關鍵人 (man/woman) 和其他關鍵字**
根據以上例題：ingredients、man、concern about（男子對哪個成分感到擔心？）

→ **解題步驟二：找到選項和圖表內容的關聯性。**
根據以上例題：只須看選項和圖表相關聯的四個成分，及其相對應的劑量（數字），如下圖框起來的部分，其他多餘資訊不用看。

Nutrition Information
Serving size: 200 grams
Calories: **150**

Amount per serving

Fat	5 grams
Protein	11 grams
Sugar	32 grams
Sodium	40 milligrams

→ **解題步驟三：聽到關鍵人說出關鍵字，搭配圖表答題**
根據以上例題：關鍵人 (man) 一定不會提到圖表中的四個成分，而是提到擔心的「劑量」（數字）。所以同學們要把重心放在右邊的劑量，也就是關鍵字，當聽到相關數字，馬上對照左邊的成分，答案即出現。

Questions 1 through 3 refer to the following conversation and graph. (50)

(美式男聲) ❶ The latest sales figures for our new vacuum cleaner are out. After we ran our TV advertisement in May, we saw an increase in sales in all cities.

(美式女聲) That's great news. ❷ But I think our best-performing market for this vacuum cleaner has even more potential than we expected. So I suggest we focus on social media ads there next month to reach people who may not have seen our ad on TV.

(美式男聲) Are you sure we can afford that? Our budget is very tight this quarter.

(美式女聲) I'm sure Finance will approve it, but could you write up a new budget request for those ads?

(美式男聲) ❸ Sure. I can start on that right now.

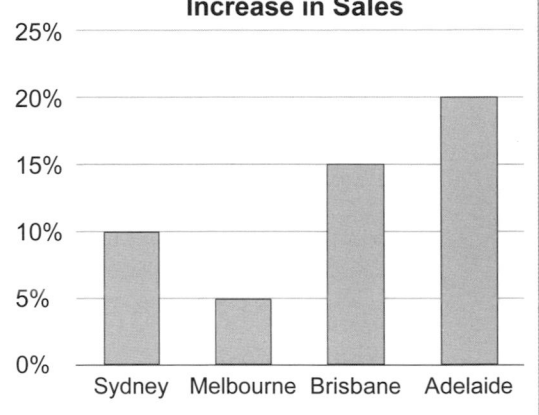

Increase in Sales

問題 1 至 3 請參考以下對話和圖表。

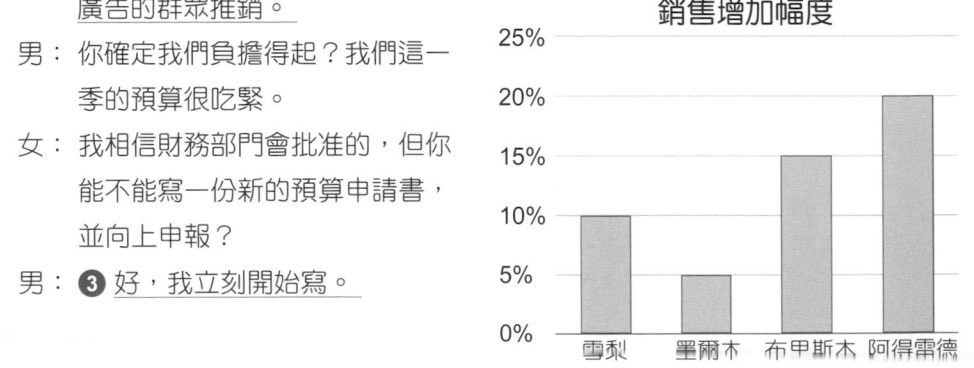

男： ❶ 我們新吸塵器的最新銷售數據出來了。我們在五月播放電視廣告後，各城市的銷售量都有上升。

女： 真是好消息。❷ 但我想這吸塵器在表現最佳的市場，前景比我們所預期還要好，所以我建議下個月可以將重心放在社群媒體網站，向沒有看到電視廣告的群眾推銷。

男： 你確定我們負擔得起？我們這一季的預算很吃緊。

女： 我相信財務部門會批准的，但你能不能寫一份新的預算申請書，並向上申報？

男： ❸ 好，我立刻開始寫。

銷售增加幅度

1. Which department do the speakers most likely work in?
   (A) Sales
   (B) IT
   (C) Finance
   (D) Purchasing

   說話者可能是哪個部門？
   (A) 業務部門
   (B) 資訊部門
   (C) 財務部門
   (D) 採購部門

解說 職務題，線索為：「我們新吸塵器的最新銷售數據出來了。我們在五月播放電視廣告後，各城市的銷售量都有上升。」，說話者在討論銷售數據和銷售量，所以答案是 (A)。

2. Look at the graphic. In which city will the company probably launch a social media campaign?
   (A) Sydney
   (B) Melbourne
   (C) Brisbane
   (D) Adelaide

   請看圖表，該公司可能會在哪座城市展開社群媒體廣告活動？
   (A) 雪梨
   (B) 墨爾本
   (C) 布里斯本
   (D) 阿得雷德

解說 根據圖表題『秒殺三步驟』，步驟一：題目問在哪座城市展開社群媒體廣告活動，步驟二：找選項和圖表關聯處（四座城市），步驟三：音檔絕對不會唸到城市的名稱，而是唸相對應的百分比，所以要仔細聆聽和百分比相關的內容（銷售增加幅度）。原文中女子提到「但我想這吸塵器在表現最佳的市場，前景比我們所預期還要好，所以我建議下個月可以將重心放在社群媒體網站，向沒有看到電視廣告的群眾推銷」，當聽到表現最佳的市場，得知是百分比最高 (20%) 的城市，所以答案是 (D)。

3. What does the man say he will do?
   (A) Approve an advertising campaign
   (B) Start a new business
   (C) Write a budget proposal
   (D) Compile data from websites

   男子說他接下來會怎麼做？
   (A) 批准廣告活動
   (B) 展開新業務
   (C) 寫預算申請書
   (D) 收集網站資料

解說 動作題，要聽表示動作的常用句型，正解在「男子最後一個說話處」，提到 I can：「好，我立刻開始寫」，表示男子聽從女子的要求，寫一份預算申請書，所以答案是 (C)。

單字 approve (v.) 批准、同意

(美式男聲) Hi, I'm looking to buy a TV. I was thinking about getting one of those HDTVs, but I don't know much about them.

(英式女聲) Basically HDTV gives you much higher resolution. ❹ We have many types of HDTVs, ranging from 29 inches to 56 inches. ❺ I should also add that for all TV purchases over $2,000, you get a ●**free** DVD player and 10% off any speaker set you wish to buy with your TV.

(美式男聲) Wow, that's a pretty good deal. ❻ However, my budget is $1,500 maximum. I'm not too sure about getting speakers yet; I just want to get the largest screen that falls within that price.

(英式女聲) OK, I've got an excellent choice for you. Take a look at this one. This is an LED flat screen and comes with a two-year warranty.

(美式男聲) OK, that's perfect. Do you take credit card?

Casa Hi-Tech Store

Flat Panel Screen Size	Price
29 inches	$899
38 inches	$1299
42 inches	$1499
56 inches	$2099

單字 resolution (n.) 解析度 / purchase (n./v.) 購買，採購
warranty (n.) 保固、保證書

問題 **4** 至 **6** 請參考以下對話和圖表。

男： 嗨，我想買電視，我在考慮買那種高畫質電視，但我不是很瞭解這類電視。

女： 高畫質電視基本上解析度比較高。❹ 我們有許多不同類型的高畫質電視，從 29 吋到 56 吋都有。❺ 我要補充一下，凡購買售價超過 2000 元的電視，可以獲得一台 DVD 播放器，加購音響系統還可以打九折。

男： 哇，很划算，❻ 但我的預算最多是 1500 元，我還不確定要不要買音響，我只想在預算內購買螢幕尺寸最大的電視。

女： 好，我可以提供你很不錯的選擇。看一下這個，這是薄型平面顯示器，附有兩年保固。

男： 好，那就選這個了，你們收信用卡嗎？

卡沙高科技商店

薄型平面螢幕尺寸	價格
29 吋	$899
38 吋	$1299
42 吋	$1499
56 吋	$2099

4. Where is the conversation probably taking place?

   (A) An electronics store
   (B) An auto repair shop
   (C) A movie theater
   (D) An office equipment store

   對話的場合可能是在哪裡？

   (A) 電器用品店
   (B) 汽車修理店
   (C) 電影院
   (D) 辦公室用品店

> **解說** 地點題，透過「上下文」判斷，線索為：「我們有許多不同類型的高畫質電視」，另外還可聽出店中有 DVD 播放器和音響系統，綜合這些商品內容，可知地點為電器用品店，所以答案是 (A)。

5. What will the man get if he makes a purchase over $2,000?

   (A) A 10% discount on a future purchase
   (B) A free microphone
   (C) A complimentary DVD player
   (D) A $10 gift voucher

   男子若購買 2000 元以上，可以獲得什麼？

   (A) 下次購物可享九折
   (B) 一支免費的麥克風作為贈品
   (C) 一台免費的 DVD 播放器
   (D) 一張十元禮券

> **解說** 一般細節題，聽到關鍵字 $2,000 相關內容即正解：「我要補充一下，凡購買售價超過 2000 元的電視，可以獲得一台 DVD 播放器，加購音響系統還可以打九折」。所以答案是 (C)。
>
> **單字** complimentary (a.) 贈送的
>
> **同義替換** complimentary = free

6. Look at the graphic. What size of screen will the man buy?

   (A) 29 inches
   (B) 38 inches
   (C) 42 inches
   (D) 56 inches

   請看圖表，男子會買哪種尺寸的電視？

   (A) 29 吋
   (B) 38 吋
   (C) 42 吋
   (D) 56 吋

> **解說** 根據圖表題『秒殺三步驟』，步驟一：題目問男子會買哪種尺寸的電視，步驟二：找選項和圖表關聯處（四種尺寸），步驟三：音檔絕對不會唸到尺寸，而是唸相對應的價錢（數字）。原文中男子提到「但我的預算最多是 1500 元，我還不確定要不要買音響，我只想在預算內購買螢幕尺寸最大的電視」，當聽到預算 1500 元，可買到的最大尺寸，趕快對照圖表左邊，得知是 42 吋的電視，所以答案是 (C)。

NOTE

1. Where most likely does the woman work?

(A) At an interior decorating service

(B) At a public relations agency

(C) At a printing company

(D) At an insurance agency

2. What does the woman inquire about?

(A) Product number

(B) Business hours

(C) Printing quantity

(D) Payment method

3. What does the man suggest the woman do?

(A) Schedule an appointment

(B) Visit a website

(C) Provide some information

(D) Place an order online

4. What is the purpose of the call?

(A) To explain a delay in delivery

(B) To provide a reminder

(C) To confirm a meeting location

(D) To promote a product

5. What problem does the woman mention?

(A) Her meeting has been canceled.

(B) Her appliance has broken down.

(C) She will be busy all day.

(D) She has another engagement.

6. What does the man say about the installation service?

(A) It will require a fee.

(B) It will take less than two hours.

(C) It will be rescheduled to another day.

(D) It is no longer available.

7. What problem does the man have?

(A) The item he purchased is defective.

(B) The shoe size is incorrect.

(C) The shipping has been delayed.

(D) The warranty has expired.

8. According to the woman, why can't the order been canceled?

(A) It has already been sent.

(B) It is a discount item.

(C) The computer system is not working.

(D) The man is not eligible for a refund.

9. What does the woman say she will send the man?

(A) A reimbursement

(B) A full refund

(C) A return shipping label

(D) An extended warranty

10. What does the woman ask about?

    (A) The cost of a study course

    (B) The price of a trip abroad

    (C) The address of a website

    (D) The length of a class

11. What does the woman say she will do?

    (A) Inquire about financial aid

    (B) Talk to a career consultant

    (C) Submit an application

    (D) Apply for a loan

12. According to the man, what advantage does the college offer?

    (A) Small class sizes

    (B) Reduced tuition

    (C) Convenient class times

    (D) Advanced level courses

13. What does the woman say she will do later in the week?

    (A) Go out to dinner

    (B) Host an award banquet

    (C) Take a business trip

    (D) Attend a ceremony

14. What does the woman mean when she says, "Oh, that much?"?

    (A) She is worried she can't get the gown cleaned in time.

    (B) She is surprised by the cost of expediting a service.

    (C) She doesn't expect it to take so long to clean a gown.

    (D) She doubts whether the stain can be removed.

15. What does the man suggest the woman do?

    (A) Ask employees to work overtime

    (B) Put in a rush order

    (C) Change the work schedule

    (D) Ask for a deadline extension

16. What type of business does the man work for?

(A) An insurance company

(B) An auto repair shop

(C) A car rental company

(D) An automobile dealership

17. What is most important to the woman when purchasing a car?

(A) Warranty

(B) Mileage

(C) Safety

(D) Price

18. What does the man encourage the woman to do?

(A) Visit another branch

(B) Take a test ride

(C) Replace broken parts

(D) Pay a deposit

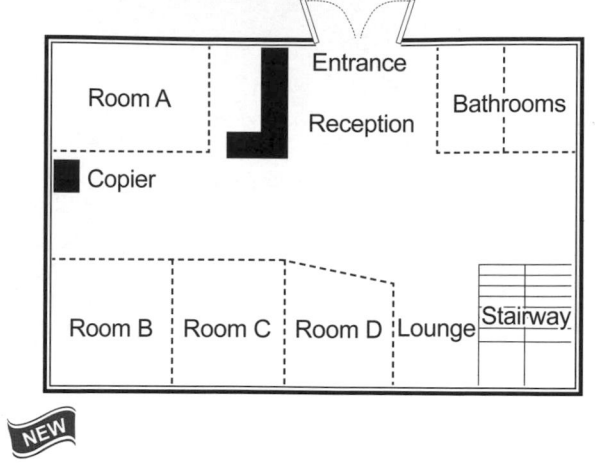

 NEW

19. What does the woman say about Mr. Rodriquez?

(A) He is on sick leave.

(B) He is out to lunch.

(C) He is on a business trip.

(D) He has left the company.

20. Look at the graphic. Where will the man leave the packages?

(A) Room A

(B) Room B

(C) Room C

(D) Room D

21. What does the man request of the woman?

(A) That she sign a contract

(B) That she give him directions

(C) That she sign for a delivery

(D) That she take a message

NOTE

Questions 1 through 3 refer to the following conversation.

(美式女聲) Hi. ❶ This is Susan Lee from Interpublic Communications. I'm planning an ad campaign for the Ultra Music Festival, ❷ and I'm looking for a printing company that can supply a very large quantity of posters and flyers. We need them this week. Can you handle that kind of order?

(英式男聲) We take jobs of almost any size. We can have as many as 20,000 ready by Friday.

(美式女聲) I see. We probably won't need that many. Maybe just four or five thousand. I can't be sure until I know our exact budget.

(英式男聲) OK. Well, thanks for considering us for the job. ❸ You can (回)**check out** our price list on our website. We offer big discounts for bulk orders.

問題 1 至 3 請參考以下對話。

女：嗨，❶ 我是國際公共傳播的蘇珊李。我在為超世代音樂節規劃廣告活動，❷ 我在找印刷公司印製大量海報和傳單。我們這週就需要。你們能接這種訂單嗎？

男：我們可以接任何數量的訂單。我們週五前可以印製二萬份。

女：這樣啊，我們可能不需要這麼多。也許只要四、五千份。等我知道預算後才能確定。

男：好，謝謝你考慮讓我們接訂單。❸ 你可以到我們網站查看價目表，對於大批訂單我們會提供優惠價。

(單字) poster (n.) 海報 / flyer (n.) 傳單 / bulk order 大量訂購

1. Where most likely does the woman work? 女子最有可能在哪裡工作？
   (A) At an interior decorating service (A) 室內裝潢服務
   (B) At a public relations agency **(B) 公關公司**
   (C) At a printing company (C) 印刷公司
   (D) At an insurance agency (D) 保險公司

解說 職務題，線索為：「我是國際公共傳播的蘇珊李。我在為超世代音樂節規劃廣告活動」，表示女子的公司專門為活動做廣告宣傳，所以答案是 (B)。

單字 interior (a.) 內部的

2. What does the woman inquire about? 女子在詢問什麼？
   (A) Product number (A) 產品編號
   (B) Business hours (B) 營業時間
   (C) Printing quantity **(C) 印刷數量**
   (D) Payment method (D) 付費方式

解說 詢問 / 要求題，要聽詢問資訊的句型。女子：「我在找印刷公司印製大量海報和傳單」，所以答案是 (C)。

3. What does the man suggest the 男子建議女子
   woman do? 做什麼？
   (A) Schedule an appointment (A) 安排預約
   (B) Visit a website **(B) 造訪網站**
   (C) Provide some information (C) 提供一些資訊
   (D) Place an order online (D) 上網訂購

解說 建議題，正解在最後面，表建議的常用句型。男子提到 You can：「你可以到我們網站查看價目表，大批訂單有優惠」，所以答案是 (B)。

同義替換 check out = visit

Questions 4 through 6 refer to the following conversation.

(美式男聲) This is Doug calling from Appliance Mart. ❹ I want to remind you that we have an appointment to install a washing machine and two televisions in your home on Sunday, May 28. Does that date still work for you?

(英式女聲) Well, I want to be there when the appliances are installed, ❺ but I have an ⓘimportant meeting that morning. I won't be back at my apartment until around 1 p.m. Would it be possible for the installation crew to come over after one?

(美式男聲) Certainly. You can expect our workers to arrive between one and three. ❻ The ⓘentire process should take approximately an hour and a half.

(英式女聲) Great. I'll be available at that time.

問題 **4** 至 **6** 請參考以下對話。

男：我是家電賣場的道格，❹ 我想提醒你，我們預約了五月 28 日星期日到府上安裝洗衣機和兩臺電視。日期沒問題嗎？

女：我希望安裝時我能在場，❺ 但那天上午我有重要會議。下午一點左右我才會回公寓，安裝工人可否在下午一點後過來？

男： 沒問題。工人會在一到三點之間過去。❻ 安裝過程大約需要一個半小時。

女： 太好了，到時我會在家。

單字 appliance (n.) 家電

4. What is the purpose of the call?

    (A) To explain a delay in delivery

    (B) To provide a reminder

    (C) To confirm a meeting location

    (D) To promote a product

這通電話的目的是？

    (A) 解釋送貨遲到

    (B) 提醒預約

    (C) 確認會議地點

    (D) 推銷產品

解說 主旨題，答案在**前兩句**：「我想提醒你，我們預約了五月 28 日星期日到府上安裝洗衣機和兩臺電視」，所以答案是 (B)。

單字 reminder (n.) 提醒

5. What problem does the woman mention?

    (A) Her meeting has been canceled.

    (B) Her appliance has broken down.

    (C) She will be busy all day.

    (D) She has another engagement.

女子提到什麼問題？

    (A) 她的會議取消了。

    (B) 她的家電故障了。

    (C) 她一整天都沒空。

    (D) 她還有其他預約。

解說 疑難雜症題，要聽女子提及**負面字眼**：「但那天上午我有重要會議。下午一點左右我才會回公寓」，表示有事情，不能在原本約定的時間赴約，所以答案是 (D)。

同義替換 important meeting = another engagement

6. What does the man say about the installation service?

    (A) It will require a fee.

    (B) It will take less than two hours.

    (C) It will be rescheduled to another day.

    (D) It is no longer available.

男子說了什麼有關安裝服務的事？

    (A) 需要收費。

    (B) 需要不到兩小時。

    (C) 重新安排日子。

    (D) 不再提供安裝服務。

解說 一般細節題，聽男生提及**安裝事宜**，即正解：「安裝過程大約需要一小時半」，所以答案是 (B)。

單字 require (v.) 需要

同義替換 entire process = installation service

Questions 7 through 9 refer to the following conversation.

(美式男聲) Hello, my name is Mark Davis. I placed an order last week for a pair of high heels that I was going to give to my wife as a gift. ❼ I think I bought the wrong size, though, so I'd like to cancel the order.

(美式女聲) One moment, please. ❽ I'm sorry, but that item has already ⦿**shipped**. You'll need to wait until it arrives and then return it. But don't worry. We can still give you a full refund.

(美式男聲) Okay, thanks. I'm surprised my order was shipped so soon after I placed it. By the way, do I still have to pay for shipping?

(美式女聲) Unfortunately, yes. According to our policy, customers are required to pay for return shipping. ❾ I'll send you a return shipping label by e-mail. Can you give me your e-mail address, please?

問題 7 至 9 請參考以下對話。

男： 哈囉，我叫馬克戴維斯。我上週訂購一雙高跟鞋，是要送給我妻子的禮物。❼ 但我想我買錯尺寸了，所以想取消訂單。

女： 請等一下。❽ 抱歉，但商品已經寄出了。你要等收到後再退還。但別擔心，我們會全額退款。

男： 好，謝謝。真訝異我才下完訂單就這麼快寄出。對了，我還要付運費嗎？

女： 很不幸，是的。根據我們的政策，顧客退貨要付運費。❾ 我會用電郵寄退貨標籤給你。請告訴我你的電郵地址好嗎？

單字 item (n.) 項目 / refund (n.) 退款

7. What problem does the man have?　　　　男子有什麼問題？

   (A) The item he purchased is defective.　　(A) 他買的商品有瑕疵。

   (B) The shoe size is incorrect.　　**(B) 鞋子尺寸錯誤。**

   (C) The shipping has been delayed.　　(C) 送貨延遲。

   (D) The warranty has expired.　　(D) 保固過期。

解說 疑難雜症題，要聽男子提及**負面字眼**：「我想我買錯尺寸了，所以想取消訂單」，所以答案是 (B)。

單字 defective (a.) 有缺陷的、不完美的 / expire (v.) 到期、過期

8. According to the woman, why can't the order been canceled?　　根據女子所說，為何不能取消訂單？

   (A) It has already been sent.　　**(A) 商品已經寄出。**

   (B) It is a discount item.　　(B) 這是折價商品。

   (C) The computer system is not working.　　(C) 電腦系統故障。

   (D) The man is not eligible for a refund.　　(D) 不符合退款資格。

解說 一般細節題，聽女子提到**無法取消訂單的原因**即正解：「抱歉，但商品已經寄出了」。所以答案是 (A)。

單字 eligible (a.) 合乎資格的

同義替換 ship = send

9. What does the woman say she will send the man?　　女子說會寄給男子什麼？

   (A) A reimbursement　　(A) 補償退款

   (B) A full refund　　(B) 全額退款

   (C) A return shipping label　　**(C) 退貨標籤**

   (D) An extended warranty　　(D) 延長保固

解說 動作題，正解在**最後面**，表動作的常用句型。女子提到 I'll：「我會用電郵寄退貨標籤給你」，所以答案是 (C)。

單字 reimbursement (n.) 賠償、補償

Questions 10 through 12 refer to the following conversation.

英式女聲　Hello, ➓ I'm interested in enrolling in your hair stylist training program, but I wasn't able to find any information about 🔊tuition on your school's website.

美式男聲　Thanks for your interest in our school. Our hair stylist program is a two-semester vocational course. Tuition for a single semester is $4,300.

英式女聲　Oh, OK. To be honest, that's a little more expensive than I expected. ➒ I'll have to get a student loan from a bank. ➓ What advantages does your program have?

美式男聲　➓ Well, one thing is that we offer night classes for all of our vocational programs, which is great for students who have full-time jobs. We're also one of the top vocational schools in the state, and most of our graduates have gone on to pursue careers in their area of study.

問題 **10** 至 **12** 請參考以下對話。

女：　你好，➓ 我有興趣報名你們的髮型師培訓課，但我在你們的學校網站上找不到學費資訊。

男：　謝謝你對我們學校有興趣。我們的髮型師課程是兩個學期的職業課程。一學期的學費是 4300 元。

女：　噢，好。坦白說，比我想像中來得貴。➒ 我要向銀行申請學生貸款。➓ 你們的課程有什麼優點？

男：　➓ 我們有提供夜間職業課程，適合有全職工作的學生。我們也是全州最優秀的職業學校，我們大部分畢業生都能在相關學習領域找到工作。

單字　tuition (n.) 學費 / vocational (a.) 職業（訓練）的、就業指導的
loan (n.) 貸款

10. What does the woman ask about?　女子詢問什麼事？

    (A) The cost of a study course　**(A) 課程費用**

    (B) The price of a trip abroad　(B) 出國旅遊費用

    (C) The address of a website　(C) 網站地址

    (D) The length of a class　(D) 課程時長

解說 詢問／要求題，要聽**要求對方**提供資訊的句型，女子：「我有興趣報名你們的髮型師培訓課，但我在你們的學校網站上找不到學費資訊」表示女子想了解學費，所以答案是 (A)。

同義替換 tuition = cost

11. What does the woman say she will do?　女子說她會怎麼做？

    (A) Inquire about financial aid　(A) 詢問助學金

    (B) Talk to a career consultant　(B) 跟職業顧問談

    (C) Submit an application　(C) 遞交申請表

    (D) Apply for a loan　**(D) 申請貸款**

解說 動作題，要聽**表動作**的句型，女子提到 I'll：「我要向銀行申請學生貸款」，所以答案是 (D)。

單字 application (n.)（書面）申請

12. According to the man, what advantage does the college offer?　根據男子所說，這所大學有什麼優點？

    (A) Small class sizes　(A) 小班教學

    (B) Reduced tuition　(B) 有學費優惠

    (C) Convenient class times　**(C) 方便的上課時間**

    (D) Advanced level courses　(D) 有高階課程

解說 一般細節題，聽男子提及**學校的優點**即正解。女子問：「你們的課程有什麼優點？」男子答：「我們有提供夜間職業課程，適合有全職工作的學生」。所以答案是 (C)。

單字 advanced (a.) 進階的

Questions 13 through 15 refer to the following conversation.

(美式女聲) Hello, I need to have this evening gown cleaned. ⑬ I'm going to an award ceremony later this week and I've only just noticed that there's a big stain on the back here. Can I have it back by tomorrow evening?

(英式男聲) Yes, I can have it ready for you by 8:00 p.m. tomorrow. ⑭ It'll cost $40.

(美式女聲) Oh, that much? ⑭ But your price list says it should be $20.

(英式男聲) Well, yes, but if you need next day service, we charge double.

(美式女聲) OK, I understand. That's fine. I'll be busy tomorrow evening so I'll send my assistant to pick the gown up at 8:00. Her name is Emily.

(英式男聲) No problem. ⑮ I'll fill out the 圇**next day service request** for you.

問題 13 至 15 請參考以下對話。

女： 哈囉，我要把這件晚禮服送洗。⑬ 這星期稍晚我要參加頒獎典禮，我剛發現後面有個大污點。明天晚上能來取嗎？

男： 可以，明天晚上八點可以來取。⑭ 費用是 40 元。

女： 噢，這麼多？⑭ 但你們的價目表說是 20 元。

男： 對，但你需要隔天服務，我們會收雙倍價錢。

女： 好，我懂了。沒關係。我明天晚上會很忙，所以我會派我的助理八點來取禮服。她叫艾蜜莉。

男： 沒問題。⑮ 我會幫你填隔天服務訂單。

單字 ceremony (n.) 儀式、典禮 / charge (v.) 收費 / request (n.) 要求、請求

13. What does the woman say she will do later in the week?
    (A) Go out to dinner
    (B) Host an award banquet
    (C) Take a business trip
    (D) Attend a ceremony

女子說她這週稍晚要做什麼？
(A) 外出吃晚餐
(B) 主持頒獎晚宴
(C) 出差
(D) 參加典禮

解說 動作題，要聽**表動作**的句型。女子提到 I'm going to：「這星期稍晚我要參加頒獎典禮，我剛發現後面有個大污點」，所以答案是 (D)。

單字 banquet (n.) 宴會

NEW . What does the woman mean when she says, "Oh, that much?"?
    (A) She is worried she can't get the gown cleaned in time.
    (B) She is surprised by the cost of expediting a service.
    (C) She doesn't expect it to take so long to clean a gown.
    (D) She doubts whether the stain can be removed.

女子說「噢，這麼多」是什麼意思？
(A) 她擔心無法即時拿到洗好的禮服。
(B) 她對快速服務的價格很驚訝。
(C) 她沒想到要花這麼長時間洗禮服。
(D) 她懷疑能不能除掉污點。

解說 隱含文意題，要結合上下文，推論出題目 "Oh, that much?" 的意思，正解在：男子說「費用是40元」，女子反應「但你們的價目表說是20元」，表示女子覺得貴，所以答案是 (B)。

單字 expedite (v.) 加速

15. What does the man say he will do?
    (A) Ask employees to work overtime
    (B) Put in a rush order
    (C) Change the work schedule
    (D) Ask for a deadline extension

男子說他會怎麼做？
(A) 請員工加班
(B) 填緊急訂單
(C) 更改工作進度安排
(D) 要求延長期限

解說 動作題，要聽**表動作**的句型。男子提到 I'll：「我會幫你填隔天服務訂單」，表示可以用急件方式，客戶明天即可取貨，所以答案是 (B)。

同義替換 next day service request = rush order

Questions 16 through 18 refer to the following conversation.

（美式女聲）Hi, Mr. Bannon. This is Flora Hudson. ⑯ You showed me a used Ford Focus last week. I reviewed my financial situation and I've decided to go ahead and make the purchase.

（英式男聲）I'm sorry, Ms. Hudson. Unfortunately, ⑯ we sold that car to another customer yesterday. However, I do have a similar model that I could show you.

（美式女聲）Oh, that's too bad you sold the Ford already. ⑰ That model has an excellent safety rating, which is my top consideration in buying a car.

（英式男聲）I understand. This other model also has a five-star safety rating. The car is five years old, but it has a new battery and new brakes.

（美式女聲）And what's the mileage?

（英式男聲）Uh, let me check. Oh, yes. It has 75,000 miles on it.

（美式女聲）That's quite high for a car that's only five years old.

（英式男聲）Yes, but it's in great shape. ⑱ Why don't you come by and take it for a 🔊**test drive**? It's a real bargain at only $12,000, and it comes with a good warranty.

問題 **16** 至 **18** 請參考以下對話。

女： 嗨，班農先生。我是佛蘿拉哈森。⑯ 你上週讓我看一輛二手福特 Focus，我審視了一下我的財務狀況，決定購買那輛車。

男： 抱歉，哈森女士，⑯ 可惜昨天我們把車賣給另一位顧客。但我還有一種類似的車款，可以讓你看看。

女： 噢，可惜你賣掉那輛福特。⑰ 那種車款的安全評分很高，是我買車的首選。

男： 我懂。另一種車款的安全評分也有五顆星，車齡五年，但電池和煞車已經換新。

女： 里程數有多少？

男： 我看一下，好，有七萬五千英里。

女： 以車齡五年來說這有一點多。

男： 對，但車況很好。⑱ 你何不過來試開一下？價格真的很划算，只要一萬兩千元，而且有不錯的保固。

16. What type of business does the man work for? 男子從事什麼行業？
    (A) An insurance company　　　　　　　(A) 保險公司
    (B) An auto repair shop　　　　　　　　(B) 汽車修理廠
    (C) A car rental company　　　　　　　 (C) 租車公司
    (D) An automobile dealership　　　　　**(D) 汽車經銷商**

解說 職務題，線索為女子說：「你上週讓我看一輛二手福特 Focus，我審視了一下我的財務狀況，決定購買那輛車。」及男子的回答「可惜昨天我們把車賣給另一位顧客。但我還有一種類似的車款，可以讓你看看」。女子提到「二手車、買車」，男子提到「賣車」及提供另一種車款，所以答案是 (D)。

17. What is most important to the woman when 女子買車的最重要考量
    purchasing a car? 是什麼？
    (A) Warranty　　　　　　　　　　　　(A) 保固
    (B) Mileage　　　　　　　　　　　　　(B) 里程數
    (C) Safety　　　　　　　　　　　　　**(C) 安全**
    (D) Price　　　　　　　　　　　　　　(D) 價格

解說 一般細節題，聽女子提到**最重要的考量**即正解：「那輛車款的安全評分很高，是我買車的首選」，所以答案是 (C)。

18. What does the man encourage the woman 男子鼓勵女子
    to do? 做什麼？
    (A) Visit another branch　　　　　　　　(A) 造訪另一家分店
    (B) Take a test ride　　　　　　　　　**(B) 試開一下車**
    (C) Replace broken parts　　　　　　　 (C) 更換煞車零件
    (D) Pay a deposit　　　　　　　　　　 (D) 付訂金

解說 建議題，正解在**最後面**，表建議的常用句型。男子提到 Why don't you：「你何不過來試開一下？」，所以答案是 (B)。

同義替換 test drive = test ride

Questions 19 through 21 refer to the following conversation and floor plan.

美式男聲 Hi. I have a delivery here for Mr. Rodriquez.

美式女聲 OK. His office is down the hall to the right—next to the copier. Wait, I just remembered. ⑲ 回He**'s away on business**, so his office is probably locked. How many packages are there?

美式男聲 Two.

美式女聲 OK. ⑳ Why don't you put them in the mailroom? It's straight ahead—right next to the employee lounge.

美式男聲 All right. ㉑ Would you mind signing this for me?

美式女聲 Sure, no problem.

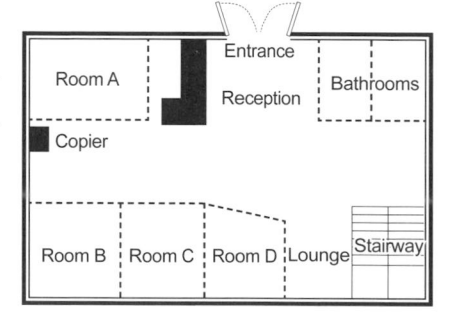

問題 **19** 至 **21** 請參考以下對話和平面圖。

男： 嗨，我有貨要送給羅格茲先生。

女： 好，他的辦公室在大廳盡頭右轉，在影印機旁邊。等等，我剛想起來，⑲ 他出差了，所以他的辦公室可能上鎖了。你有幾個包裹？

男： 兩個。

女： 好，⑳ 你何不放在收發室？前面直走，就在員工休息室旁邊。

男： 好，㉑ 能幫我簽收嗎？

女： 好，沒問題。

單字 package (n.) 包裹 / lounge (n.) 休息室

19. What does the woman say about Mr. Rodriquez?
    (A) He is on sick leave.
    (B) He is out to lunch.
    (C) He is on a business trip.
    (D) He has left the company.

女子說了關於羅格茲先生什麼事？
    (A) 他請病假。
    (B) 他外出吃午餐。
    (C) 他出差了。
    (D) 他離職了。

解說 一般細節題，聽女子提到**羅格茲先生**的相關內容即正解：「他出差了，所以他的辦公室可能上鎖了」，所以答案是 (C)。

同義替換 be away on business = be on a business trip

20. Look at the graphic. Where will the man leave the packages?
    (A) Room A
    (B) Room B
    (C) Room C
    (D) Room D

請看圖表。男子會將包裹放在哪裡？
    (A) A 室
    (B) B 室
    (C) C 室
    (D) D 室

解說 圖表題中的「樓層平面圖」是特殊題型，要注意看圖中各「地點圖示」(entrance、reception、bathroom、copier、lounge、stairway)，及仔細聽「表位置的用法」。根據圖表題「秒殺三步驟」，步驟一：題目問男生把包裹放哪裡，步驟二：找選項和圖表關聯處 (Room A, B, C, D)，步驟三：音檔絕對不會唸到 Room A, B, C, D，而是提到其他地點圖示。原文中女子提到「你何不放在收發室？前面直走，就在員工休息室旁邊。」，當聽到 next to（表位置的用法）和 lounge（地點圖示），就馬上得知是 Room D，所以答案是 (D)。

21. What does the man request of the woman?
    (A) That she sign a contract
    (B) That she give him directions
    (C) That she sign for a delivery
    (D) That she take a message

男子要求女子做什麼？
    (A) 簽合約
    (B) 為他指路
    (C) 簽收包裹
    (D) 轉交留言

解說 詢問／要求題，要聽**詢問對方**的句型（多為問句）。男子：「能幫我簽收嗎？」，所以答案是 (C)。

單字 direction (n.) 指示（此定義固定用複數）

Part **4**

簡短獨白

簡短獨白

題型介紹：

一人簡短獨白，共 10 篇，一篇 3 道題目，一題作答時間為 8 秒鐘。
聆聽獨白，回答試題本上的題目，其中有兩篇獨白要搭配圖表答
題 (此為新增題型)。

• 試題本上，每篇有 3 道題目：

題型示範：

你會聽到

(美式男聲) **Questions 71-73 refer to the following talk.**

I'd like to welcome you all to Venus Technology. My name is
William Harper and I'm the manager of operations. I'm in charge
of showing you around today. You should all have a packet with
details about company policies and workplace guidelines. If you
haven't received one, please let me know. For the first half hour,
we'll be discussing the corporate structure of Venus Technology
so you can understand how the business is organized. After
that, Jenny Valdez, our HR director, will talk to you about the
resources and opportunities available to you as employees.
Then, in the afternoon, we'll go for a walk around the office
so you can become familiar with our various departments and
facilities.

問題 71-73 請參考以下談話。

我要歡迎各位加入維納斯科技。我叫威廉哈柏，是營運經理。今天由我負責帶各位熟悉環境。你們應該都已經拿到一套關於公司政策和職場指南的資料。若沒拿到，請告訴我。前半個小時，我們要討論維納斯科技的公司結構，好讓你們瞭解公司的內部組織。之後人事部門經理珍妮佛德茲會告訴你們，做為這裡的員工，你們可運用的資源和機會。接著下午時我們會在辦公室四處逛逛，讓各位熟悉一下各部門和設施。

你會看到

71. Who most likely are the listeners?

(A) Job applicants
(B) Newly-hired employees
(C) Prospective customers
(D) Tourists

聽者最有可能是誰？

(A) 求職者
(B) 新聘員工
(C) 潛在顧客
(D) 遊客

等，共三題。

1 解題重點：

Ⓐ Part 4 高分關鍵：同 Part 3，在音檔播放前，快速審閱 3 道題目，掌握題型。在音檔播放時，仔細**聆聽出題點**，就能輕鬆篩選重點。

Ⓑ 熟練「五大題型」的解題點，也就是常見答案句型，即可精準定位答案，讓答題事半功倍。請繼續看以下章節，就知道「五大題型」如何解題囉！

Ⓒ 破解「六大必考主題」：Part 4 共有六種文章類型，而每種都有固定劇情套路，也代表有固定喜歡出題的地方。Olivia 幫大家整理出「必考點」，讓考生們聽到就直覺反應這裡一定考！

Ⓓ Part 4 特色：同 Part 3，題順 = 文順，也就是**答案會依序出現**。因此按順序聽，掌握文章發展非常重要。

Ⓔ 注意「同義表達」：聽力非常喜歡單字的同義替換。**原文聽到的內容，選項通常會換句話說，用相同字的選項通常是陷阱。**所以背單字一定要連同義字一起背，解題才會快速。

Ⓕ **不要邊聽邊畫卡**，很容易分心。應該先在答案卡做記號（例：鉛筆點一下），等所有答案都確定後，一口氣畫 3 題。

2 題目類型：五大題型 Ⓐ ~ Ⓔ (Pp.149~153)

Ⓐ 主旨題：正解在「前兩句」

題型 1. What is the purpose of the meeting/announcement/talk?
會議 / 公告 / 談話的目的是什麼？

2. What is the radio broadcast/advertisement mainly about?
廣播 / 廣告的主要內容是什麼？

解說 獨白的前兩句即為主題。一開始掌握主題，對後面的文意理解非常
重要。所以聽到音檔開始念 Questions 71 through 73 refer to the
following talk. 時，就要專心聽了。無論前一篇是否寫完，都要專注聽
每篇的前兩句。

Ⓑ 細節題：正解在「關鍵字」

題型 1. **What** does the speaker say about the **weather**?
說話者對天氣有什麼看法？

2. **Where** is the **main office** located? 公司總部在哪裡？

3. **How long** does the **renovation** take? 裝修需要多久時間？

解說 迅速找到題目關鍵字後，聆聽文章，關鍵字出現即為正解。
同時，也要注意聽關鍵字的同義替換，例：weather 可替換為 rain
shower（陣雨）、fog（霧）等相關字；main office（總公司）可替
換為 head office、headquarters（總部）等同義字。

C 推論題：正解在「最後面」

題型 1. What will happen at the end of the event?
   活動最後會發生什麼事？

2. What will the listeners most likely do next?
   聽眾接下來會做什麼？

3. What does the speaker say he will do?
   說話者說他會做什麼？

解說 推論題的題目會有「將要做什麼、將會發生什麼事」等關鍵字，答案一定在文章快結束時，通常聽到 speaker 提到 "I'll..., You'll..., We're going to..." 等即將要去做的句型（未來式時態），即為正解。

解題重點 「建議、提議」題型：正解在「最後面」

題型 1. What does the speaker **suggest** the listeners do on **Saturday**? 說話者建議聽眾星期六做什麼？

2. What are the customers **asked to do**? 顧客被要求做什麼？

3. What does the woman **encourage** the listeners **to do**?
   女子鼓勵聽眾做什麼？

解說 建議題為推論題的一種，因為答案也在「最後面」。說話者在最後通常會「建議／提醒／鼓勵／要求」聽眾做某些事。

當聽到以下句型，即為正解。

「建議題」常見答案句型

1. **Please...** 請…

   Please take some time over the next days to familiarize yourselves with their sales techniques.

   接下來幾天，請大家利用時間熟悉他們的銷售技巧。

2. **Remember/Don't forget/Be sure/Make sure...** 記住 / 務必…

   Remember, for the most up-to-date weather forecast, **be sure to** download the WFL app onto your mobile device.

   記住，想要最新的氣象預報，手機務必要下載 WFL 應用程式。

3. 命令句（原形動詞開頭的句子）

   For more information, **call** Randall's Home Management today to schedule an appointment.

   想了解更多資訊，今天就打到蘭德爾住家管理安排會面事宜。

4. **You should/We recommend/We suggest...** 你應該 / 我們建議…

   Why don't you... 你何不…？

   It's supposed to be hot today, so **we suggest** you put on some sunscreen and drink more water.

   今天應該會很熱，所以我們建議你擦些防曬，還有多喝水。

D 隱含文意題型

> **題型** What does the **speaker** mean when she says, "**I couldn't have done it without my team**"? 說話者說「若沒有我的團隊，我就無法做到」是什麼意思？

> **解說** 此題型在考考生是否了解上下文意。一定要先預覽，且牢記題目的「隱含文意句」，聽到「關鍵句」時，連結前後文，統整聽到的內容。

E 圖表題型

> **題型**

Look at the graphic. What does the speaker **want the listeners to discuss**?

(A) Web-site design

(B) Prices and fees

(C) Meal services

(D) Helpfulness of staff

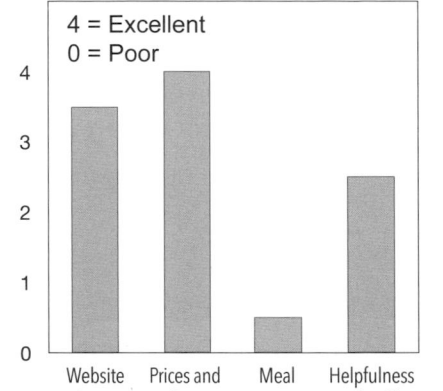

請看圖表，說話者想讓聽眾討論什麼？

(A) 網站設計

(B) 價格和費用

(C) 餐點服務

(D) 員工樂於助人

（此為官方指南例題）

> **解說** 同 Part 3，考生需同時專注圖表和聽文章，並整合內容作答。不僅閱讀速度要快，解析資訊的能力也很重要。因此，洪欣老師獨創『秒殺三步驟』，讓大家考試不慌亂，迅速抓住圖表解題線索。

秒殺三步驟：

→ **解題步驟一：預覽題目，找出關鍵字**

根據以上例題：可找出 listeners、discuss 這幾個關鍵字，意思為「聽眾要討論什麼？」

→ **解題步驟二：找到選項和圖表內容的關聯性。**

根據以上例題：只須看選項和圖表相關聯的四個討論主題（橫坐標），及其相對應的分數（縱座標數字），其他多餘資訊不用看。

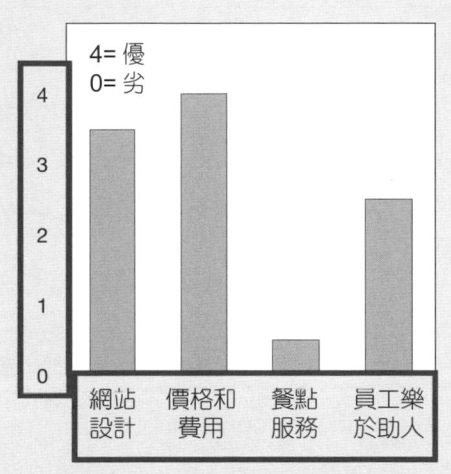

→ **解題步驟三：聽到關鍵字，搭配圖表答題**

根據以上例題：講者一定不會提到圖表中的四個主題，而是提到相對應的「分數（數字）」，例：討論如何改善最低分的那項 (with lowest rating)，答案就是 meal services。所以同學們要把重心放在縱座標的分數，也就是關鍵字，當聽到相關數值，馬上對照橫座標的主題，答案即出現。

3 六大必考主題 Ⓐ ~ Ⓕ (Pp.154~191)

Ⓐ News Report 新聞報導

- 內容：天氣報導、路況報導、商業 / 地方新聞

- 必考點

1. Weather report 天氣報導

a) usually bad 通常是壞天氣
b) current/later situation 目前和稍晚情況
c) 建議：stay at home 待在家、take a coat 帶外套、
   put on sunscreen 擦防曬、stay tuned 鎖定頻道

2. Road condition 路況報導

a) traffic jam/congestion 塞車、reduce to a single lane 縮減成一線道、
   accident 車禍、under construction 施工中、
   close to all traffic 全面封閉
b) 建議：detour 繞道、take another route 改道

3. Business/Local news 商業 / 地方新聞

a) 各種類型新聞，單字量較大

b) 常見主題：acquisition 收購、merger 合併、opening 開幕、
proposal 提案、expand 拓展、company policy 公司政策、
future project 未來發展、product launch 產品上市

NOTE

Questions 1 through 3 refer to the following radio broadcast. (53)

(美式男聲) Hello, this is John McKinley with the WKYZ weather forecast. ❶ The national weather service has issued a warning that the heavy rain expected to start Friday morning will last all day, resulting in foggy conditions early the next morning. ❷ The fog will most likely have lifted by noon on Saturday, which is good news for the Road Running Race to be held in the afternoon. ❸ Pedestrians are encouraged to dress in brightly colored clothing if you plan to be near busy roads on Saturday morning. For the most up-to-date weather conditions, download the WKYZ app onto your mobile device.

問題 1 至 3 請參考以下廣播。

大家好，我是 WKYZ 天氣預報的約翰麥金利。❶ 全國天氣服務處發佈警告，預計週五上午開始將有豪雨，並將持續一整天，導致隔天早上有霧。❷ 星期六中午前大部分的霧會散去，這對將在下午舉辦的路跑比賽來說是好消息。❸ 如果有行人計畫星期六上午到繁忙街道附近，建議穿著顏色鮮豔的衣服。欲知最新天氣狀況，請用行動裝置下載 WKYZ 應用程式。

單字 broadcast (n.) 廣播節目、電視節目 / forecast (n./v.) 預測、預報
issue (v.) 發佈 / lift (v.) （霧氣）散去 / up-to-date (a.) 最新的

1. What is predicted for Friday?
   (A) Fog
   (B) Sun
   (C) Rain
   (D) Snow

星期五的天氣預報是什麼？
   (A) 有霧
   (B) 晴天
   (C) 雨天
   (D) 下雪

> **解說** 新聞報導類的「細節題」，聽到 Friday，答案即出現：「全國天氣服務處發佈警告，預計週五上午開始將有豪雨，並將持續一整天」，所以答案是 (C)。

2. When is the road race scheduled to begin?
   (A) On Friday morning
   (B) On Saturday evening
   (C) On Saturday afternoon
   (D) On Sunday afternoon

路跑比賽計畫何時開始？
   (A) 星期五上午
   (B) 星期六晚上
   (C) 星期六下午
   (D) 星期日下午

> **解說** 新聞報導類的「細節題」，聽到 road race，答案即出現：「星期六中午前大部分的霧會散去，這對將在下午舉辦的路跑比賽來說是好消息」，所以答案是 (C)。

3. What are people advised to do?
   (A) Bring an umbrella
   (B) Wear bright clothes
   (C) Stay away from busy roads
   (D) Call the station with questions

說話者建議大家怎麼做？
   (A) 帶雨傘
   (B) 穿顏色鮮豔的衣服
   (C) 避免到繁忙的街道
   (D) 有問題可致電廣播電台

> **解說** 商業新聞類的「建議題」，聽文章最後面「建議」的句型 are encouraged to...：「如果有行人計畫星期六上午到繁忙街道附近，建議穿著顏色鮮豔的衣服」，所以答案是 (B)。

Questions 4 through 6 refer to the following broadcast. 🎧54

(英式男聲) It's Doug Russell with your 5 p.m. traffic update. **❹** There are long delays along Carter Boulevard due to 🔊**maintenance work** in the area. The traffic lights at the Carter Boulevard-Wharton Road intersection are being repaired after damage from last night's rainstorm. **❺** Commuters are advised to 🔊**take another route**, if possible. Traffic in all other areas is flowing smoothly. If you're out on the roads and notice any delays, please call and let us know at FM100 radio. **❻** Next, you'll hear all the latest 🔊**news headlines** with Cynthia Holmes.

問題 4 至 6 請參考以下廣播。

我是道格羅素,為大家播報下午 5 點最新交通新聞。**❹** 卡特大道因該區進行維修工程而出現長時間交通延遲。卡特大道和沃頓路交叉口的紅綠燈因昨晚暴風雨受損,現正搶修中。**❺** 建議通勤族盡可能改道。其他地區的交通情況都很順利。你若在開車,發現有延遲情況,請打電話到 FM100 廣播電台告訴我們。**❻** 接下來請聽辛蒂亞洪斯的最新頭條新聞。

單字 maintenance (n.) 維修 / commuter (n.) 通勤者 / route (n.) 路線

4. What is causing a delay?

    (A) An accident
    (B) Heavy traffic
    (C) Bad weather
    (D) Repair work

交通延遲的原因是什麼？

    (A) 車禍
    (B) 塞車
    (C) 天氣惡劣
    (D) 整修工程

> **解說**　新聞報導類的「細節題」，聽到「delay」，答案即出現：「卡特大道因
> 該區進行維修工程而出現長時間交通延遲」，所以答案是 (D)。

同義替換 maintenance work = repair work

5. What are commuters asked to do?

    (A) Take an alternate road
    (B) Use public transportation
    (C) Make a lengthy detour
    (D) Delay trips until traffic clears

說話者要通勤族怎麼做？

    (A) 改道
    (B) 搭乘大眾運輸
    (C) 繞遠路
    (D) 延後上路，等交通暢通

> **解說**　新聞報導類的「建議題」，聽文章最後面，有「建議」的句型 are
> advised to 即正解：「建議通勤族盡可能改道」，所以答案是 (A)。

單字 alternate (a.) 供替換的 / detour (n.) 繞道

同義替換 take another route = take an alternate road

6. What will listeners hear next?

    (A) Some commercials
    (B) A weather forecast
    (C) A news report
    (D) An exclusive interview

聽眾接下來會聽到什麼？

    (A) 商業廣告
    (B) 天氣預報
    (C) 新聞報導
    (D) 獨家採訪

> **解說**　「推論題」，聽文章最後面「未來式」的句型 you'll：「接下來請聽辛蒂
> 亞洪斯的最新頭條新聞」，所以答案是 (C)。

單字 commercial (n.) 商業廣告 / exclusive (a.) 獨家的

同義替換 news headlines = news report

Questions 7 through 9 refer to the following broadcast. (55)

(美式女聲) In business news today, ❼ a British company has manufactured the world's first "smart ▣scooter." Adventure Motors unveiled the Eco S1 at the World Motor Show in London last night. ❽ Not only does the scooter produce zero emissions, it doesn't need any external fuel source. ❽ The rechargeable batteries are the cleanest and most convenient way to provide enough power for the scooter to run for days. The vehicle has been in development for nearly four years, and cost over $200 million to complete. ❾ It is expected to be on the market in ▣half a year.

問題 7 至 9 請參考以下廣播。

今日商業新聞，❼ 一間英國公司製造出世界第一輛「電動機車」。冒險汽車公司昨晚在倫敦世界車展中推出 Eco S1。❽ 這輛電動車不但是零排放，更不需要外部燃料來源。❽ 可充電電池可為電動機車提供騎乘數日的足夠電力，是最乾淨也最方便的供電方式。這輛電動車已研發了近四年，生產成本超過二億元，❾ 預計在半年內上市。

單字　manufacture (v.) 製造 / emission (n.) 排放物
　　　fuel (n./v.) 燃料；為添加燃料 / rechargeable (a.) 可充電的

7. What's the news report mainly about? 新聞報導主要是關於什麼？

    (A) An environmental protection event   (A) 環保活動

    (B) A new vehicle model   **(B) 新車型**

    (C) A listed company   (C) 上市公司

    (D) An electronic device   (D) 電子裝置

解說 商業新聞類的「主題」，要聽「前兩句」：「一間英國公司製造出世界第一輛「電動機車」，所以答案是 (B)。

單字 listed company 上市公司

同義替換 scooter = vehicle

8. What is mentioned about the Eco S1? 關於 Eco S1，說話者提到什麼？

    (A) It is manufactured in London.   (A) 是在倫敦製造的。

    (B) It is fueled by gasoline.   (B) 以石油當燃料。

    (C) It may cause air pollution.   (C) 可能導致空氣污染。

    (D) It is powered by electricity.   **(D) 以電為動力。**

解說 商業新聞類的「細節題」，聽到電動機車 Eco S1 相關內容，答案即出現：「可充電電池可為電動機車提供騎乘數日的足夠電力，是最乾淨也最方便的供電方式」，所以答案是 (D)。

9. When will the Eco S1 be available? Eco S1 何時上市？

    (A) In four years   (A) 四年內

    (B) In one year   (B) 一年內

    (C) In six months   **(C) 六個月內**

    (D) In one month   (D) 一個月內

解說 商業新聞類的「細節題」，聽到「上市時間」，答案即出現：「預計在半年內上市」，所以答案是 (C)。

單字 available (a.) 可買到的、可取得的

同義替換 half a year = six months

⓫ Public Announcement 公共通告

- 內容：機場、機艙、車站、賣場、公司內部會議

- 必考點（以下考點會依文章順序出現）

1. 地點

題型 **Where** is the announcement being made?

解說 多益喜歡考公告發生在哪裡，多聽幾個字以判斷正確答案。例：聽到 airline（飛機）、flight（航班）、passengers（乘客）、boarding gate/pass（登機門 / 登機證）、turn off all electronic devices（關掉電子裝置）等字眼，即可判斷是在機場或飛機上。

2. 目的 / 主題

題型 What is the **purpose** of the announcement?
公告的目的是什麼？

解說 搭配前一章節的五大題型，答案在「前兩句」。
例：Welcome to this month's staff meeting. I'm pleased to announce our company's merger with Sedona Corp. 歡迎參加本月員工會議。我很高興宣布公司將與席多納公司合併。
→公告目的在前兩句：宣布和某公司的合併事宜。

3. 對象（聽眾）

題型 **Who** most likely are the listeners? 聽眾最有可能是誰？

解說 對象通常是員工、購物民眾或乘客,答案在「前兩句」。

例:Attention Superway Grocery shoppers. Head to the produce section for fresh fruit and vegetables. They're on sale today for half price! 超威雜貨賣場的購物民眾請注意,農產品區有新鮮蔬果,今天半價出售!

→公告開頭常用 attention 請大家注意,賣場公告對象即購物民眾。

4. 具體事項

題型 What special feature is mentioned about the new digital keys?
新的數位電子鑰匙有什麼特殊功能?

解說 常見內容包含公司會議(內部訓練),政策 / 策略宣佈,維修工程通知,登機 / 機上注意事項,賣場公告宣布商品促銷、特價或營業時間結束。

例:The new digital keys will be linked exclusively to your employee ID, so we will be able to track who enters and leaves the building at any time. 新的數位電子鑰匙和員工身分證件連結,所以我們於任何時刻皆可以追蹤誰進入與離開大樓。

5. 要求事項 / 建議(建議常見句型)

題型 What does the speaker ask the listeners to do?
說話者要聽眾做什麼?

解說 搭配前一章節的五大題型,答案在文章最後面的「建議題常見句型」。

例:**Please** use the bathroom facilities on one of the other floors on these days.

→答案在 Please 後面,建議員工這幾天使用別的樓層的廁所。

Questions 1 through 3 refer to the following announcement. (56)

英式女聲 **①** Attention all American Airlines passengers bound for Seattle. Due to heavy snow storms, flight 888 to Seattle has been rescheduled. Our new estimated time of departure is 7 o'clock this evening. We apologize for any inconvenience that this may cause you. **②** Each passenger on the rescheduled flight will receive 回**a coupon for 100 dollars off** a future flight anywhere in North America. In the meantime, **③** please feel free to relax in our passenger lounge, where 回**beverages and snacks** are available at no charge. Again, we apologize for the inconvenience. Thank you for your patience.

問題 **1** 至 **3** 請參考以下公告。

① 所有飛往西雅圖的美國航空乘客請注意，因暴風雪來襲，飛往西雅圖的 888 號航班時間有更動。起飛時間已更改為今天晚上 7 點鐘。抱歉造成您的不便。**②** 航班時間更動的乘客可獲得一百元折價券，可用於未來飛往北美任何地方的航班。在這段時間，**③** 乘客歡迎到候機室休息，那裡有免費飲料和點心。我們再次為造成您的不便表示歉意，感謝您的耐心等待。

單字 estimated (a.) 估計的 / departure (n.) 離開 / coupon (n.) 折價券、優惠券

1. Where is the announcement being made?   公告是在哪裡發佈？

   (A) At an airport   **(A) 機場**
   (B) At a bus terminal   (B) 巴士總站
   (C) At a train station   (C) 火車站
   (D) At a travel agent's office   (D) 旅行社辦公室

> **解說**   公告類的「地點」，要多聽幾個關鍵字判斷：「所有飛往西雅圖的美國航空乘客請注意，因暴風雪來襲，飛往西雅圖的 888 號航班時間有更動」，聽到 airline、passengers、flight 等字眼，即可判斷是在機場，所以答案是 (A)。

2. What is American Airlines offering?   美國航空提供什麼？

   (A) A refund for tickets   (A) 機票退費
   (B) A free trip to Seattle   (B) 免費飛往西雅圖的航班
   (C) A discount on a future flight   **(C) 未來航班的折扣**
   (D) A meal voucher   (D) 餐券

> **解說**   公告類的「具體事項」，聽和「補償」相關的內容即正解：「航班時間更動的乘客可獲得一百元折價券，可用於未來飛往北美任何地方的航班」，所以答案是 (C)。

> **同義替換** a coupon for 100 dollars off = a discount on a future flight

3. What can listeners do in the passenger lounge?   聽眾可在候機區做什麼？

   (A) Obtain a refund   (A) 領取退款
   (B) Have free refreshments   **(B) 享用免費茶點**
   (C) View their flight schedule   (C) 看到新的班機時刻表
   (D) Access a boarding gate   (D) 通往登機門

> **解說**   公告類的「具體事項」，聽和 passenger lounge 相關的內容即正解：「在這段時間，乘客歡迎到候機室休息，那裡有免費飲料和點心」，所以答案是 (B)。

> **同義替換** beverages and snacks = refreshments

Questions 4 through 6 refer to the following announcement and schedule. 57

美式男聲

Program	
Presenter	**Time**
Mr. Chang	10:00-10:50
Panel Discussion	11:00-12:00
LUNCH BREAK	12:00-13:00
Dr. Fitzsimmons	13:00-14:00
Ms. Lee	14:10-15:00

節目表	
講者	**時間**
張先生	10:00-10:50
小組討論	11:00-12:00
午餐時間	12:00-13:00
費茲蒙斯博士	13:00-14:00
李女士	14:10-15:00

Thank you for attending the 2nd Annual Milestone Conference. My name is Richard Arnold and I'll be chairing this event. There is an exciting line-up of presentations today. Our first talk, Creating Personal Connections, which will be delivered by Victor Chang, is due to start at 10:00. ❹ We'll then have a panel discussion on team building techniques at 11:00. At 12:00, we'll have a one-hour lunch break. ❺ And please note that there will be a switch in times for the last two presenters. Our one o'clock presenter, Dr. Fitzsimmons, is stuck at the airport, and the soonest flight he can catch won't get him here until 2:00. ❻ If you want to know about the schedule in more detail, please pick up a copy of the program from the **registration desk**.

問題 4 至 6 請參考以下公告和時間表。

感謝參加第二屆年度里程碑會議。我叫李察阿諾，是這場會議的主席。今天會有一系列精彩的報告。第一場演講「創造個人人脈」，講者是維多張，預定 10 點鐘開始。❹ 接著 11 點鐘小組討論，主題為「打造團隊」。12 點鐘將有一小時的午餐休息時間。❺ 請注意最後兩位講者的時間將會對調。原本 1 點鐘的講者費茲蒙斯被困在機場，他搭最快的班機要在 2 點鐘才能到達這裡。❻ 若想知道更詳細的時間表，請到登記處領取節目表。

單字 chair (v.) 主持（會議）/ line-up (n.) 陣容 / registration (n.) 登記、報名

4. What most likely is the topic of the panel discussion?

小組討論的主題可能是什麼？

(A) **Improving relationships between colleagues**

(A) **改善同事關係**

(B) Reducing corporate expenses

(B) 減少公司開支

(C) Holding effective meetings

(C) 舉行有效會議

(D) Construction techniques

(D) 建築技術

解說 公告類的「具體事項」，聽和 panel discussion 相關的內容即正解：「接著 11 點鐘小組討論，主題為「打造團隊」，和同事間的互動有關，所以答案是 (A)。

5. Look at the graphic. Who will be the final presenter?

請看圖表，最後一位講者是誰？

(A) Mr. Chang

(A) 張先生

(B) **Dr. Fitzsimmons**

(B) **費茲蒙斯博士**

(C) Mr. Arnold

(C) 阿諾先生

(D) Ms. Lee

(D) 李女士

解說 根據圖表題『秒殺三步驟』，步驟一：題目問最後一位講者是誰，步驟二：找選項和圖表關聯處（四位講者的名字），步驟三：音檔絕對不會直接唸到名字，而是提到右邊欄位的時間。原文中說話者提到「請注意最後兩位講者的時間將會對調」，就馬上得知最後一位講者是 Dr. Fitzsimmons，所以答案是 (B)。

6. What are listeners asked to do?

聽眾被要求做什麼？

(A) Switch seats after the lunch break

(A) 午休後換座位

(B) **Get a program at the registration area**

(B) **到登記處索取時間表**

(C) Give a presentation on a selected subject

(C) 針對選定的主題演講

(D) Share printed programs with others

(D) 跟其他人共用列印出來的節目表

解說 公告類的「要求事項 / 建議題」，要聽文章最後面「建議」的句型 please... :「若想知道更詳細的時間表，請到登記處領取節目表」，所以答案是 (B)。

同義替換 registration desk = registration area

ⓒ Guided Tour 觀光導覽

- 內容：導遊介紹觀光景點

- 必考點（以下考點會依文章順序出現）

1. 參觀地點

題型 **Where** is the talk **taking place**?

解說 考這裡是哪個觀光景點，多聽幾個字以判斷正確答案。

例：聽到 Welcome to the National Museum, exhibit 歡迎光臨國家博物館、展覽館等字眼，即可判斷是在博物館。聽到 factory（工廠）、blow glass（吹玻璃）、craftsmanship（工藝）等字眼，即可判斷是在玻璃工廠。

2. 說話者身分

題型 **Who** is probably **speaking**? 說話者可能是誰？

解說 答案在「前兩句」。通常會聽到 My name is Olivia, and I'll be guiding you⋯. 我叫奧利維亞，我會帶你們⋯。

→說話者 Olivia 即是導遊。

3. 行程安排

題型 **Where** will the listeners probably **go next**?
聽眾接下來會去哪裡？

解說 導遊會開始介紹接下來要去哪些地方參觀、用餐或休息。

例：We'll start by going straight to the factory's production area, where you'll see our craftspeople creating beautiful glass objects.
我們先直接去工廠的生產區，看工匠製造美麗的玻璃器皿。

→表示接下來會去玻璃生產區參觀。

4. 景點 / 展覽物品

題型 **What** is **unusual** about the Carl Johnson exhibit?
卡爾強生的展覽有何特殊之處？

解說 景點或展覽物品的特色 / 特殊之處 (special feature) 為必考。
例：This exhibit features life-size statues made of glass.
這個展覽以真人大小的玻璃雕像為特色。

5. 注意事項（建議常見句型）

題型 What does the speaker mean when she says, "this is a private collection"? 說話者說「這是私人收藏」是什麼意思？

解說 介紹完景點，導遊會說明注意事項，例：禁止拍照、攝影、飲食，準時集合等…。
例：Refrain from making any noise. 避免製造噪音。（命令句）

6. 下一步（建議常見句型）

題型 What activity does the speaker **suggest** that the listeners **do later**? 說話者建議聽眾等一下做什麼活動？

解說 答案在文章最後的「建議句型」，導遊會建議遊客往下個景點移動，通常是前往紀念品商店 (gift shop) 購物或餐廳 (cafeteria、restaurant) 用餐休息。
例：If you wish to make a purchase before you leave, remember we offer a ten percent discount on items you buy here at the factory gift shop.
你若希望在離開前買紀念品，記得在我們工廠紀念品商店購物有九折優惠。
→表示導遊最後建議到工廠的紀念品商店購物。

Questions 1 through 3 refer to the following tour information. (58)

(美式女聲) Welcome everyone. ❶ My name is Candice, and I'll be guiding you through our special exhibit of 19th century French paintings. Before we enter through the main gate, I have a few reminders. Please remember that touching of the artworks is strictly prohibited. ❷ And we don't allow photography inside the museum, so I apologize to those who have brought cameras. But don't worry, though. ❸ When our tour is over, we encourage you to visit the museum gift shop on the first floor, just across from the cafeteria, where you can purchase souvenirs and postcards. Thank you all for your attention, and I hope you have a wonderful time during your visit.

問題 1 至 3 請參考以下旅遊資訊。

歡迎各位。❶ 我叫坎狄絲，我會帶你們參觀 19 世紀法國繪畫特展。在進入大門前，我要提醒各位幾件事，請記住，美術館內嚴禁觸碰藝術品，❷ 也不准照相，因此我要向帶照相機的人說聲不好意思。但別擔心，❸ 等我們導覽結束，我們鼓勵大家參觀美術館一樓的紀念品商店，就在餐廳對面，可以購買紀念品、明信片。感謝各位專心聽講，祝各位能夠享受這次的美術館行程。

單字 prohibit (v.) 禁止 / souvenir (n.) 紀念品

1. Where is the talk being given? 談話在何處進行？
   (A) At a photo studio (A) 照相館
   (B) At an art museum **(B) 美術館**
   (C) At a trade exhibition (C) 貿易展覽館
   (D) At a boutique store (D) 精品店

   解說 觀光導覽類的「參觀地點」，仔細聽可判斷「地點」的關鍵字：「我叫坎狄絲，我會帶你們參觀 19 世紀法國繪畫特展」，聽到 special exhibit 和 French paintings，可判斷在美術館，所以答案是 (B)。

   單字 boutique (n.) 精品店

2. Why does the speaker apologize? 說話者為何道歉？
   (A) Artwork cannot be purchased. (A) 無法購買藝術品。
   (B) Photography is not allowed. **(B) 不准照相。**
   (C) Eating and drinking are prohibited. (C) 禁止飲食。
   (D) Visiting hours are limited. (D) 參觀時間有限制。

   解說 觀光導覽類的「注意事項」，仔細聽文章致歉部分（apologize）的相關內容：「我們也不允許照相，因此我要向帶照相機的人說聲不好意思」，所以答案是 (B)。

3. What does the speaker suggest the listeners do? 說話者建議聽眾做什麼？
   (A) Sign up for a guided tour (A) 報名導覽
   (B) Take a show program (B) 領取表演節目表
   (C) Rent an audio guide (C) 租語音導覽
   (D) Make a purchase **(D) 購物**

   解說 觀光導覽類的「下一步」，仔細聽文章最後的「建議句型」，we encourage you... 通常是購物：「等我們導覽結束，我們鼓勵大家參觀美術館一樓的紀念品商店，就在餐廳對面，可以購買紀念品、明信片」，所以答案是 (D)。

Questions 4 through 6 refer to the following tour information and park map.

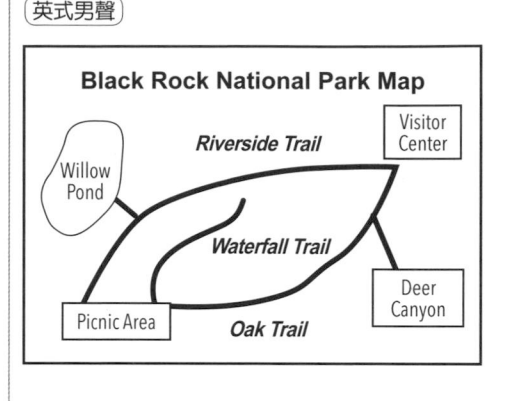

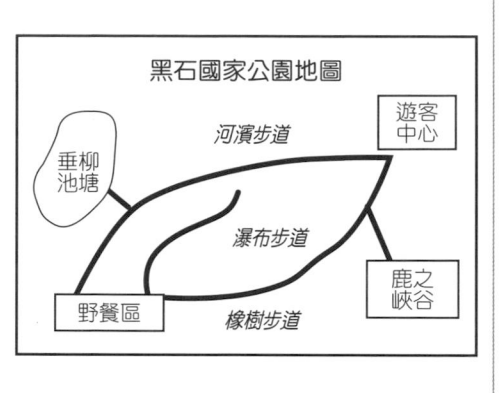

Hello. Welcome to the Visitor Center at Black Rock National Park. ❹ My name's Alan and I'll be guiding your hike today. ❺ Normally we'd be taking Riverside Trail to the picnic area, but the second half of that trail is closed due to damage from the storm last month. So instead, we'll be starting out on Riverside Trail and switching to Waterfall Trail, as you can see here on the map. We'll take a break for lunch at the Picnic Area, and then we'll take Oak Trail back to our starting point. ❻ It's supposed to be rainy today, so it's a good idea to bring **raincoats or umbrellas** with you.

問題 **4** 至 **6** 請參考以下旅遊資訊和公園地圖。

你們好，歡迎來到黑石國家公園的遊客中心。❹ 我叫艾倫，是今天大家健行的導遊。❺ 平時我們會走河濱步道前往露營區，但這條步道因上個月受到暴風雨侵襲，後半段已封閉。所以我們一開始會先走河濱步道，然後改走瀑布步道，從地圖上可以看到。我們抵達野餐區就休息吃午餐，接著再走橡樹步道回到起點。❻ 今天應該會下雨，所以最好隨身攜帶雨衣或雨傘。

單字　hike (n.) 健行 / trail (n.) 小徑、步道 / be supposed to... 應該…

4. Who most likely is the speaker?　　　　　　說話者可能是誰？
   (A) A tourist　　　　　　　　　　　　　(A) 遊客
   (B) A hiker　　　　　　　　　　　　　　(B) 健行者
   (C) A park ranger　　　　　　　　　　**(C) 公園管理員**
   (D) A school teacher　　　　　　　　　　(D) 學校老師

解說 觀光導覽類的「說話者身分」，答案一定是導遊：「歡迎來到黑石國家公園的遊客中心。我叫艾倫，是今天大家健行的導遊」，聽到 visitor Center、Black Rock National Park 和 guide 這幾個字，可判斷是國家公園的工作人員，所以答案是 (C)。

單字 ranger (n.) 公園管理員

5. Look at the graphic. Where will the listeners be not allowed to go?　　　　　請看圖表，聽眾不能去哪裡？
   (A) The Visitor Center　　　　　　　　(A) 遊客中心
   (B) Willow Pond　　　　　　　　　　**(B) 垂柳池塘**
   (C) The Picnic Area　　　　　　　　　　(C) 野餐區
   (D) Waterfall Trail　　　　　　　　　　(D) 瀑布步道

解說 根據圖表題『秒殺三步驟』，步驟一：題目問聽眾不能去哪裡，步驟二：找選項和圖表關聯處（四個景點），步驟三：音檔絕對不會直接唸到景點名稱，而是提到步道。原文中說話者提到「平時我們會走河濱步道前往露營區，但這條步道因上個月受到暴風雨侵襲，後半段已封閉。所以我們一開始會先走河濱步道，然後改走瀑布步道，從地圖上可以看到。我們抵達野餐區就休息吃午餐，接著再走橡樹步道回到起點」，根據步道相關內容，答案是 (B)。

6. What does the man encourage the listeners to do?　　　　男子鼓勵聽眾做什麼？
   (A) Have snacks and drinks　　　　　　(A) 吃點心和飲料
   (B) Wear hiking boots　　　　　　　　(B) 穿登山靴
   (C) Bring rain gear　　　　　　　　**(C) 帶雨具**
   (D) Purchase postcards　　　　　　　　(D) 購買明信片

解說 觀光導覽類的「下一步」，仔細聽文章最後的「建議句型」：「今天應該會下雨，所以最好隨身攜帶雨衣或雨傘」，所以答案是 (C)。

同義替換 raincoats or umbrellas = rain gear

D Advertisement 商業廣告

- 內容：商業廣告 / 廣播

- 必考點（以下考點會依文章順序出現）

1. 引起注意 → 目的

題型 What is being advertised? 廣告內容是什麼？

解說 廣告的目的就是「賣產品或服務」，一開始會用較聳動的台詞吸引觀眾注意，通常是「問句」，主題即在「前兩句」。

例：Are you looking for a professional house cleaning service with reasonable prices? Then you should call Allen's House Cleaning.
你想找專業且價格合理的居家清潔服務？那麼你一定要打給艾倫居家清潔公司。
→ 此廣告是在賣居家清潔服務。

2. 說話者身分、對象

題型 What kind of business is A&L? A&L 是什麼產業？
Who is the intended audience for this advertisement?
廣告的對象是誰？

解說 考說話者是哪種產業或公司和對象是誰。聽「前兩句」可得知什麼公司在賣什麼產品 / 服務，即可知道說話者身分及對象。

例：Is your construction company trying to expand? Do you find it hard to compete with other businesses because your equipment is old and inefficient? Then Millennium Tools has the products you've been looking for.
你的建設公司想擴張嗎？你覺得設備又舊又沒效率會難以跟其他產業競爭嗎？那麼千禧工具行有你想要的產品。
→ 可聽出說話者在賣工程相關設備，對象是建設公司的老闆。

3. 產品、服務特色及功能

題型 What feature of the product does the speaker emphasize?
說話者強調什麼產品功能？

解說 廣告很愛考商品／服務特色 special feature，例：lightweight（輕巧）、
water-resistant（防水）、convenient（方便）、efficient（有效率）、
fit into any bag（適合放入各種袋子）等⋯。

4. 建議（建議常見句型）

題型 What are listeners encouraged to do now?
說話者鼓勵聽眾做什麼？

解說 說明完特色，建議聽眾購買、參加抽獎、參觀產品展示等⋯。
例：If you buy a Sony E-Reader this month, you'll receive a coupon
for a free download of an electronic book.
如果你本月購買索尼公司的電子閱讀器，你將獲得可免費下載一本電
子書的優惠券。
→建議這個月購買，就可免費下載一本電子書。

5. 促銷方式、時間

題型 According to the speaker, what is offered with a purchase?
根據說話者，購買後會提供什麼？

解說 購買或參加活動後，會獲得何種優惠（折扣、贈品、免運、安裝服務
等⋯），例：All items are marked down 20%. 所有產品下殺八折，
或限時優惠，例：The sale will only be held this Saturday. 特賣只在
這星期六舉行。

Questions 1 through 3 refer to the following advertisement and list. (60)

（英式女聲）

Hello, ❶ Mother Annie's Kitchenware is celebrating its
（回）**10th year** with a sale! This weekend only, you can
get amazing discounts on everything from cooking
utensils to electric appliances and pots and pans. Make

秒殺 3 步驟

sure you stop by our store on Saturday evening, and ❷ you can find
our featured (回)**glassware** at rock-bottom prices. You won't want to
miss it! A full list of special offers for this weekend is available at the
entrance. ❸ And when you come to the store, don't forget to pick up
a free ticket for the raffle. We'll be offering fifty $100 gift vouchers to
customers who enter the drawing. So join us this weekend for some
great bargains!

Mother Annie's Kitchenware Discounts	
Cooking utensils	20%
Electric appliances	30%
Pots and pans	40%
❷ (回)Drinking glasses	50%

安妮媽媽廚具 折扣	
廚具	八折
電器設備	七折
鍋盤	六折
水杯	五折

問題 1 至 3 請參考以下廣告和清單。

大家好，❶ 安妮媽媽廚具正舉辦十週年特賣會！只有這個週末，所有產品都有
優惠折扣，從炊具到電器設備和鍋盤。記得週六晚上到我們商店，❷ 你可以找
到別具特色的超低價玻璃器皿。千萬別錯過！門口有本週末的完整特價清單。
❸ 來店裡時別忘了領一張免費抽獎券。我們為參加抽獎的顧客提供 50 份一百
元禮券。所以這週末請到我們商店購買物美價廉的產品！

單字 raffle (n.) 抽獎（活動）/ drawing (n.) 抽獎
bargain (n.) 便宜貨、特價商品

1. Why is the store having a sale?　　商店為什麼舉辦特賣？
   (A) To promote a grand opening　　(A) 開幕促銷
   (B) To get rid of old stock　　　 (B) 清倉
   (C) To advertise a new brand　　　(C) 推廣新品牌
   (D) To celebrate an anniversary　**(D) 慶祝週年慶**

> **解說** 商業廣告類的「目的」，要聽「前兩句」：「正舉辦十週年特賣會」，所以答案是 (D)。
> **單字** stock (n.) 商店庫存、存貨
> **同義替換** 10th year = anniversary

2. Look at the graphic. What is the discount　請看圖表，特色商品打
   on the featured product?　　　　　　　　幾折？
   (A) 20%　　　(A) 八折
   (B) 30%　　　(B) 七折
   (C) 50%　**(C) 五折**
   (D) 40%　　　(D) 六折

> **解說** 根據圖表題『秒殺三步驟』，步驟一：題目問特色商品打幾折。步驟二：找選項和圖表關聯處（四種折扣），步驟三：音檔絕對不會念到折扣數字，而是念左邊相對應的商品名稱。原文中說話者提到「你可以找到別具特色的超低價玻璃器皿」，得知特色商品是玻璃器皿，也就是圖表中的 drinking glasses（五折），所以答案是 (C)。
> **同義替換** glassware = drinking glasses

3. What does the speaker recommend　說話者建議聽眾
   listeners do?　　　　　　　　　　做什麼？
   (A) Obtain tickets　　**(A) 領取抽獎券**
   (B) Get a brochure　　　(B) 領小冊子
   (C) Go on a website　　 (C) 瀏覽網站
   (D) Attend a demonstration　(D) 參加展示

> **解說** 商業廣告類的「建議」，要聽文章「最後面」的常見建議句型 don't forget to：「來店裡時別忘了領一張免費抽獎券。」，所以答案是 (A)。
> **單字** brochure (n.) 小冊子

Questions 4 through 6 refer to the following advertisement. (61)

(美式男聲) ④ Is your office a little tired-looking? Would you like your business to be more accessible to clients? Relocate to the Golden Twin Tower on Penn Avenue. The Golden Twin Tower is a brand-new office building. The lobby has a spectacular view of Morrison Park, which is bound to impress your clients. It's also fully equipped with modern features such as interactive meeting rooms and conference facilities. ⑤ Most importantly, the property is 🔊conveniently located within walking distance of several subway stations. So what are you waiting for? ⑥ The available spaces are filling up fast. You can see photos and floor plans on our website at www.thegoldentwintower.com. To inquire about a lease, call WonderLand Real Estate at 021-785-633 to schedule an appointment.

問題 4 至 6 請參考以下廣告。

④ 你的辦公室是不是有點看膩了？想讓客戶更容易找到你的公司嗎？可以搬到賓州大道的金雙子塔。金雙子塔是全新的辦公大樓。從大廳可以看到莫里森公園的壯觀景致，一定能給你的客戶留下深刻印象。辦公室也配備現代化功能，例如互動會議室和會議設施。⑤ 最重要的是，此物件的地點便利，距離幾個地鐵站只有幾步之遙。所以你還在等什麼？⑥ 空位很快會搶租一空。請上我們的網站瀏覽照片和平面圖，網址是 www.thegoldentwintower.com。欲諮詢租賃事宜，請致電仙境房地產預約看房時間，電話是 021-785-633。

單字 accessible to 易接近的 / relocate (v.) 搬遷 / bound to 一定會
fully equipped 配備齊全的 / fill up 填滿

4. What is being advertised?
   (A) New apartments
   (B) An office complex
   (C) Office supplies
   (D) A convention center

廣告的內容是什麼？
   (A) 新公寓
   (B) 辦公大樓
   (C) 辦公用品
   (D) 會議中心

解說 商業廣告類的「目的」，一開始會用較聳動的台詞吸引觀眾注意，通常是「問句」，主題即在「前兩句」：「你的辦公室是不是有點看膩了？想讓客戶更容易找到你的公司嗎？可以搬到賓州大道的金雙子塔。金雙子塔是全新的辦公大樓」，說話者提到 office、office building 等字眼，所以答案是 (B)。

5. According to the advertisement, what is the main attraction of the property?
   (A) A location convenient to public transportation
   (B) A large conference room
   (C) The spacious lobby
   (D) The affordable price

根據廣告，此物業的主要魅力是什麼？
   (A) 靠近大眾運輸的便利地點
   (B) 大會議室
   (C) 寬敞的大廳
   (D) 價格實惠

解說 商業廣告類的「商品特色」，要仔細聽「大樓主要特色」的相關內容：「最重要的是，此物件的地點便利，距離幾個地鐵站只有幾步之遙」，所以答案是 (A)。

單字 affordable (a.) 價格實惠的

同義替換 conveniently located within walking distance of several subway stations = convenient to public transportation

NEW
6. Why does the speaker say, "what are you waiting for?"?
   (A) To offer assistance
   (B) To motivate the listener
   (C) To answer a customer inquiry
   (D) To promote an event

說話者為何說：「你還在等什麼」？
   (A) 提供協助
   (B) 鼓勵聽眾
   (C) 回答顧客詢問
   (D) 推廣活動

解說 隱含文意題，要結合上下文，推論出題目 "what are you waiting for?" 的意思，正解在：「空位很快會搶租一空」，鼓勵聽眾趕快租下，不要再等了，所以答案是 (B)。

單字 inquiry (n.) 詢問

E Business Talk 商務演說

- 內容：介紹（公司、課程、活動、新系統、產品、演講者、退休員工）、銷售業績報告、新進員工訓練課程、頒獎宴會、慶功宴、開幕典禮

- 必考點（以下考點會依文章順序出現）

1. 目的

題型 **What** is the **purpose** of the talk? 這場講話的目的是什麼？

解說 開頭會先感謝大家參加（Thank you for attending today's seminar on time management. 感謝各位參加今天的時間管理研討會。），以及介紹主講者（Our guest speaker today is Mark Wilson, author of the new book, *Time is Money*, which has been a bestseller for three months. 今天的演講來賓是馬克威爾森，是新書《時間就是金錢》的作者，這本書已三個月榮登暢銷榜。），再開始說明今天的主題或目的，答案在「前兩句」。

2. 說話者身分、對象

題型 1. **Who** is probably **speaking**? 說話者可能是什麼身分？
2. **Who** most **likely** are the **listeners**? 聽眾最有可能是誰？

解說 聽「前兩句」可推論說話者身分或對象是誰。
例：On behalf of Maple Technologies, I'd like to welcome you all to the company. We're happy to have you join our big family. 我代表楓樹科技公司歡迎各位加入公司，很高興各位加入我們的大家庭。
→由此開頭兩句，可推論說話者身分是楓樹科技公司職員，在對新進員工說話。

3. 具體說明

題型 **What** must the employees **do** when entering the building?
員工進入大樓時要做什麼？

解說 接下來開始進行演說，常見內容為：演說者經歷介紹、公司簡介、新
產品／系統介紹、銷售業績報告、新進員工訓練內容等…。
例：The company has performed well over the last three months,
earning a 10 percent rate of return.
公司在過去三個月表現很好，報酬率為百分之十。

4. 下一步推論（建議常見句型）

題型 1. **Wha**t will happen **last**? 最後會發生什麼事？
2. **What** does the **speaker ask a volunteer to do**?
說話者請志願者做什麼？

解說 答案在文章最後面：推論題／建議題宣布接下來要做什麼或建議聽眾
怎麼做，答案在「即將要去做」及「建議」的常見句型。
例：At the end of the press conference, we'll take some time to
answer questions from you in the media.
記者會最後，我們會回答媒體的問題。

Questions 1 through 3 refer to the following talk. (62)

(英式女聲) ❶ ▣ **At the start of next week**, we'll be upgrading the company's telephone system. It is hoped that this change will greatly improve efficiency in teleconference meetings and interdepartmental projects. ❷ All voice messages saved in the previous system will be ▣**erased**, however, which means that you need to review any saved messages before Monday so as not to lose any important information. Also, please remember that technicians will be visiting our office next Monday morning from 8 A.M. to 10 A.M. to install the new equipment. ❸ So please don't schedule any calls to clients during that time. For any critical calls that must be made on Monday morning, please speak with your department head to make special arrangements.

問題 **1** 至 **3** 請參考以下演說。

❶ 下週開始，我們會將公司各辦公室間的電話系統升級。希望這次更新能大幅改善電話會議和各部門間企畫案的效率。❷ 所有儲存在舊系統的語音訊息會被刪除，所以你們要在週一以前再檢查所有已儲存的訊息，以免流失重要訊息。另外請記住，技師會在下週一上午 8 時至 10 時到我們辦公室安裝新設備。❸ 所以這段時間請不要安排跟客戶通電話。若有必須在週一上午撥打的重要電話，請跟部門主管商談以做特殊安排。

單字 teleconference (n.) 電話會議 / efficiency (n.) 效率 / critical (a.) 重要的

1. When will the change take effect?
   (A) Before the end of the week
   (B) Early the following week
   (C) Right after the meeting
   (D) Sometime next month

   何時會更換電話系統？
   (A) 本週末之前
   (B) 下週開始
   (C) 會議過後
   (D) 下個月

> **解說** 商務演說類的「具體說明」，仔細聽和「更換的時間」相關的描述：「下週開始，我們會將公司各辦公室間的電話系統升級」，所以答案是 (B)。

> **單字** take effect 生效

> **同義替換** at the start of next week = early the following week

NEW

2. What does the speaker mean when she says, "you need to review any saved messages"?
   (A) He wants to remind the employees that the messages will be deleted.
   (B) He wants to suggest a way of solving a technical problem.
   (C) He wants to make sure the upgrade won't take long.
   (D) He wants to make sure employees can make important calls during installation.

   說話者說的「要再檢查所有已儲存的訊息」是什麼意思？
   (A) 想提醒員工訊息會被刪除。
   (B) 想建議解決技術問題的方法。
   (C) 確保不會花太多時間更新系統。
   (D) 確保員工能在安裝期間打重要電話。

> **解說** 隱含文意題，要結合上下文，推論出題目 "you need to review any saved messages" 的意思，正解在：「所有儲存在舊系統的語音訊息會被刪除，所以你們要在週一以前再檢查所有已儲存的訊息，以免流失重要訊息」，提醒員工訊息會被刪除，所以答案是 (A)。

> **同義替換** erase = delete

3. What are listeners asked to do during the upgrade?
   (A) Move to another office
   (B) Delay making calls to clients
   (C) Keep to their normal work schedule
   (D) Install new telephone software

   聽眾被要求在升級期間做什麼？
   (A) 搬去其他辦公室
   (B) 延後打電話給客戶
   (C) 維持平時工作安排
   (D) 安裝新電話軟體

> **解說** 商務演說類的「建議」，仔細聽文章最後面表「建議」的句型 please...：「所以這段時間請不要安排跟客戶通電話」，所以答案是 (B)。

Questions 4 through 6 refer to the following talk and chart. 🎧63

美式女聲

❹ All right, everyone, thanks for coming today to hear our breakdown of this year's flash drive market shares. We're still among the top four flash drive makers, but ❺ we need to pay attention to Kingston's rapid growth—they just considerably surpassed our 18% market share. These high levels of growth are mainly attributed to their new marketing strategy. ❻ Kingston is 回**bringing down the prices** of its lower-end products in an effort to entice consumers into the flash drive market in the hope that they will later be able to "upsell" them to high-end products. ❻ We think this strategy could also help us attract new users, so next quarter we're going to try it out with some select items. We expect our market share to expand beyond 18% and catch up with them.

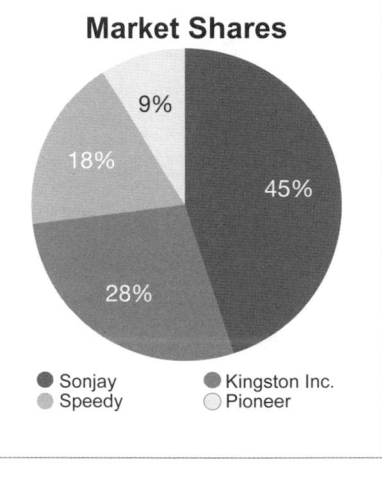

Market Shares

9%
18%
45%
28%

● Sonjay ● Kingston Inc.
● Speedy ○ Pioneer

問題 **4** 至 **6** 請參考以下演說和圖表。

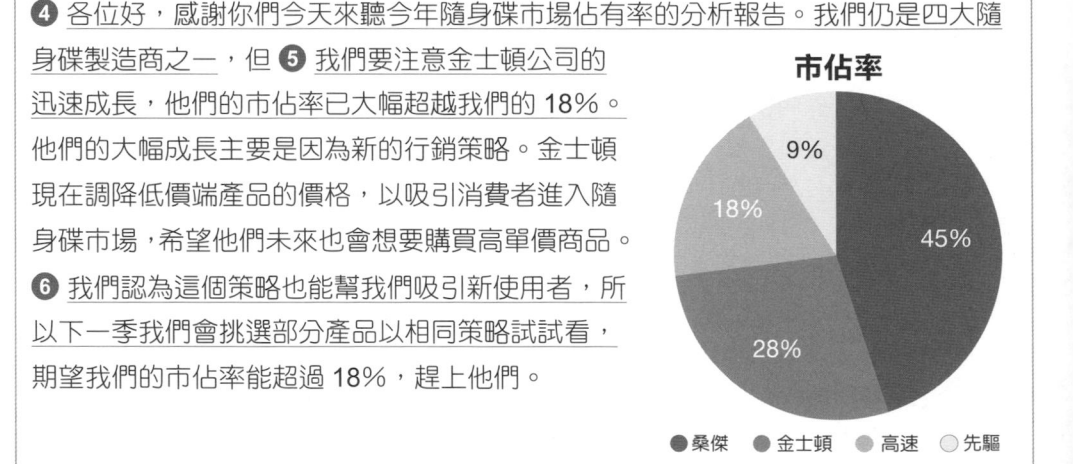

❹ 各位好，感謝你們今天來聽今年隨身碟市場佔有率的分析報告。我們仍是四大隨身碟製造商之一，但 ❺ 我們要注意金士頓公司的迅速成長，他們的市佔率已大幅超越我們的 18%。他們的大幅成長主要是因為新的行銷策略。金士頓現在調降低價端產品的價格，以吸引消費者進入隨身碟市場，希望他們未來也會想要購買高單價商品。❻ 我們認為這個策略也能幫我們吸引新使用者，所以下一季我們會挑選部分產品以相同策略試試看，期望我們的市佔率能超過 18%，趕上他們。

市佔率

9%
18%
45%
28%

● 桑傑 ● 金士頓 ● 高速 ○ 先驅

單字 breakdown (n.) 分析 / market share 市佔率 / surpass (v.) 超過
attribute to 把…歸因於 / entice sb. 吸引某人
upsell (v.) 往上推銷（試圖說服顧客購買額外或者更昂貴的產品）

4. Who is probably speaking?　　　　　　　說話者可能是什麼身分？
   (A) A business news reporter　　　　　　(A) 商業新聞記者
   (B) A marketing analyst　　　　　　　　(B) 行銷分析師
   (C) A flash drive manufacturer　　　　**(C) 隨身碟製造商**
   (D) A film producer　　　　　　　　　　(D) 電影製作人

解說 商務演說類的「說話者」，答案在「前兩句」即出現。「各位好，感謝你們今天來聽今年隨身碟市場佔有率的分析報告。我們仍是四大隨身碟製作商之一」，說話者提及：flash drive market shares 和 flash drive makers，所以答案是 (C)。

5. Look at the graphic. What company does　請看圖表，說話者在哪間
   the speaker work for?　　　　　　　　　公司上班？
   (A) Sonjay　　　　　　　　　　　　　　(A) 桑傑
   (B) Kingston Inc.　　　　　　　　　　　(B) 金士頓
   (C) Speedy　　　　　　　　　　　　　**(C) 高速**
   (D) Pioneer　　　　　　　　　　　　　　(D) 先驅

解說 根據圖表題『秒殺三步驟』，步驟一：題目問說話者在哪間公司上班，步驟二：找選項和圖表關聯處（四間公司），步驟三：音檔絕對不會唸到這四間公司，而是提到市佔率（百分比）。原文中說話者提到「我們要注意金士頓公司的迅速成長，他們的市佔率已大幅超越我們的18%」，就馬上得知是說話者公司市佔率為 18%，所以答案是 (C)。

6. According to the speaker, what will the　根據說話者，公司下一季會
   company do next quarter?　　　　　　　做什麼？
   (A) Lay off employees　　　　　　　　　(A) 裁員
   (B) Reduce manufacturing costs　　　　(B) 降低製造成本
   (C) Develop new products　　　　　　　(C) 開發新產品
   (D) Decrease product prices　　　　　**(D) 調降產品價格**

解說 商務演說類的「下一步」，即推論題，仔細聽文章表示即將要去做的句型：We're going to 最後面和 next quarter 等字眼：「我們認為這個策略也能幫我們吸引新使用者，所以下一季我們會挑選部分產品以相同策略試試看」，上文提到金士頓調降低價端產品的價格，以吸引消費者，高速之後也想用同樣方法，所以答案是 (D)。

同義替換 bringing down the prices = decrease product prices

F Telephone Message 電話留言

- 內容：電話語音留言

- 必考點（以下考點會依文章順序出現）

1. 說話者身分、對象

題型 1. Where is the woman calling from? 女子從哪裡打電話過來？
2. Who most likely is Ms. Dai? 戴女士最有可能是誰？

解說 來電者表明身份，以及說明要找誰，答案在「前兩句」。
例：Hello, Ms. Dai. **This is** Maria Nakanishi calling on behalf of Mitsutomo Studios.
喂，戴女士，我是瑪麗亞中西，代表三友工作室打電話過來。
或 **Thank you for calling** the customer service center at Omega Home Network Systems.
感謝你打來歐美加家庭網絡系統的顧客服務中心。
或 Hello, **you've reached** Smith and Jones, Ltd.
你好，這裡是史密斯和瓊斯公司。
→表示已進入某公司的語音系統。

2. 目的

題型 1. What is the woman calling about? 女子打電話來的目的是什麼？
2. Why did Trevor Davis call? 翠佛戴維斯為何打電話來？

解說 表明打電話目的，答案在「前兩句」，答案慣用句型：
I'm calling about... 我打電話來是為了…
I'm calling to... 我打來是…

3. 建議（建議常見句型）

1. What information does the speaker request?
說話者要求什麼資訊？

2. What are callers asked to do?
打電話者要求做什麼？

答案在文章最後面，要求或建議聽留言的人（對象）怎麼做。

例：For more information, or to ask about a technical problem or billing matter, please hold to be connected with a customer service representative.

需要更多資訊或詢問技術、帳單等問題，請稍等，我們會為您轉接到客服人員。

NOTE

Questions 1 through 3 refer to the following telephone message. (64)

(英式女聲) Hello. ❶ <u>You've reached the Dr. White's Clinic. You've</u> <u>called after our normal hours of operation.</u> We're open from 8:00 a.m. to 5:00 p.m. on weekdays, and from 9:00 to 12:00 on Saturday. For general inquiries, please call back during business hours tomorrow. ❷ <u>Please note that we no</u> <u>longer take appointments over the phone. Dr. White's Clinic</u> <u>has recently set up an online ⊚**reservation** service for the</u> <u>convenience of our patients.</u> To access this service, visit our official website at www.drwhiteclinic.com. ❸ <u>If you are</u> <u>currently experiencing an emergency, please stay on the</u> <u>line, and you will ⊚**be transferred** to an emergency after-</u> <u>hours dental clinic.</u> Thank you.

問題 1 至 3 請參考以下電話訊息。

你好，❶ <u>這裡是懷特醫生診所，現在不是我們的上班時間。</u>我們的上班時間為平日上午 8 點至下午 5 點，週六上午 9 點至中午 12 點。若是一般問題，請於明天上班時間來電。❷ <u>請注意我們不再透過電話預約。為方便病患，懷</u> <u>特醫生診所最近已建立網路預約服務。</u>欲使用此服務，可瀏覽我們的官方網站，網址是 www.drwhiteclinic.com。❸ <u>你若現在需要看急診，請不要掛斷</u> <u>電話，我們會為你轉接在非上班有急診服務的牙醫診所。</u>謝謝。

1. Who most likely is the speaker?　　　說話者可能是什麼身分？

　(A) A patient　　　　　　　　　　　(A) 病患

　(B) A customer service representative　(B) 客服代表

　(C) A clinic staff　　　　　　　　**(C) 診所員工**

　(D) Recording technician　　　　　　(D) 錄音技師

> **解說** 電話留言類的「說話者」，答案在「前兩句」的常見句型：Hello, you have reached….「你好，這裡是懷特醫生診所，現在不是我們的上班時間」，說話者最有可能為牙醫診所的答錄機，所以答案是 (C)。

2. What has changed at the clinic?　　　診所有什麼變動？

　(A) The booking system　　　　　**(A) 預約方式**

　(B) The business hours　　　　　　　(B) 營業時間

　(C) The website design　　　　　　　(C) 網站設計

　(D) The clinic location　　　　　　　(D) 診所地點

> **解說** 一般細節題，仔細聽「診所變動」的相關內容：「請注意我們不再透過電話預約。為方便病患，懷特醫生診所最近已建立網路預約服務」，表示預約方式已改變，所以答案是 (A)。

同義替換 reservation = booking

3. What are callers asked to do in case of emergency?　　　致電者若要看急診該怎麼做？

　(A) Speak to a telephone operator　　(A) 告知接線生

　(B) Leave a message　　　　　　　　(B) 留言

　(C) Wait to be connected　　　　　**(C) 不要掛斷等待轉接**

　(D) Call during business hours　　　　(D) 在營業時間打來

> **解說** 電話留言類的「建議」，要聽文章最後面，表示「建議」的句型，please... 此題也有關鍵字 emergency：「你若現在需要看急診，請不要掛斷電話，我們會為你轉接在非上班有急診服務的牙醫診所」，所以答案是 (C)。

同義替換 be transferred = be connected

Questions 4 through 6 refer to the following telephone message. (65)

(美式男聲) Hello, Ms. Perkins. ❹ This is Josh Turner at EZ Press. I'm calling about the graphic design position you applied for last week. ❺ We've had look at your application materials, and your credentials seem very impressive. I'd like to schedule an interview with you for Thursday morning at 10 o'clock. It should take an hour or so. Please bring a portfolio so that I can have a more extensive look at your design work. ❻ Please call me back at 018-528-317 to let me know if you can come in on Thursday. I look forward to meeting with you.

問題 4 至 6 請參考以下電話訊息。

您好，帕金斯女士。❹ 我是喬許杜納，代表 EZ 報刊打電話過來。我打來是為了你上週應徵的平面設計職位。❺ 我們看了你的應徵資料。你的資歷似乎令人印象非常深刻。我想跟你安排面試，時間是週四上午 10 點。應該會需要大約一小時。請帶你的作品集過來，好讓我更瞭解你的設計作品。❻ 請回電告知你是否願意週四過來，電話是 018-528-317。我期待與你見面。

單字 credential (n.) 資歷 / impressive (a.) 令人印象深刻的
portfolio (n.) （藝術）作品集 / extensive (a.) 廣泛的、大量的

4. Why did Josh Turner call?　　　　喬許杜納為何打電話來？
    (A) To invite employees to apply for a　(A) 邀請員工應徵
        position　　　　　　　　　　　　職缺
    (B) To reschedule a meeting　　　　(B) 重新安排會議
    (C) To request a telephone number　(C) 詢問電話號碼
    (D) To arrange a job interview　　**(D) 安排工作面試**

> **解說**　電話留言類的「目的」，答案在「前兩句」的常見句型 : I'm calling about… :「我是喬許杜納，代表 EZ 報刊打電話過來。我打來是為了你上週應徵的平面設計職位。我們看了你的應徵資料。你的資歷似乎令人印象非常深刻。我想跟你安排面試，」，所以答案是 (D)。

5. What does the speaker mean when　說話者說的「你的資格似乎
    he says, "your credentials seem very　令人印象非常深刻」是什麼
    impressive."?　　　　　　　　　　意思？
    (A) He's congratulating the woman for　(A) 恭喜聽電話者
        getting a job　　　　　　　　　　被錄取
    (B) He's acknowledging her　　　**(B) 認可專業**
        professional qualifications　　**資格**
    (C) He's welcoming a new colleague　(C) 歡迎新同事
    (D) He's celebrating a successful contract　(D) 慶祝合約簽訂成功

> **解說**　隱含文意題，要結合上下文，推論出題目 "your credentials seem very impressive." 的意思，正解在 :「我們看了你的應徵資料。你的資歷似乎令人印象非常深刻。我想跟你安排面試，時間是週四上午 10 點」，表示認同其資歷，想邀請來面試，所以答案是 (B)。

> **單字**　acknowledge (v.) 認可

6. What should Ms. Perkins do next?　帕金斯女士接下來該做什麼？
    (A) Confirm her appointment　　**(A) 確認是否要在約定時間到場**
    (B) Send comments about the agenda　(B) 寄送對於議程的意見
    (C) Bring a copy of her résumé　　(C) 帶她的履歷過去
    (D) Call to place an order　　　　(D) 打電話過去訂購

> **解說**　電話留言類的「建議」，要聽文章最後面，表「建議」的句型 please... :「請回電告知你是否願意週四過來」，表示要請應徵者確認見面時間，所以答案是 (A)。

1. What is the announcement mainly about?

(A) Repair of the bathroom facilities

(B) Loss of power to the building

(C) Replacement of some pipes

(D) Leaks in the plumbing system

2. When will the work likely be completed?

(A) On Monday

(B) On Wednesday

(C) On Friday

(D) On Tuesday

3. What are employees asked to do on affected days?

(A) Use an alternate restroom

(B) Come to the office later

(C) Avoid the office kitchen

(D) Turn off their computers

4. What is the purpose of the speech?

(A) To introduce a new employee

(B) To present an employee award

(C) To thank team members

(D) To announce a retirement

5. In what field does Mr. White work?

(A) Advertising

(B) Production

(C) Accounting

(D) Marketing

6. What is mentioned about Mr. White?

(A) He was recruited from another company.

(B) He has been working part-time.

(C) He has been promoted.

(D) He is going to graduate this year.

7. What is the report mainly about?

(A) An upcoming conference

(B) An expansion plan

(C) A new government policy

(D) A newly-opened facility

8. What is mentioned as being available at the Apex Convention Center?

(A) Dining facilities

(B) Presentation software

(C) On-site hotel rooms

(D) A fitness center

9. Who is Craig Harvey?

(A) A local official

(B) An architect

(C) A mayor

(D) A journalist

10. What are the hotel's guests least satisfied with?

(A) The quality of their service

(B) The comfort of their rooms

(C) Their prices and fees

(D) The cleanliness of their facilities

11. What does the speaker imply when she says, "everyone can see our ratings online"?

(A) She wants the company to build a website.

(B) She encourages people to book rooms online.

(C) She is happy the hotel information is easily accessible.

(D) She is worried about damage to the hotel's reputation.

12. What does the speaker suggest?

(A) Organizing a training program

(B) Hiring more customer service staff

(C) Starting an incentive scheme

(D) Reviewing customer complaints

13. Who most likely are the listeners?

(A) Accountants

(B) Market analysts

(C) Consultants

(D) Investors

14. What does the speaker mean when he says, "These excellent results wouldn't have been possible without each and every one of you"?

(A) He believes additional staff will be required.

(B) He has not worked with the team before.

(C) All the team members made important contributions.

(D) It will be possible to achieve the sales target.

15. What has the speaker promised to do?

(A) Give a pay raise

(B) Reimburse travel expenses

(C) Negotiate a contract

(D) Provide a financial reward

NOTE

Questions 1 through 3 refer to the following announcement.

(美式女聲) Excuse me, everyone. I have a quick announcement to make. ❶ Starting this afternoon, there will be maintenance staff working on our floor every day. They're going to repair the plumbing system, as a number of the pipes have begun to rust. There are no leaks now, but ❶ we've decided to replace the rusty pipes before they begin to leak. ❷ The work should be 回finished by Friday, but on Tuesday, Wednesday and Thursday there may be some noise and disruption. Also, ❸ please use the restroom facilities on one of the other floors until the repairs are completed. I'll notify everyone by e-mail when the work's finished.

問題 1 至 3 請參考以下公告。

不好意思，各位。很快宣布一件事。❶ 從今天下午開始，我們這一樓每天都會有維修人員來工作。由於有許多水管已經開始生鏽，所以他們會修理水管系統。現在雖然沒有漏水，不好意思，各位。很快宣布一件事。❶ 但我們決定先行更新生鏽的水管，以免日後漏水。❷ 應該會在週五前完工，但週二、週三和週四可能會有點吵雜和干擾。另外 ❸ 在維修完工前，請用其他樓層的廁所。等完工時，我會用電郵通知各位。

單字 plumbing (n.) 水管、管路系統 / pipe (n.) 管子、管道 / rust (v.) 生鏽 leak (n./v.) 漏水 / notify (v.) 告知

1. What is the announcement mainly about?　公告的主要內容是什麼？
   (A) Repair of the bathroom facilities　(A) 修理廁所設備
   (B) Loss of power to the building　(B) 大樓停電
   (C) Replacement of some pipes　**(C) 更換水管**
   (D) Leaks in the plumbing system　(D) 水管漏水

解說 公告類的「主題」，要聽「前兩句」：Starting this afternoon, there will be maintenance staff working on our floor every day. They're going to repair the plumbing system.「從今天下午開始，我們這一樓每天都會有維修人員來工作。他們會修理水管系統」，所以答案是 (C)。

單字 replacement (n.) 替換、更換

2. When will the work likely be completed?　何時能完工？
   (A) On Monday　(A) 週一
   (B) On Wednesday　(B) 週三
   (C) On Friday　**(C) 週五**
   (D) On Tuesday　(D) 週二

解說 公告類的「具體事項」，聽和 completed 相關的內容即正解：The work should be finished by Friday.「應該會在週五前完工」，所以答案是 (C)。

同義替換 finished = completed

3. What are employees asked to do on affected days?　維修期間員工被要求做什麼？
   (A) Use an alternate restroom　**(A) 用其他廁所**
   (B) Come to the office later　(B) 晚一點到辦公室
   (C) Avoid the office kitchen　(C) 避免用辦公室廚房
   (D) Turn off their computers　(D) 關掉電腦

解說 公告類的「要求事項 / 建議題」，要聽文章最後面「建議」的句型：please use the restroom facilities on one of the other floors until the repairs are completed.「在維修完工前，請用其他樓層的廁所」，所以答案是 (A)。

Questions 4 through 6 refer to the following speech.

(美式男聲) ❹ Good evening, and thank you for coming to our annual awards ceremony. Our first award tonight is for New Recruit of the Year. This year we had an outstanding group of graduate recruits, so this was a tough decision to make. Nevertheless, there was one candidate who stood head and shoulders above the rest. ❺ Steve White joined us this year as a marketing assistant, and has showed a high level of dedication to his work. He always completes his tasks on or ahead of schedule and to a consistently high standard. ❻ Steve has learned so quickly that he's already earned a promotion. We expect great things from this young man in the future. Everyone, please give Steve a warm round of applause!

問題 **4** 至 **6** 請參考以下演講。

❹ 晚安,謝謝各位參加我們的年度頒獎典禮。今晚第一個要頒發的獎項是年度新進員工獎。今年我們有一群剛畢業的傑出新員工,所以是很艱難的決定。不過仍有一位人選脫穎而出。❺ 史帝夫懷特今年剛加入我們,擔任行銷助理,對工作表現出高度的奉獻精神。他總是按時或提前完成任務,始終保持高水準。❻ 史帝夫學習得很快,已經獲得晉升。我們期待這位年輕人在未來有更優秀的表現。請各位給史帝夫熱烈的掌聲!

單字 recruit (n./v.) 新員工;招聘 / stand head and shoulders above 脫穎而出 dedication (n.) 奉獻 / promotion (n.) 升遷 / applause (n.) 掌聲

4. What is the purpose of the speech? 演講的目的是什麼？

    (A) To introduce a new employee (A) 介紹新員工

    (B) To present an employee award (B) **頒發員工獎**

    (C) To thank team members (C) 感謝團隊成員

    (D) To announce a retirement (D) 宣布退休

解說 商務演說類的「目的」，要聽「前兩句」：Good evening, and thank you for coming to our annual awards ceremony. Our first award tonight is for New Recruit of the Year.「晚安，謝謝各位參加我們的年度頒獎典禮。今晚第一個要頒發的獎項是年度新進員工獎」，所以答案是 (B)。

5. In what field does Mr. White work? 懷特先生在哪個領域工作？

    (A) Advertising (A) 廣告

    (B) Production (B) 生產

    (C) Accounting (C) 會計

    (D) Marketing (D) **行銷**

解說 商務演說類的「細節題」，仔細聽 Mr. White 的工作內容即為正解：Steve White joined us this year as a marketing assistant, and has showed a high level of dedication to his work.「史帝夫懷特今年剛加入我們，擔任行銷助理，對工作表現出高度的奉獻精神」，行銷助理即在行銷部門，所以答案是 (D)。

6. What is mentioned about Mr. White? 演講提到懷特先生什麼事？

    (A) He was recruited from another (A) 他是從其他公司
        company. 挖角來的。

    (B) He has been working part-time. (B) 他是兼職員工。

    (C) He has been promoted. (C) **他獲得晉升。**

    (D) He is going to graduate this year. (D) 他今年要畢業了。

解說 商務演說類的「細節題」，仔細聽和 Mr. White 相關的描述，判斷出正確答案：Steve has learned so quickly that he's already earned a promotion.「史帝夫學習得很快，已經獲得晉升」，所以答案是 (C)。

Questions 7 through 9 refer to the following report.

(英式男聲) ❼ The city government today ⊙**unveiled** the new Apex Convention Center. Located in the downtown area, the center is a modern structure designed to hold large international events. ❽ It offers conference facilities and meeting rooms equipped with everything necessary for multimedia presentations. The center also offers a complete suite of office productivity software, complimentary wireless Internet access and two banquet halls. ❾ Craig Harvey, ⊙**director of the city's infrastructure department**, told the media that the convention center could become an important city landmark. Its design features majestic twin towers overlooking the city. For more information about the Apex Convention Center, visit the city government's website at www.apexcity.gov.us.

問題 7 至 9 請參考以下報導。

❼ 市政府今天啟用新的高峰會議中心。會議中心的地點在市中心,是為了舉辦大型國際活動而設計的現代建築,提供會議設施,❽ 會議室配備多媒體講座所需的一切設備。會議中心也包括一套完整的辦公室生產力軟體,免費無線網路和兩間宴會聽。❾ 市府公共建設部門主任柯雷格哈維告訴媒體,會議中心會成為重要的城市地標,設計特色是俯瞰城市的宏偉雙塔。欲知更多關於高峰會議中心的資訊,可瀏覽市政府網站:www.apexcity.gov.us。

單字 multimedia (a.) 多媒體的 / suite (n.) 軟體套裝 / productivity (n.) 生產率
Internet access(連線)上網 / infrastructure (n.) 基礎建設

7. What is the report mainly about? 這篇報導主要是關於什麼？
   (A) An upcoming conference (A) 即將舉行的會議
   (B) An expansion plan (B) 拓展計畫
   (C) A new government policy (C) 新的政府政策
   (D) A newly-opened facility **(D) 新啟用的場所**

解說 商業新聞類的「主題」，要聽「前兩句」：The city government today unveiled the new Apex Convention Center. Located in the downtown area「市政府今天啟用新的高峰會議中心」，所以答案是 (D)。

同義替換 unveil = newly open

8. What is mentioned as being available at 報導中提到高峰會議中心
   the Apex Convention Center? 有什麼？
   (A) Dining facilities (A) 餐飲設施
   (B) Presentation hardware **(B) 講座硬體**
   (C) On-site hotel rooms (C) 實地旅館房間
   (D) A fitness center (D) 健身中心

解說 商業新聞類的「細節題」，仔細聽 Apex Convention Center 提供的服務和設備，並歸納答案：雖然文中使用的是 software（軟體），但和講座相關的設備都屬於硬體 (hardware)，「提供會議設施，會議室配備多媒體簡報所需的一切設備。會議中心也包括一套完整的辦公軟體，免費無線網路和兩間宴會廳」，所以答案是 (B)。

9. Who is Craig Harvey? 誰是柯雷格哈維？
   (A) A local official **(A) 地方官員**
   (B) An architect (B) 建築師
   (C) A mayor (C) 市長
   (D) A journalist (D) 記者

解說 商業新聞類的「細節題」，聽到 Craig Harvey 即答案：Craig Harvey, director of the city's infrastructure department「市府公共建設部門主任柯雷格哈維」，所以答案是 (A)。

同義替換 director of the city's infrastructure department = local official

Questions 10 through 12 refer to the following telephone message.

(英式女聲) Hi, Ethan. It's Dana. I was just going over our hotel's online ratings, and they're a lot lower than I'd hoped. ⑩ Customers had complaints about all kinds of things, but the biggest issue seems to be that our (回)**staff members just aren't very helpful**. We need to remember that everyone can see our ratings online. ⑪ We've got a lot of competition, and we want to make sure travelers continue to choose us for their accommodation. ⑫ To address this issue, I think we should (回)**start giving bonuses** to the employees who consistently receive high customer ratings. And we could honor an employee of the month each month.

問題 **10** 至 **12** 請參考以下電話留言。

嗨，伊森，我是達娜。我剛剛在看我們旅館的網上評分，比我所希望的還低。⑩ 顧客抱怨了各種事情，但最大的問題是我們的員工服務不佳。我們要記住，所有人都會看到我們在網路上的評分。⑪ 我們有很多競爭對手，我們要讓旅客繼續選擇住宿我們旅館。⑫ 為解決這問題，我想我們應該開始為持續獲得高顧客評分的員工提供獎金。我們每個月可獎勵該月最佳員工。

(單字) ratings (n.) 評級、等級 / accommodation (n.) 住處 / bonus (n.) 獎金

10. What are the hotel's guests least satisfied with? 旅館客人最不滿意什麼？

(A) **The quality of their service**　　(A) 服務品質

(B) The comfort of their rooms　　(B) 房間的舒適度

(C) Their prices and fees　　(C) 價格和費用

(D) The cleanliness of their facilities　　(D) 設施的乾淨度

解說 一般細節題，仔細聽「客戶最不滿」的內容：「顧客抱怨了各種事情，但最大的問題是我們的員工服務不佳。」 所以答案是 (A)。

同義替換 staff members just aren't very helpfule = the quality of their service

NEW

11. What does the speaker imply when she says, "everyone can see our ratings online"?　　「所有人都會看到我們在網上的評分」是在暗示什麼？

(A) She wants the company to build a website.　　(A) 她希望公司能架設網站。

(B) She encourages people to book rooms online.　　(B) 她鼓勵大家上網訂房。

(C) She is happy the hotel information is easily accessible.　　(C) 她很高興旅館資訊可以輕易取得。

(D) **She is worried about damage to the hotel's reputation.**　　(D) 她擔心旅館的名聲受損。

解說 隱含文意題，要結合上下文，推論出題目「我們有很多競爭對手，我們要讓旅客繼續選擇住宿我們旅館」，暗示網路的評價會影響客戶的決定，所以答案是 (D)。

12. What does the speaker suggest?　　講者建議什麼？

(A) Organizing a training program　　(A) 組織訓練課程

(B) Hiring more customer service staff　　(B) 聘請更多客服人員

(C) **Starting an incentive scheme**　　(C) 開辦獎金計畫

(D) Reviewing customer complaints　　(D) 審閱顧客投訴

解說 電話留言類的「建議」，要聽文章最後面，表「建議」的句型：「為解決這問題，我想我們應該開始為持續獲得高顧客評分的員工提供獎金」，建議公司進行獎勵機制以提升服務品質，所以答案是 (C)。

同義替換 start giving bonuses = starting an incentive scheme

Questions 13 through 15 refer to the following talk.

(美式男聲) I'd like to thank you all for your outstanding efforts. The project has been a huge success. Our client told me at our meeting that we're the best team that they've ever worked with. ⑬ With our consulting services, they were able to cut their expenses by 25% and increase their sales by 20% in just five months. ⑭ I have no doubt that many of you put in a lot of overtime during the contract period. These excellent results wouldn't have been possible without each and every one of you. ⑮ Therefore, I've arranged for all of you to 🔊 **receive generous bonuses** for your great work.

問題 **13** 至 **15** 請參考以下演說。

我想謝謝各位非凡的努力。這項專案大獲全勝。我們的客戶在會議上告訴我，我們是他們合作過最棒的團隊。⑬ 因為我們的諮詢服務，他們得以在僅僅五個月內減少 25%開支，增加 20%銷售額。 ⑭ 我相信你們當中有許多人在合約期間經常加班。沒有各位，就不會有這樣優秀的成果。 ⑮ 因此我已經為各位準備優渥的獎金，獎勵你們優秀的表現。

單字 outstanding (a.) 傑出的 / consulting (n.) 諮詢
overtime (n./a.) 加班、超時 / generous (a.) 大量的、豐富的

13. Who most likely are the listeners?　　　聽者可能是誰？
    (A) Accountants　　　　　　　　　　　(A) 會計
    (B) Market analysts　　　　　　　　　　(B) 市場分析師
    (C) Consultants　　　　　　　　　　　**(C) 顧問**
    (D) Investors　　　　　　　　　　　　　(D) 投資人

解說 商務演說類的「對象」，答案在「前幾句」即出現。「因為我們的諮詢服務，他們得以在僅僅五個月內減少 25% 開支，增加 20% 銷售量」，說話者提及：客戶讚賞我們的諮詢服務，所以答案是 (C)。

NEW
14. What does the speaker mean when he says,　講者說「沒有各位，就
    "These excellent results wouldn't have been　不會有這優秀的成果」
    possible without each and every one of you"?　是什麼意思？
    (A) He believes additional staff will be　　(A) 他認為需要增加
        required.　　　　　　　　　　　　　　　員工。
    (B) He has not worked with the team before.　(B) 他以前沒跟這團隊合作過。
    (C) All the team members made important　**(C) 團隊所有人都做出重要**
    contributions.　　　　　　　　　　　　**貢獻。**
    (D) It will be possible to achieve the sales　(D) 有可能達到銷售目標。
        target.

解說 隱含文意題，要結合上下文，推論出題目 "These excellent results wouldn't have been possible without each and every one of you" 的意思，正解在：「我相信你們當中有許多人在合約期間經常加班」，表示因每個人的努力付出，造就今天成功的專案，所以答案是 (C)。

15. What has the speaker promised to do?　　講者保證什麼？
    (A) Give a pay raise　　　　　　　　　　(A) 加薪
    (B) Reimburse travel expenses　　　　　(B) 補貼出差費
    (C) Negotiate a contract　　　　　　　　(C) 協商合約
    (D) Provide a financial reward　　　　　**(D) 提供獎金**

解說 商務演說類的「下一步」，仔細聽文章最後面，宣布接下來要做什麼：「因此我已經為各位準備優渥的獎金，獎勵你們優秀的表現」，所以答案是 (D)。

單字 pay raise 加薪 / reimburse 補償 / reward 酬謝、獎勵、報償

同義替換 receive generous bonuses = provide a financial reward

Part **5**

實戰模擬測驗

本模擬試題的形式比照正式測驗，但分量縮減，
所以測驗時間為 35 分鐘。

答案卡位於 p. 277，可剪下劃記。

Part 1

Directions: For each question in this part, you will hear four statements about a picture in your test book. When you hear the statements, you must select the one statement that best describes what you see in the picture. Then find the number of the question on your answer sheet and mark your answer. The statements will not be printed in your test book and will be spoken only one time.

1.

(A) (B) (C) (D)

2.

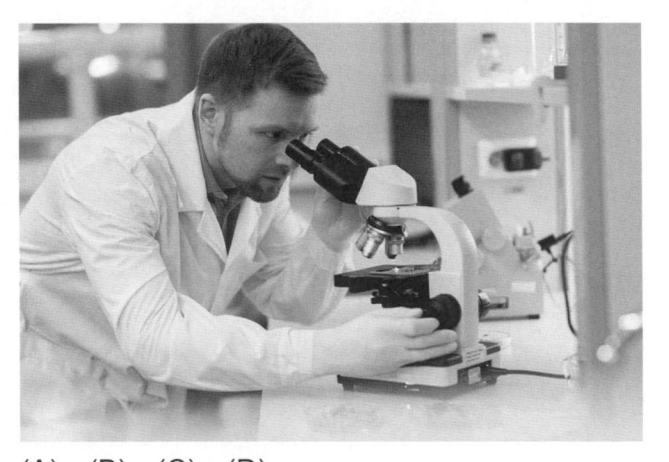

(A) (B) (C) (D)

3.

(A)　(B)　(C)　(D)

4.

(A)　(B)　(C)　(D)

5.

(A)　(B)　(C)　(D)

6.

(A)　(B)　(C)　(D)

Part 2

Directions: You will hear a question or statement and three responses spoken in English. They will not be printed in your test book and will be spoken only one time. Select the best response to the question or statement and mark the letter (A), (B), or (C) on your answer sheet.

7.   Mark your answer on your answer sheet.

8.   Mark your answer on your answer sheet.

9.   Mark your answer on your answer sheet.

10.   Mark your answer on your answer sheet.

11.   Mark your answer on your answer sheet.

12.   Mark your answer on your answer sheet.

13.   Mark your answer on your answer sheet.

14.   Mark your answer on your answer sheet.

15.   Mark your answer on your answer sheet.

16.   Mark your answer on your answer sheet.

11.   Mark your answer on your answer sheet.

17.   Mark your answer on your answer sheet.

18.   Mark your answer on your answer sheet.

19.   Mark your answer on your answer sheet.

20.   Mark your answer on your answer sheet.

21.   Mark your answer on your answer sheet.

22.   Mark your answer on your answer sheet.

23.   Mark your answer on your answer sheet.

24.   Mark your answer on your answer sheet.

Part 3

Directions: You will hear some conversations between two or more people. You will be asked to answer three questions about what the speakers say in each conversation. Select the best response to each question and mark the letter (A), (B), (C), or (D) on your answer sheet. The conversation will not be printed in your test book and will be spoken only one time.

25. What is the man inquiring about?

(A) The name of a performance

(B) Discounted tickets for a show

(C) The registration fee for a fair

(D) The schedule for an upcoming movie

26. What does the woman imply about the discounted tickets?

(A) They won't be available until next month.

(B) They are valid only for weekdays.

(C) They can be used at different locations.

(D) They will soon be completely sold out.

27. What does the woman mean when she says, "Be sure to check it out."?

(A) The man should read a publication.

(B) The man should reserve a seat.

(C) The man should check the calendar.

(D) The man should rent a video.

28. What type of business do the speakers work for?

(A) A sportswear manufacturer

(B) A publishing company

(C) An advertising agency

(D) A fitness center

29. What is one of the features of the sports watch?

(A) Its affordable price

(B) Its resistance to water

(C) Its compact design

(D) Its light weight

30. What does the man ask the woman to do?

(A) Post a help-wanted ad

(B) Find potential clients

(C) Find some athletes

(D) Research a competitor

31. Who most likely is the woman?

   (A) A housekeeper
   (B) A maintenance worker
   (C) A front desk receptionist
   (D) A hotel security guard

32. What problem does the man mention?

   (A) The room next door is too noisy.
   (B) The air-conditioner isn't working properly.
   (C) He can't get hot water in the bathroom.
   (D) His room hasn't been cleaned.

33. What does the woman offer to do?

   (A) File a customer complaint
   (B) Issue a refund
   (C) Reduce a price
   (D) Provide a gift certificate

34. What are the speakers mainly discussing?

(A) A remodeling project

(B) A product launch

(C) A room reservation

(D) A store floor plan

35. What does the woman say about the dining room?

(A) It has a large dining table.

(B) It covers a large area.

(C) It doesn't have enough space.

(D) It needs more decorations.

36. What compensation does the woman recommend?

(A) A gift voucher

(B) A free meal

(C) A refund

(D) A special offe

Article	Deadline
"Exploring Formosa"	May 15
"Have Fun in Taipei"	May 15
"MRT Tours"	July 23
"Taiwan by Train"	August 30

37. What does the woman ask the man to do?

(A) Proofread a publication

(B) Increase the word count of an article

(C) Correct a mistake in a document

(D) Modify the content of an article

38. Look at the chart. Which article's deadline will be extended?

(A) "Exploring Formosa"

(B) "Have Fun in Taipei"

(C) "MRT Tours"

(D) "Taiwan by Train"

39. What does the man say he will do?

(A) Send a final draft

(B) Finish an assignment

(C) Delegate tasks to another writer

(D) Travel in a tour group

Branch Sales

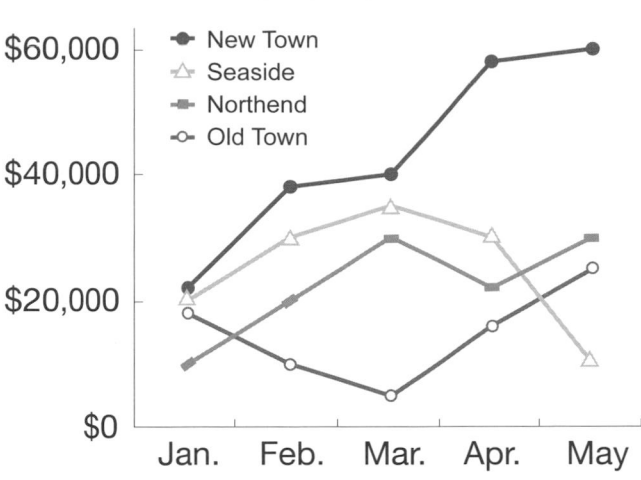

40. What does the woman plan to do?

(A) Submit a new budget proposal

(B) Upgrade some office equipment

(C) Promote some of her staff

(D) Hire additional workers

42. Look at the graphic. Which branch does the woman work at?

(A) New Town

(B) Seaside

(C) Northend

(D) Old Town

41. According to the man, what has the company recently done?

(A) It has opened a new branch.

(B) It has held an annual sale.

(C) It has downsized its workforce.

(D) It has reduced its spending.

43. What is the advertisement for?

    (A) A house cleaning service
    (B) A cleaning product
    (C) A household appliance
    (D) A dust cloth

44. What does the speaker mean when he says, "it'll be spotless in just seconds!"?

    (A) The cleaner can't remove all the spots.
    (B) The surface will be clean immediately.
    (C) It takes time to clean the cloth.
    (D) The wet cloth will dry fast.

45. What are some listeners encouraged to do?

    (A) Pick up product samples
    (B) Obtain raffle tickets
    (C) Sign up for a free trial
    (D) Participate in a demonstration

46. Where is the talk being given?

(A) At a clothing factory

(B) At a shoe manufacturer

(C) At an antique store

(D) At a department store

47. What is special about the factory?

(A) Its production method

(B) Its automated equipment

(C) Its guided tours

(D) Its convenient location

48. What will listeners do at the end of the tour?

(A) Receive free samples

(B) Join in a hands-on experience

(C) Sign up for a class

(D) Make a purchase

49. What is the radio broadcast mainly about?

(A) Worldwide cooking

(B) Food carnivals

(C) Healthy eating habits

(D) Overseas travel

50. What has Paul Jackson recently done?

(A) Produced a TV program

(B) Written an article

(C) Made a film

(D) Opened a restaurant

51. What does the speaker suggest listeners do?

(A) Watch a preview

(B) Listen to a radio show

(C) Download a documentary

(D) Contact a film company

Life Shield Co.

	Bronze	Silver	Gold	Elite
Price	$1,000	$1,300	$1,800	$2,600
Backup System	No	Yes	Yes	Yes
Data Archive	4 weeks	12 weeks	24 weeks	52 weeks

52. What is the purpose of the talk?

(A) To provide training for clients

(B) To launch a new system

(C) To compete with other companies

(D) To promote a new product

53. Which security package does the speaker recommend?

(A) Bronze

(B) Silver

(C) Gold

(D) Elite

54. Why is Elite the most expensive package?

(A) It includes a year of data storage.

(B) It offers a backup system.

(C) It provides high-tech surveillance.

(D) It is the newest product available.

Lawson Engineering
Office Supplies Order Form

Order Number: 903H2

Item	Units ordered
Office chairs	6
Drafting tables	3
Personal computers	5
Adjustable lamps	8

55. Where is the man likely calling from?

(A) A furniture store

(B) A stationery store

(C) An office supply store

(D) An office building

56. Which quantity will the listener probably adjust?

(A) 6

(B) 3

(C) 5

(D) 8

57. Why should the listener return the call?

(A) To confirm a delivery date

(B) To discuss sales numbers

(C) To verify the units ordered

(D) To explain survey results

實戰模擬測驗 答案與解説

Part 1
1. (B)　　2. (B)　　3. (A)　　4. (D)　　5. (C)　　6. (C)

Part 2
7. (C)　　8. (C)　　9. (B)　　10. (B)　　11.(A)　　12. (C)　　13. (C)　　14. (B)　　15. (B)

16. (B)　17. (A)　18. (B)　19. (C)　20. (B)　21. (B)　22. (A)　23. (B)　24. (A)

Part 3
25. (B)　26. (D)　27. (A)　28. (C)　29. (B)　30. (C)　31.(C)　32. (D)　33. (D)

34. (A)　35. (B)　36. (D)　37. (D)　38. (B)　39. (A)　40. (D)　41.(D)　42. (A)

Part 4
43. (B)　44. (B)　45. (D)　46. (B)　47. (A)　48. (B)　49. (A)　50. (C)　51. (A)

52. (D)　53. (B)　54. (A)　55. (D)　56. (C)　57. (C)

Part 1

1.

美式男聲

(A) She's turning on a light.

(B) She's using a photocopier.

(C) She's opening a cabinet.

(D) She's checking out some books.

(A) 她在開燈。

(B) 她在用影印機。

(C) 她在開櫥櫃。

(D) 她在借書。

> **解說** 此為人物題的單人圖片，要注意「人物、動作、地點」。(B) 兩個重點描述皆正確：女子、使用影印機，為正確答案。(A) 錯在動作描述：並沒有把燈打開，所以刪除。(C) 錯在動作描述：沒有打開櫥櫃，所以刪除。(D) 錯在動作描述：不是在借書，不能選。

> **單字** photocopier (n.) 影印機 / check out 結帳離開，此為借書之意

2.

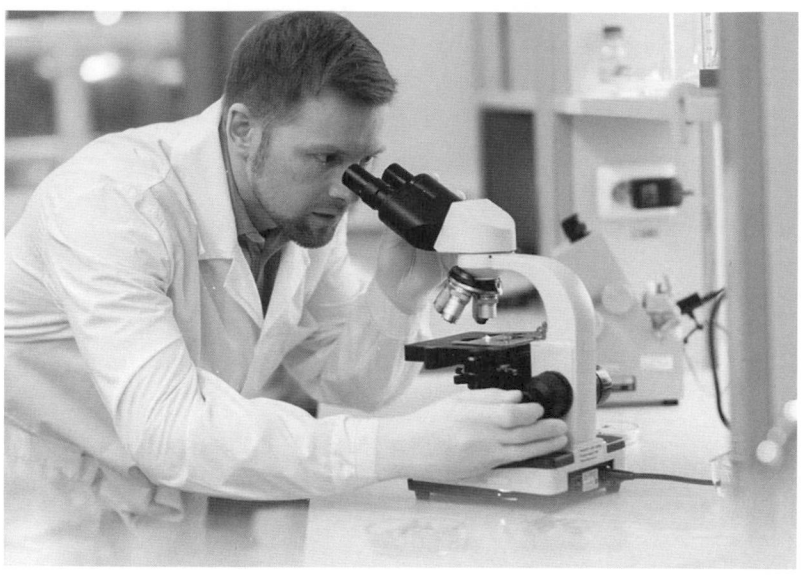

英式女聲

(A) He's looking into the telescope.

(B) He's using laboratory equipment.

(C) He's adjusting the microphone.

(D) He's putting on a pair of gloves.

(A) 他在看望遠鏡。

(B) 他在用實驗器材。

(C) 他在調整麥克風。

(D) 他在戴手套。

解說 此為人物題的單人圖片，要注意「人物、動作、地點」。(B) 兩個重點描述皆正確：男子、使用實驗室儀器，為正確答案。(A) 錯在專有名詞：望遠鏡不正確，所以刪除。(C) 錯在動作描述：調整麥克風不正確，所以刪除。(D) 錯在動作描述：正戴上手套，應該改為：He's wearing a pair of gloves. 他正戴著手套。

單字 telescope (n.) 望遠鏡 / laboratory (n.) 實驗室，可簡稱為 lab microphone (n.) 麥克風

3.

美式女聲

(A) **The vehicles are lined up by the curb.**

(B) The traffic lights are being installed.

(C) Cars are driving down the street.

(D) The leaves have fallen off the trees.

(A) 一排車輛停在路邊。

(B) 正在安裝交通號誌燈。

(C) 汽車在街道上行駛。

(D) 葉片從樹上落下。

解說　此為景物題，要「注意動、靜態、事物位置」。(A) 為靜態描述：被排列停靠在路邊，為正確答案。(B) 錯在動態：正在安裝不正確，且沒有看到交通號誌燈，所以刪除。(C) 錯在動態：正在行駛不正確，所以刪除。(D) 有圖有真相：樹葉很茂盛，沒有掉落。

單字　vehicle (n.) 車輛 / traffic light 紅綠燈

4.

英式男聲

(A) Fruit is scattered all over the floor.

(B) Crates are stacked in a corner.

(C) A shopper is carrying a basket of groceries.

(D) A vendor is selling produce.

(A) 水果散落一地。

(B) 角落堆著木箱。

(C) 顧客拿著一籃食品雜貨。

(D) 小販在賣農產品。

> 解說　此為人物題的兩人以上圖片，要「注意共同、分別動作」。(D) 攤販在販賣農產品，為正確答案。(A) 眼見為憑：水果沒有散落在地上，所以刪除。(B) 眼見為憑：沒有木箱被堆放在角落，所以刪除。(C) 錯在個別動作：購物者沒有提著一籃食品雜貨，所以刪除。

> 單字　crate (n.) 木箱

5.

美式女聲

(A) The women are arranging shoes for display.

(B) The women are trying on clothing.

(C) Some clothing is hanging on the racks.

(D) There are folded shirts sitting on a shelf.

(A) 女子在擺放要展示的鞋子。

(B) 女子在試穿衣服。

(C) 一些衣服掛在衣架上。

(D) 架子上放著摺疊好的襯衫。

解說 此為人物題的兩人以上圖片，要注意「共同、分別動作」。(C) 衣服掛在架子上，為正確答案。(A) 錯在共同動作：沒有在擺放要展示的鞋，所以刪除。(B) 錯在共同動作：是挑選而非試穿衣服，所以刪除。(D) 眼見為憑：沒有摺起來的衣服在架上，不能選。

單字 display (n.) 展示 / hang (v.) 懸掛、吊掛 / fold (v.) 摺

6.

美式男聲

(A) People are waiting in line for tickets.

(B) The stage has been set up indoors.

(C) Some people are watching a performance.

(D) People are entering the concert hall.

(A) 有人在排隊買票。

(B) 舞台是搭建在室內。

(C) 有些人在觀看 表演。

(D) 有人正在進入音樂廳。

解說　此為人物題的多人圖片，要注意「共同、分別動作」。(C) 共同動作：正在看表演，為正確答案。(A) 錯在共同動作：排隊買票不正確，所以刪除。(B) 眼見為憑：舞台不是設置在室內，所以刪除。(D) 錯在共同動作：沒有人正在進入音樂廳，不能選。

單字　set up 設立 / performance (n.) 表演 / concert hall 音樂廳

Part 2

7. (美式女聲) What's the best way to get in touch with you?

(英式男聲) (A) Take the highway, it's faster.

(B) Friday is best for me.

(C) You can reach me at this number.

怎麼跟你聯絡最好？

(A) 走這條高速公路比較快。

(B) 週五比較方便。

(C) 你可以打這個電話號碼。

> **解 說** 本題關鍵字：best way，問「最好的方式」。(C) 電話聯絡，是正確答案。(A) 相似音陷阱：best way 和 highway。(B) 回答時間，與題意不符，重複字陷阱：best。

> **單字** highway (n.) 高速公路 / get in touch 聯絡

8. (英式女聲) Where can I find the color cartridges?

(美式男聲) (A) Double-sided copies, please.

(B) Yes, I can do it for you.

(C) On the other end of the aisle.

彩色墨水在哪裡？

(A) 請幫我雙面影印。

(B) 好，我來幫你。

(C) 在走道另一端。

> **解 說** 本題關鍵字：Where can，問「地點」。(C) 是正確答案。(A) 不符合題意。(B) 不可以有「Yes/No」的回答，直接刪除。

> **單字** cartridge (n.) 墨水匣 / aisle (n.) 走道

9. (美式男聲) When will the charity event be held?

(美式女聲) (A) At the community center.

(B) The last Saturday of the month.

(C) Yes, Ms. Brown organized everything.

慈善活動何時舉行？

(A) 在社區中心。

(B) 那個月的最後一個週六。

(C) 對，全是布朗女士安排的。

解 說 本題關鍵字：When will，問「時間」。(B) 是正確答案。(A) 回答地點，不能選。(C) 不可以有「Yes/No」的回答，直接刪除。

單字 charity (n.) 慈善 / community (n.) 社區 / organize (v.) 安排、籌畫

10. (英式女聲) How soon can we expect the package?

(美式男聲) (A) Much sooner than expected.

(B) At the end of the week.

(C) Yes, it's all packed.

包裹多快會送到？

(A) 比預期快很多。

(B) 這週末。

(C) 對，都打包好了。

解 說 本題關鍵字：soon，問「多快」（時間）。(B) 是正確答案。
(A) 重複字陷阱：expect 和 expected，時態也不正確（題意是指 package 還沒送到，而選項是已收到）。(C) 不可以有「Yes/No」的回答，直接刪除。

單字 pack (v.) 打包

11. (美式女聲) They're going to have someone fill in for you while you're on leave, right?

(美式男聲) **(A) That's what I heard.**

(B) Yes, I feel good.

(C) Remember to fill out the leave request form.

你請假時，他們應該會找人幫你代班吧？

(A) 我聽說是這樣。

(B) 是的，我感覺很好。

(C) 記得填請假單。

解 說 (A) 是正確答案。(B) 不符合題意，相似音陷阱：fill 和 feel，不能選。(C) 不符合題意，重複字陷阱：fill in 和 fill out，不能選。

單字 fill in for 臨時代替 / leave request 請假申請

12. (英式女聲) What do you think of the new coffee maker?

(英式男聲) (A) I think that would be a good idea.

(B) I'm willing to buy it.

(C) It's better than I expected.

你覺得新咖啡機怎麼樣？

(A) 我覺得這主意很棒。

(B) 我願意買。

(C) 比我預期的還好。

解 說 本題關鍵字：what 和 think，問「覺得如何」。(C) 回答感受，是正確答案。(A) 不符合題意，重複字陷阱：think，不能選。(B) 不符合題意，題目問使用後的看法。

13. (美式女聲) Did you call the restaurant to confirm our reservation?

(美式男聲) (A) Yes, they called about our reservation.

(B) Let's try the new Chinese restaurant.

(C) Sorry, I've been busy all day.

你有打給餐廳確認訂位嗎？

(A) 對，他們打來問訂位的事。

(B) 我們試試新的中國餐館。

(C) 抱歉，我一整天都很忙。

解說 (C) 是正確答案，sorry 即為否定。(A) 不符合題意，主詞 they 不正確，重複字陷阱：call 和 called，不能選。(B) 不符合題意，重複字陷阱：restaurant，不能選。

14. (美式女聲) Why don't you buy some coffee for the meeting?

(美式男聲) (A) No thanks. I've quit drinking coffee.

(B) How many people will be attending?

(C) It will be held in the third-floor conference room.

你何不替會議買些咖啡？

(A) 不用，謝謝，我戒掉咖啡了。

(B) 有多少人會出席？

(C) 在三樓的會議室舉行。

解說 本題關鍵字：why don't you，提出「建議」。(B) 是正確答案，反問通常是正解。(A) 不符合題意，不是問對方要喝咖啡嗎？重複字陷阱：coffee，不能選。(C) 回答地點，不能選。

單字 quit (v.) 停止

15. (英式男聲) Could you tell me how often I have to submit status reports?

(美式女聲) (A) The deadline is next Friday.

(B) At least once a week.

(C) You have to report to the project manager.

你能告訴我多久要交一次現況報告嗎？
(A) 截止日期是下週五。
(B) 至少一週一次。
(C) 你要向專案經理報告。

解 說 子句型的題目，本題關鍵字：how often，問「頻率」。(B) 回答頻率，是正確答案。(A) 回答一個時間點，不能選。(C) 不符合題意，重複字陷阱：report，不能選。

單字 status report 進度報告 / deadline (n.) 截止日期、最後期限

16. (美式男聲) Which computer monitor did you decide to buy?

(美式女聲) (A) I bought it at a home appliance store.

(B) The one with the highest resolution.

(C) No, it's broken.

你決定要買哪個電腦螢幕？
(A) 我是在家電用品商店買的。
(B) 解析度最高的那臺。
(C) 不，那臺壞了。

解 說 本題關鍵字：computer monitor，問「電腦螢幕」。(B) 是正確答案，the one 指的是「電腦螢幕」，是常見答案。(A) 回答地點，不符合題意。(C) 聽到 No，直接刪掉。

17. 美式男聲 How do I stop this shredding machine?

美式女聲 **(A) The power switch is on the right.**

(B) It stopped running a few days ago.

(C) It needs to be repaired immediately.

我要怎麼讓這臺碎紙機停下來？

(A) 電源開關在右邊。

(B) 它幾天前故障了。

(C) 需要立刻修理。

解說 本題關鍵字：how stop，問「如何停止」。(A) 是正確答案。
(B) 不符合題意，重複字陷阱：stop，不能選。(C) 不符合題意。

單字 shredding machine 碎紙機 / switch (n) 開關

18. 英式女聲 Should I submit my estimate right away, or is next week okay?

美式女聲 (A) No, I'll be here all week.

(B) There's no rush. Take your time.

(C) All right. I'm on my way.

我該立刻提交估價單嗎？或是下週也行？

(A) 不，我整個星期都在這裡。

(B) 不急，慢慢來。

(C) 好，我現在過去。

解說 本題關鍵字：立刻提交估價單？或是下週也行？問「兩個選擇」。
(B) 選擇其一回答，並換句話說，是正確答案。(A) 不符合題意，
重複字陷阱：week，不能選。(C) 不符合題意，相似音陷阱：way
和 away，不能選。

單字 rush (n.) 緊急、匆忙

19. (英式男聲) You completed the customer survey, didn't you?

(美式女聲) (A) We guarantee quality after-sales service.

(B) Ed has been working hard on the market survey.

(C) No, I'll do it tomorrow.

你把客戶問卷調查填寫完成了，對吧？
(A) 我們保證提供高品質的售後服務。
(B) 艾德最近都在忙著處理市場調查。
(C) 不，我明天會去做。

解說　附加問句型的題目，本題關鍵字：completed, didn't you，問「你完成了嗎？」。(C) 是正確答案。(A) 不符合題意，相似音陷阱：survey 和 service，不能選。(B) 不符合題意，重複字陷阱：survey，不能選。

單字　guarantee (v.) 保證 / quality (adj.) 優質的
after-sales service 售後服務

20. (美式男聲) Should we use TV or Internet ads in our marketing campaign?

(美式女聲) (A) Let's order it online.

(B) Either would be effective.

(C) Yes, that's a great idea.

我們這次行銷活動應該使用電視或網路廣告嗎？
(A) 我們上網訂購吧。
(B) 任何一種都很有效。
(C) 對，那是好主意。

解說　本題關鍵字：電視或網路廣告？問「兩個選擇」。(B) 回答兩種都很有效，是正確答案，either 是常見答案。(A) 不符合題意，選項 online 和題目 Internet 相關，用來誤導考生。(C) 沒有回答哪一個，不能選。

21. 英式男聲 Remember that our client is visiting the plant tomorrow.

美式女聲 (A) I don't know who's coming.

(B) What time will he arrive?

(C) We're planning on joining the year-end party.

記住，我們客戶明天要來工廠參訪。

(A) 我不知道誰會來。

(B) 他幾點會到？

(C) 我們正打算參加尾牙。

解說 (B) 是正確答案，反問通常是正解。(A) 不符合題意。(C) 不符合題意，相似音陷阱：plant 和 plan，不能選。

單字 plant (n.) 工廠 / plan on 打算

22. 美式女聲 Who will lead the budget review committee?

美式男聲 **(A) Mr. Benson will be in charge.**

(B) I don't think we have enough in the budget.

(C) I hope they approve the budget.

誰會帶領預算審核委員會？

(A) 班森先生會負責。

(B) 我想我們預算不夠。

(C) 希望他們能批准預算。

解說 本題關鍵字：Who will，問「是誰」。(A) 是正確答案。(B) (C) 皆不符合題意，且為重複字陷阱：選項內有 budget 這個字，不能選。

單字 budget 預算 / review committee 審查委員會

23. 英式女聲 Do you know how to use this new time clock?

美式女聲 (A) No, she doesn't use it.

(B) Let's look at the manual.

(C) It went very well.

你知道怎麼用這個新的打卡鐘嗎？

(A) 不，她沒有使用。

(B) 我們看一下說明書。

(C) 這進展得很順利。

解說 子句型的題目，本題關鍵字：how to use，問「如何使用」。
(B) 是正確答案。(A) 不符合題意，重複字陷阱：use，不能選。
(C) 不符合題意。

24. 美式女聲 Why didn't you buy the tickets online?

美式男聲 **(A) I couldn't log on to the website.**

(B) Sorry, but his line is busy right now.

(C) No, thanks for reminding me.

你為何不上網買票？

(A) 我無法登入網站。

(B) 抱歉，但他的電話正忙線中。

(C) 不，謝謝你提醒我。

解說 本題關鍵字：why didn't buy，問「沒有買的原因」。(A) 是正確
答案，通常省略 because。(B) Sorry 即為 No，直接刪除。(C) 聽
到 No，直接刪除。

單字 The line is busy. 忙線中 / remind (v.) 提醒

Part 3

Questions 25 through 27 refer to the following conversation.

美式男聲	Hello, ㉕ I saw a poster advertising 🔊**half-price admission** for Saturday performances of Swan Lake at the Terrace Theater this month.
美式女聲	Yes, that's right, but this Saturday and the next are already sold out. There are still seats available on the 23rd and 30th, though.
美式男聲	Oh, I see. Um... I'm not sure I can make it on those days. Let me check my schedule and think it over.
美式女聲	All right, ㉖ but if you want to get the discount rate, you should reserve as soon as possible. The show only runs through the end of this month, and at this price the remaining tickets 🔊**won't last long**.
美式男聲	Thank you for reminding me. I'll get back to you as soon as possible.
美式女聲	No problem. ㉗ And please feel free to take a copy of our monthly newsletter, *Terrace Show*s. It has the full programs, show times and price information for this month. Be sure to check it out.
美式男聲	Great—thanks.

問題 25 至 27 請參考以下對話。

男：	你好，㉕ 我看到海報廣告說，這個月每週六在露臺劇院的天鵝湖表演，門票都是半價。
女：	對，沒錯，但這週六和下週六的票都賣光了，但 23 號和 30 號還有位子。
男：	這樣啊⋯我不知道那兩天有沒有空。我先看看我的行程表再考慮。
女：	好，㉖ 但你若想要折扣，要儘早訂位。這齣戲只演到本月底，這價位的票很快就會賣完。
男：	謝謝你提醒我。我會盡快回覆你。
女：	沒問題。㉗ 請拿一份我們的每月通訊，《露臺表演》，上面有列出本月所有節目、表演時間和價格資訊。請務必看一下。
男：	太好了，謝謝。

單字 last 持續 / newsletter 每月通訊 / program 節目單、節目

25. What is the man inquiring about?
    (A) The name of a performance
    (B) Discounted tickets for a show
    (C) The registration fee for a fair
    (D) The schedule for an upcoming movie

男子詢問什麼事？
(A) 表演的名稱
(B) 表演的折扣票
(C) 博覽會的報名費
(D) 即將上映的電影時間表

解說 詢問／要求題，要聽「詢問資訊」的句型，男子：「我看到海報廣告說，這個月每週六在露臺劇院的天鵝湖表演，門票都是半價」，表示男子想問半價門票的資訊，所以答案是 (B)。

單字 registration fee 報名費、註冊費

同義替換 half-price admission = discounted tickets

26. What does the woman imply about the discounted tickets?
    (A) They won't be available until next month.
    (B) They are valid only for weekdays.
    (C) They can be used at different locations.
    (D) They will soon be completely sold out.

女子暗示折扣票券會怎樣？
(A) 下個月才會有票。
(B) 只有週間才能用。
(C) 可以在不同地點用。
(D) 很快就會賣完。

解說 一般細節題，聽女子提及「折扣門票」即正解：「但你若想要折扣，要儘早訂位。這齣戲只演到本月底，這價位的票很快就會賣完」，所以答案是 (D)。

單字 sold out 賣光了

同義替換 won't last long = will soon be completely sold out

27. What does the woman mean when she says, "Be sure to check it out."?
    (A) The man should read a publication.
    (B) The man should reserve a seat.
    (C) The man should check the calendar.
    (D) The man should rent a video.

女子說「請務必看一下」是什麼意思？
(A) 男子應該看一下刊物。
(B) 男子應該訂位。
(C) 男子該看一下行事曆。
(D) 男子應該租錄影帶。

解說 隱含文意題，要結合上下文，推論出題目 "Be sure to check it out" 的意思，正解在：「請拿一份我們的每月通訊，《露臺表演》，上面有列出本月所有節目、表演時間和價格資訊」，表示女子強烈推薦看一下每月通訊，所以答案是 (A)。

單字 publication 刊物

Questions 28 through 30 refer to the following conversation with three speakers.

英式男聲　Hi, guys. ㉘ Orange HiTech contacted us to do some promotional work for them. Before I accept, I'd like your input. Do you think we can market them?

英式女聲　They're ㉙ famous for their sports watches. Their latest product can record your heart rate and running speed, and then transmit the data to your smartphone.

美式男聲　Yes, I just bought one. ㉙ It's stylish, 🔊**waterproof** and functional. Most importantly, as a global brand, they basically sell themselves.

英式男聲　Then let's do it. I'd like to give Orange HiTech an outline of our marketing strategy when I call them back. Any ideas?

英式女聲　We could find some runners from the National Track Team to wear the watch during a race.

美式男聲　Then we could transmit their data to a screen for the audience to watch in real time.

英式男聲　Great idea. I'll bring that up when I call them. For now, ㉚ Charlotte, could you get in touch with the National Track Team and see if you can find some 🔊**runners** for us?

英式女聲　I'll do that right now.

問題 28 至 30 請參考以下三人對話。

男 1：嗨，各位。 ㉘ 橙子高科技聯絡我們，希望我們替他們做宣傳工作。我在接訂單前想聽聽你們的意見，你們覺得我們能幫他們行銷嗎？

女　：他們的 ㉙ 運動手錶很有名。他們的最新產品能紀錄心跳頻率和跑步速度，然後將數據傳到智慧手機。

男 2：對，我剛買了一支， ㉙ 很時尚、防水且功能齊全。最重要的是，這是全球品牌，基本上就能自我推銷。

男 1：那我們就接訂單吧。當我回覆橙子高科技時，那時就會提供他們大致的行銷策略，各位有什麼想法？

女　：我們可以從國家田徑隊找幾個田徑選手在比賽時戴他們的手錶。

男 2：然後把他們的數據即時傳到螢幕給觀眾看。

男 1：好主意，我打給他們時會提這個意見。現在 ㉚ 請夏洛特聯絡國家田徑隊，看能不能找到幾個選手？

女　：我立刻去聯絡。

單字　transmit 傳送 (v.) / waterproof 防水 (a.) / outline (n.) 大綱、概要

28. What type of business do the speakers work for? 講者是從事什麼行業？
    (A) A sportswear manufacturer   (A) 運動服製造商
    (B) A publishing company   (B) 出版公司
    (C) An advertising agency   **(C) 廣告公司**
    (D) A fitness center   (D) 健身中心

解說 職務題，線索為：「橙子高科技聯絡我們，希望我們替他們做宣傳工作。
我在接訂單前想聽聽你們的意見，你們覺得我們能幫他們行銷嗎？」，內
容提到「宣傳、行銷」，所以答案是 (C)。

單字 publish (v.) 出版

29. What is one of the features of the sports watch? 運動手錶有什麼特色？
    (A) Its affordable price   (A) 價格親民
    (B) Its resistance to water   **(B) 防水**
    (C) Its compact design   (C) 小巧設計
    (D) Its light weight   (D) 輕巧

解說 一般細節題，聽「運動手錶的特色」即正解。女子說：「他們的最新產品
能紀錄心跳頻率和跑步速度，然後將數據傳到智慧手機」。男子說：「很
時尚、防水且功能齊全」。所以答案是 (B)。

單字 resistance (n.) 抵抗 / compact (a.) 小巧的

同義替換 waterproof = resistance to water

30. What does the man ask the woman to do? 男子要女子做什麼？
    (A) Post a help-wanted ad   (A) 張貼徵人廣告
    (B) Find potential clients   (B) 找潛在客戶
    (C) Find some athletes   **(C) 找幾位運動員**
    (D) Research a competitor   (D) 研究競爭對手

解說 詢問／要求題，要聽「要求對方」的句型多為問句：Could you...? :「現
在請夏洛特聯絡國家田徑隊，看能不能找到幾個選手？」表示男生要求女
生去找一些運動員，所以答案是 (C)。

單字 help-wanted 徵才 / potential (a.) 潛在的 / athlete (n.) 運動員

同義替換 runner = athlete

Questions 31 through 33 refer to the following conversation.

美式男聲 Excuse me. ㉛ I have a complaint about the service here.

英式女聲 ㉛ I'm sorry to hear that. What seems to be the problem, sir?

美式男聲 Well, I'm a regular guest at your hotel, and I've never had any problems in the past. ㉜ But this time, I've had to call housekeeping every day to ask them to clean my room.

英式女聲 First, I'd like to say how sorry I am. I can see how this must have affected your stay with us. I'll speak to housekeeping straight away. I want to make sure this never happens again. Since you've been so inconvenienced, ㉝ I'd be glad to offer you a 🔊voucher—two free nights for your next stay at our hotel. You can use it any time you wish.

美式男聲 Oh, that would be great! I am so glad that we could work this out. I do want to keep coming back here.

問題 31 至 33 請參考以下對話。

男：不好意思，㉛ 我想投訴服務。

女：㉛ 很遺憾聽到你這麼說，先生，請問有什麼問題嗎？

男：我是你們旅館的常客，以前從來沒遇到問題。㉜ 但這次我每天都必須打給總務部門，叫他們來打掃我的房間。

女：首先，我想說我很抱歉。我瞭解這一定影響到您的住宿品質。我會立刻跟清潔人員談，以確保此事不會再發生。因為造成您的不便，㉝ 所以我想提供您現金禮券，讓你下次入住我們旅館時可享有兩晚免費住宿。優惠券可以在任何時間使用。

男：噢，那就太好了！很高興我們能解決這問題。我下次還會想入住這裡。

單字 housekeeping (v.)（飯店）總務部門 / voucher 禮券、折價券

31. Who most likely is the woman? 女子可能是什麼身分？
    - (A) A housekeeper　　　　　　　(A) 清潔人員
    - (B) A maintenance worker　　　　(B) 維修人員
    - **(C) A front desk receptionist**　**(C) 服務台接待員**
    - (D) A hotel security guard　　　　(D) 旅館警衛

解說 職務題，線索為：「不好意思，我想投訴服務」及「很遺憾聽到你這麼說，先生，請問有什麼問題嗎？」男子提到「投訴抱怨」，女子提到「遺憾」及想了解問題，所以答案是 (C)。

32. What problem does the man mention? 男子提到什麼問題？
    - (A) The room next door is too noisy.　(A) 隔壁房間太吵。
    - (B) The air-conditioner isn't working properly. (B) 空調故障。
    - (C) He can't get hot water in the bathroom.　(C) 浴室沒有熱水。
    - **(D) His room hasn't been cleaned.**　**(D) 他的房間沒打掃。**

解說 疑難雜症題，要聽男生提及「負面字眼」：「但這次我每天都必須打給清潔人員，叫他們來打掃我的房間」，表示抱怨飯店的清潔服務，所以答案是 (D)。

33. What does the woman offer to do? 女子有什麼提議？
    - (A) File a customer complaint　　(A) 填顧客投訴單
    - (B) Issue a refund　　　　　　　(B) 退款
    - (C) Reduce a price　　　　　　　(C) 減價
    - **(D) Provide a gift certificate**　**(D) 提供禮券**

解說 建議題，正解在「女子最後一個說話處」，表建議的常用句型：I'd be glad to offer you a voucher—two free nights for your next stay at our hotel.「我想提供你現金禮券，讓你下次入住我們旅館時可享有兩晚免費住宿」，表示以提供禮券的方法，來補償客戶，所以答案是 (D)。

單字 file 提出（訴訟等…）

同義替換 voucher = gift certificate

Questions 34 through 36 refer to the following conversation.

(美式男聲) 34 How are the restaurant ⓘ**renovations** coming along, Alyssa? Do you think we'll be ready to open again by Saturday?

(美式女聲) No. 35 The shipment of new floor boards hasn't even arrived yet. And because the floor space is so big, it's going to take a week to finish the project.

(美式男聲) OK. 36 In that case, what should we do about all the dinner reservations we have for the weekend?

(美式女聲) 36 How about calling everyone who has a reservation and offering them a ⓘ**30% discount** on their next visit to make up for their inconvenience?

問題 34 至 36 請參考以下對話。

男： 34 艾麗莎，餐廳裝修得怎樣？你覺得我們能在週六重新開張嗎？

女： 不行，35 新地板還沒送到。因為地板空間太大，工程需要一星期才能完成。

男： 好，36 那這樣的話，這週末的訂位要怎麼辦？

女： 36 不如打給所有訂位顧客，提供他們下次惠顧時七折優惠，以彌補他們的不便？

單字 floor board 地板

34. What are the speakers mainly discussing?　講者主要在討論什麼？

　(A) A remodeling project　　**(A) 裝修工程**
　(B) A product launch　　(B) 推出產品
　(C) A room reservation　　(C) 訂位
　(D) A store floor plan　　(D) 商店平面圖

解說　主旨題，正解在「前兩句」：How are the restaurant renovations coming along, Alyssa?「艾麗莎，餐廳裝修得怎樣？」，所以答案是 (A)。

同義替換　renovation = remodeling

35. What does the woman say about the restaurant?　女子說了什麼關於餐廳的事？

　(A) It has a large dining table.　　(A) 有很大的餐桌。
　(B) It covers a large area.　　**(B) 場地很大。**
　(C) It doesn't have enough space.　　(C) 沒有足夠空間。
　(D) It needs more decorations.　　(D) 需要更多裝潢。

解說　一般細節題，聽女子提到「餐廳」的相關內容即正解：The shipment of new floor boards hasn't even arrived yet. And because the floor space is so big, it's going to take a week to finish the project.「新地板還沒送到。因為地板空間太大，工程需要一星期才能完成。」，所以答案是 (B)。

36. What compensation does the woman recommend?　女子推薦什麼補償方案？

　(A) A gift voucher　　(A) 禮券
　(B) A free meal　　(B) 免費用餐
　(C) A refund　　(C) 退款
　(D) A special offer　　**(D) 優惠**

解說　建議題，正解在「女子最後一個說話處」，表建議的常用句型：How about calling everyone who has a reservation and offering them a 30% discount on their next visit to make up for their inconvenience?「不如打給所有訂位顧客，提供他們下次惠顧時七折優惠，以彌補他們的不便？」，所以答案是 (D)。

單字　gift voucher 禮券 / special offer 優惠
同義替換　30% discount = special offer

Questions 37 through 39 refer to the following conversation and chart.

(美式女聲) Hi, Brett. This is Samantha, your editor at Asia Travel Magazine. Do you have a minute?

(英式男聲) Sure. What's up?

(美式女聲) ❸❼ I'd like to ask you to ⓐ**make some revisions** to your "Exploring Formosa" article. There are several topics I'd like you to add.

(英式男聲) I'd be happy to revise the article for you, but I'm not sure I'll have enough time. ❸❽ I have another article due that same day.

(美式女聲) ❸❽ Yes, I see that on your assignment chart. There's no need to rush. Let's extend the deadline for your other article by a week— that way you can take your time on the Formosa article.

(英式男聲) OK, that would be great. By the way, ❸❾ I've completed the ⓑ**final version** of "Travelling Southern Taiwan." I'll send it to you later today for comment.

Article	Deadline
"Exploring Formosa"	May 15
"Have Fun in Taipei" ❸❽	May 15
"MRT Tours"	July 23
"Taiwan by Train"	August 30

問題 37 至 39 請參考以下對話和圖表。

女： 嗨，布雷特。我是莎曼珊，是你在《亞洲旅遊雜誌》的編輯。你現在有空嗎？

男： 當然，什麼事？

女： ❸❼ 我想請你修改一下你寫的文章《探索福爾摩沙》。 我想請你加幾個主題。

男： 我很樂意修改文章，但我不確定我時間夠不夠。❸❽ 我還有一篇文章要在同一天交。

女： ❸❽ 對，我看到你的工作表了。不用急。你的另一篇文章可以延後一星期交，這樣你就有時間修改福爾摩沙這篇。

男： 好，那就太好了。對了，❸❾ 我已經完成《南台灣旅遊》最終版。我今天稍晚會寄給你評論一下。

文章	交稿日期
探索福爾摩沙	5 月 15 日
台北好好玩 ❸❽	5 月 15 日
捷運之旅	7 月 23 日
搭火車遊台灣	8 月 30 日

單字 revision (n.) 修改 / extend (v.) 延長

37. What does the woman ask the man to do?　女子要男子做什麼？
   (A) Proofread a publication　(A) 校對一份刊物
   (B) Increase the word count of an article　(B) 增加文章的字數
   (C) Correct a mistake in a document　(C) 訂正文件中的錯誤
   (D) Modify the content of an article　**(D) 修改文章內容**

解說 詢問 / 要求題，要聽「要求對方」的句型，女子：I'd like to ask you make some revisions to your "Exploring Formosa" article. There are several topics I'd like you to add. 女子提到修改文章，加一些主題進去，所以答案是 (D)。

單字 proofread (v.) 校對 / modify (v.) 修改

同義替換 make some revisions = modify

38. Look at the chart. Which article's deadline will be extended?　請看圖表，哪一篇文章的期限要延長？
   (A) "Exploring Formosa"　(A) 探索福爾摩沙
   (B) "Have Fun in Taipei"　**(B) 台北好好玩**
   (C) "MRT Tours"　(C) 捷運之旅
   (D) "Taiwan by Train"　(D) 搭火車遊台灣

解說 根據圖表題『秒殺三步驟』，步驟一：題目問哪一篇文章的期限要延長，步驟二：找選項和圖表關聯處（article 文章標題），步驟三：音檔絕對不會唸到文章標題，而是提到右欄截止日相關的內容。原文中男子提到 I have another article due that same day. 及女子提到 Yes, I see that on your assignment chart. There's no need to rush. Let's extend the deadline for your other article by a week. 當聽到 due the same day 和 extend the deadline for your other article，就馬上得知是 "Have Fun in Taipei"，所以答案是 (B)。

39. What does the man say he will do?　男子說他會做什麼？
   (A) Send a final draft　**(A) 寄出最終草稿**
   (B) Finish an assignment　(B) 完成工作
   (C) Delegate tasks to another writer　(C) 將工作委派給其他作家
   (D) Travel in a tour group　(D) 參加團體旅遊

解說 要聽表動作的句型，男子提到 I'll：I've completed the final version of "Travelling Southern Taiwan." I'll send it to you later today for comment. 表示會寄稿子給對方看，所以答案是 (A)。

單字 draft (n.) 草稿

同義替換 final version = final draft

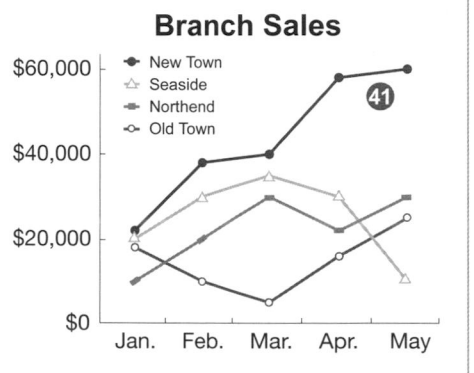

Questions 40 through 42 refer to the following conversation and graph.

(美式男聲) Hi, Natalie. My assistant mentioned that you're looking for some extra staff.

(美式女聲) That's right. ⑳ I'm hoping to ⓜ**add six salespeople** to help handle the upcoming rush season at my branch. I heard you have some part-time employees that might be willing to take on more work temporarily. Could you send me their telephone numbers?

(美式男聲) No problem. ㊶ But ⓜ**budgets have been cut** recently, so I think management may turn down your request for more staff.

(美式女聲) I already have approval, actually. ㊷ Management made a special exception in this case because sales have grown at our branch every month since I took over in January.

問題 **40** 至 **42** 請參考以下對話和圖表。

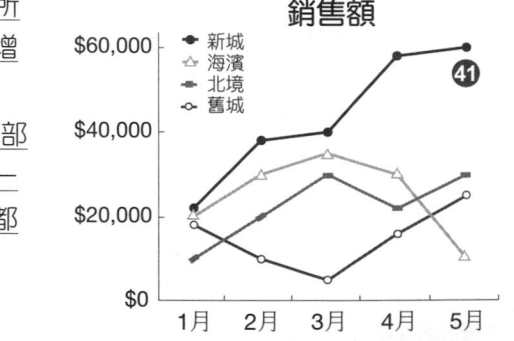

男：嗨，娜塔莉，我的助理說你還要多請幾位員工。

女：沒錯。⑳ 我想增加六名銷售員來幫我的分店應付即將到來的旺季。聽說你有一些兼職員工可能願意多接一些臨時工作。你能把他們的電話號碼給我嗎？

男：沒問題。㊶ 但最近刪減了預算，所以我想管理部門可能會拒絕讓你增加員工。

女：其實我已經獲得批准了。㊷ 管理部門替我開了特例，因為自從我在一月接任分店以來，每月的銷售量都有增加。

單字 rush (n.) 繁忙 / take on 承擔 / turn down 回絕，拒絕 / approval (n.) 贊成、同意

40. What does the woman plan to do?
    (A) Submit a new budget proposal
    (B) Upgrade some office equipment
    (C) Promote some of her staff
    (D) Hire additional workers

女子計畫做什麼？
    (A) 提交新的預算提案
    (B) 升級辦公室設備
    (C) 晉升她的員工
    (D) 多聘幾位員工

解說 動作題，要聽表動作的句型，女子提到 I'm hoping to：「我想增加六名銷售員來幫我的分店應付即將到來的旺季」，女子打算增加員工，所以答案是 (D)。

同義替換 add six salespeople = hire additional workers

41. According to the man, what has the company recently done?
    (A) It has opened a new branch.
    (B) It has held an annual sale.
    (C) It has downsized its workforce.
    (D) It has reduced its spending.

根據男子所說，公司最近做了什麼？
    (A) 開新分店。
    (B) 舉辦年度拍賣。
    (C) 刪減人力。
    (D) 刪減支出。

解說 一般細節題，聽男子提到和公司相關的內容即正解：「但最近刪減了預算，所以我想管理部門可能會拒絕讓你增加員工。」，所以答案是 (D)。

單字 downsize (v.) 縮編 / workforce (n.) 人力 / reduce (v.) 減少

同義替換 budgets have been cut = reduce its spending

42. Look at the graphic. Which branch does the woman work at?
    (A) New Town
    (B) Seaside
    (C) Northend
    (D) Old Town

請看圖表。女子在哪間分店工作？
    (A) 新城
    (B) 海濱
    (C) 北境
    (D) 舊城

解說 根據圖表題『秒殺三步驟』，步驟一：題目問女子在哪間分店工作，步驟二：找選項和圖表關聯處（四間分店），步驟三：音檔絕對不會唸到這四間分店，而是提到曲線走勢或縱坐標的數字。原文中女子提到：「管理部門替我開了特例，因為自從我在一月接任分店以來，每月的銷售量都有增加。」，當聽到 sales have grown at our branch every month，就馬上得知是唯一曲線走勢沒有掉下來的 New Town，所以答案是 (A)。

Part 4

Questions 43 through 45 refer to the following advertisement.

美式男聲 **43** Cleaning all the different surfaces in your home is a big challenge, isn't it? Usually, you need one type of cleaner for the bathroom, another for the kitchen, and another for your furniture. Well CleanRite is different. Its powerful yet safe ingredients allow you to clean any surface in your home. **44** Just spray CleanRite on a damp cloth and wipe it over any dirty surface— it'll be spotless in just seconds! And what's more, our store's annual sale starts today. All items, including CleanRite, are 20% off. Now I'm going to ask some of you to join me on stage. **45** You're going to have the chance to ⊚**try out** this great cleaner and see just how well it works!

問題 43 至 45 請參考以下廣告。

43 在家大掃除時清理所有細節是一大挑戰,對吧?浴室通常會需要一種清潔劑,廚房則需要另一種,家具又需要另一種。但科林萊清潔劑不一樣。強大但安全的成分能讓你清潔家中任何表面。**44** 只要將科林萊噴在濕抹布上,在骯髒的表面上擦拭,幾秒鐘就清潔溜溜!還有,我們商店今天開始舉辦年度特賣。所有商品,包括科林萊都打八折。我要請幾個人上台跟我一起,**45** 你們有機會試用這厲害的清潔劑,看看它效果有多好!

單字 ingredient 成分 / damp 濕的 / spotless 極清潔的 / try out 嘗試

43. What is the advertisement for? | 這是什麼廣告？

(A) A house cleaning service　(A) 居家清潔服務

(B) A cleaning product　**(B) 清潔產品**

(C) A household appliance　(C) 家用設備

(D) A dust cloth　(D) 抹布

解說 商業廣告類的「目的」，要聽「前兩句」：「在家大掃除時清理所有細節是一大挑戰，對吧？浴室通常會需要一種清潔劑，廚房則需要另一種，家具又需要另一種」，說話者提到 cleaning、cleaner 等字眼，目的在廣告清潔用品，所以答案是 (B)。

單字 household 家用的

NEW

44. What does the speaker mean when he says, "it'll be spotless in just seconds!"? | 講者說「幾秒鐘就清潔溜溜」是什麼意思？

(A) The cleaner can't remove all the spots.　(A) 清潔劑無法清除所有髒污。

(B) The surface will be clean immediately.　**(B) 表面會立刻清乾淨。**

(C) It takes time to clean the cloth.　(C) 需要花點時間清潔抹布。

(D) The wet cloth will dry fast.　(D) 濕抹布很快就會乾。

解說 隱含文意題，要結合上下文，推論出題目 "it'll be spotless in just seconds!" 的意思，正解在：Just spray CleanRite on a damp cloth and wipe it over any dirty surface「只要將科林萊噴在濕抹布上，在骯髒的表面上擦拭」，強調幾秒內就能使任何髒污表面乾淨，所以答案是 (B)。

45. What are some listeners encouraged to do? | 聽者被鼓勵做什麼？

(A) Pick up product samples　(A) 領取試用產品

(B) Obtain raffle tickets　(B) 領取抽獎券

(C) Sign up for a free trial　(C) 報名免費試用

(D) Participate in a demonstration　**(D) 參加示範**

解說 商業廣告類的「建議」，要聽文章最後面，希望聽眾做什麼： You're going to have the chance to try out this great cleaner and see just how well it works!「你們有機會試用這厲害的清潔劑，看看它效果有多好！」，請觀眾來試用產品，所以答案是 (D)。

單字 trial 試用

同義替換 try out = participate in a demonstration

Questions 46 through 48 refer to the following talk.

英式女聲 ㊻ Welcome to the Arrow ⊙**Footwear Factory**. My name is Yolanda Evans, and I'll be your guide for today's tour. ㊻ We'll start off by going right to the production area, where you'll see how our shoes are made and packaged before being shipped to our distributors. ㊼ One thing that makes our factory special is that all our shoes are made by hand. Unlike most factories, where automated equipment does most of the work, at Arrow Footwear Factory, everything is done by a team of master craftspeople. ㊽ At the end of the tour, everyone will get the chance to ⊙**try making a pair of shoes or sandals** with the assistance of our staff members. You shouldn't miss out on this great opportunity!

問題 46 至 48 請參考以下演說。

㊻ 歡迎光臨箭鞋工廠。我叫尤蘭達伊凡斯，我是你們今天參觀工廠的嚮導。
㊻ 我們先到右邊的生產區，可以看到鞋子的製造和包裝，然後會運到我們的經銷商。㊼ 我們工廠的特別之處在於鞋子都是手工製造。大部分工廠是用自動化設備製造，箭鞋工廠則不一樣，一切都是由一群專業鞋匠製造。㊽ 參觀結束後，大家可以在員工的協助下自己嘗試製造一雙鞋子或涼鞋。千萬別錯過這絕佳機會！

單字 distributor 經銷商 / automated 自動化的 / craftspeople 工匠
sandals 涼鞋

46. Where is the talk being given? | 講話的地點是哪裡？

(A) At a clothing factory | (A) 製衣廠

(B) At a shoe manufacturer | **(B) 製鞋廠**

(C) At an antique store | (C) 古董店

(D) At a department store | (D) 百貨公司

解說 觀光導覽類的「參觀地點」，仔細聽可判斷「地點」的關鍵字： Welcome to the Arrow Footwear Factory.「歡迎光臨箭鞋工廠」，再加上 We'll start off by going right to the production area, where you'll see how our shoes are made and packaged「我們先到右邊的生產區，可以看到鞋子的製造和包裝」，透過 footwear factory 和 shoes，可判斷在製鞋工廠，所以答案是 (B)。

單字 antique 古董的

同義替換 footwear factory = shoe manufacturer

47. What is special about the factory? | 工廠的特別之處是什麼？

(A) Its production method | **(A) 生產方式**

(B) Its automated equipment | (B) 自動化設備

(C) Its guided tours | (C) 參觀導覽

(D) Its convenient location | (D) 地點便利

解說 觀光導覽類的「景點特色」，仔細聽描述「工廠特色」的內容：「我們工廠的特別之處在於鞋子都是手工製造。大部分工廠是用自動化設備製造，箭鞋工廠則不一樣，一切都是由一群專業鞋匠製造」，由此可判斷，和別的工廠最大的不同是：產品皆鞋匠手工製作，非機器製作，所以答案是 (A)。

48. What will listeners do at the end of the tour? | 聽者在參觀結束後會做什麼？

(A) Receive free samples | (A) 收到免費樣品

(B) Join in a hands-on experience | **(B) 參加手工製作體驗**

(C) Sign up for a class | (C) 報名課程

(D) Make a purchase | (D) 購物

解說 觀光導覽類的「下一步」為推論題，正解在最後「導遊推薦」的內容：At the end of the tour, everyone will get the chance to try making a pair of shoes or sandals with the assistance of our staff members.「參觀結束後，大家可以在員工的協助下自己嘗試製造一雙鞋子或涼鞋」，導遊在行程最後，推薦大家體驗手工 DIY，所以答案是 (B)。

單字 hands-on 實際動手的

同義替換 try making a pair of shoes or sandals = Join in a hands-on experience

Questions 49 through 51 refer to the following radio broadcast.

美式女聲 ㊾ Thank you for listening to the weekly broadcast of The World Kitchen, the program that takes you on a 同 **culinary** adventure exploring culinary traditions all around the world. In today's episode, ㊿ our guest is Paul Jackson, who is not only a famous chef, but also a 同 **maker of documentaries**. Mr. Jackson is with us to talk about his new work, Culinary Traditions of India, which highlights traditional Indian cuisine and culinary techniques. In the documentary, Mr. Jackson visits famous restaurants in India and interviews chefs and restaurant patrons. (51) Make sure to visit our website at www.worldkitchen.com, where you can 同 **view a trailer** for the documentary.

問題 49 至 51 請參考以下廣播。

㊾ 謝謝各位收聽每週的《世界廚房》廣播，這節目會帶你探索世界各地的傳統烹飪。今天這集的 ㊿ 嘉賓是保羅傑克森，他不僅是知名主廚，也是紀錄片製作人。傑克森先生要跟我們談談他的新作品，《印度的傳統烹飪》，傳統印度美食和烹飪技巧是這支紀錄片的特色。傑克森先生在紀錄片中造訪印度的知名餐廳，訪問主廚和餐廳常客。(51) 記得瀏覽我們的網站，網址是 www.worldkitchen.com，各位可在網站上觀看這支紀錄片的預告。

單字 culinary (a.) 烹飪的 / adventure (n.) 歷險 / chef (n.) 主廚
documentary (n.) 紀錄片 / patron (n.) 老顧客、主顧

49. What is the radio broadcast mainly about? 這廣播主要是關於什麼？

(A) Worldwide cooking **(A) 世界烹飪**

(B) Food carnivals (B) 美食嘉年華會

(C) Healthy eating habits (C) 健康飲食習慣

(D) Overseas travel (D) 海外旅遊

> **解說** 新聞報導類的「主題」，要聽「前兩句」：Thank you for listening to the weekly broadcast of The World Kitchen, the program that takes you on a culinary adventure exploring culinary traditions all around the world.「謝謝各位收聽每週的《世界廚房》廣播，這節目會帶你探索世界各地的傳統烹飪」，所以答案是 (A)。

> **單字** carnival (n.) 嘉年華會
> **同義替換** culinary = cooking

50. What has Paul Jackson recently done? 保羅傑克森最近做了什麼？

(A) Produced a TV program (A) 製作了電視節目

(B) Written an article (B) 寫了文章

(C) Made a film **(C) 製作了電影**

(D) Opened a restaurant (D) 開了餐廳

> **解說** 新聞報導類的「細節題」，聽到 Paul Jackson，答案即出現：our guest is Paul Jackson, who is not only a famous chef, but also a maker of documentaries.「今天這集的嘉賓是保羅傑克森，他不僅是知名主廚，也是紀錄片製作人」，所以答案是 (C)。

> **同義替換** maker of documentaries = made a film

51. What does the speaker suggest listeners do? 講者建議聽眾做什麼？

(A) Watch a preview **(A) 看預告片**

(B) Listen to a radio show (B) 聽廣播節目

(C) Download a documentary (C) 下載紀錄片

(D) Contact a film company (D) 聯絡電影公司

> **解說** 新聞報導類的「建議」，聽文章最後面「建議」的句型 Make sure to：Make sure to visit our website at www.worldkitchen.com, where you can view a trailer for the documentary.「記得瀏覽我們的網站，網址是 www.worldkitchen.com，各位可在網站上觀看這支紀錄片的預告」，所以答案是 (A)。

> **單字** preview (n.) 試映
> **同義替換** view a trailer = watch a preview

Questions 52 through 54 refer to a talk and a chart.

(英式男聲) Hello, everyone. 52 Thank you for inviting me here today to introduce our latest security packages. Our newest line of office security systems is designed to provide the most protection for the lowest cost, and I am sure it will meet your needs. We have developed four packages to choose from, and are confident that we can meet your security needs. After a thorough inspection of your office building, 53 I believe that our package with 回**three months** of archived data would provide you with the best value. It's not as comprehensive as the Elite package, but with state-of-the-art video surveillance and a backup system, I'm confident that it will provide all the protection you need. 54 Although Elite comes with 回**365 days of archived data**, after taking a tour of your facilities, I feel this would be more than your company needs.

Life Shield Co.

	Bronze	53Silver	Gold	Elite
Price	$1,000	$1,300	$1,800	$2,600
Backup System	No	Yes	Yes	Yes
Data Archive	4 weeks	12 weeks	24 weeks	52 weeks

問題 52 至 54 請參考以下演說和圖表。

大家好。 52 謝謝各位今天邀請我到這裡介紹我們最新的保全套組。我們最新的辦公室保全系統是為了提供消費者最低價格、最高防護所設計，相信能滿足各位的需求。我們研發了四種套組供您選擇，我們有信心能符合各位的保全需求。我們徹底檢查過貴公司大樓後， 53 相信有三個月資料庫的套組是最划算的。雖然不如菁英套組提供更全面防護，但擁有最先進的監視器和備份系統，我有信心它能提供各位所需的所有防護。 54 雖然菁英套組有 365 天資料庫，但參觀過貴公司設施後，我認為這個套組可能會超過貴公司的需求。

生命之盾公司

	銅	53銀	金	菁英
價格	$1,000	$1,300	$1,800	$2,600
備份系統	無	有	有	有
資料庫	4 週	12 週	24 週	52 週

單字 archive 存檔、歸檔 / comprehensive 無所不包的
state-of-the-art 最先進的 / surveillance 監視 / backup 備份

52. What is the purpose of the talk? 　這場講話的目標是什麼？
    (A) To provide training for clients 　(A) 為客戶提供訓練
    (B) To launch a new system 　(B) 推出新系統
    (C) To compete with other companies 　(C) 與其他公司競爭
    (D) To promote a new product 　**(D) 宣傳新產品**

解說 商務演說類的「主題」，要聽「前兩句」：「謝謝各位今天邀請我到這裡介紹我們最新的保全套組。我們最新的辦公室保全系統是為了提供消費者最低價格、最高防護所設計，相信能滿足各位的需求」，推銷公司最新的保全產品，所以答案是 (D)。

53. Which security package does the speaker 　講者推薦什麼保全
    recommend? 　套組？
    (A) Bronze 　(A) 銅
    (B) Silver 　**(B) 銀**
    (C) Gold 　(C) 金
    (D) Elite 　(D) 菁英

解說 根據圖表題『秒殺三步驟』，步驟一：題目問講者推薦什麼保全套組，步驟二：找選項和圖表關聯處（四種套組），步驟三：音檔絕對不會唸到這四種套組，而是提到價錢、有無備份系統或資料存檔的週數。原文中說話者提到：「相信有三個月資料庫的套組是最划算的」，當聽到「三個月的資料庫」，就馬上得知是銀套組，所以答案是 (B)。

同義替換 three months = 12 weeks

54. Why is Elite the most expensive package? 　為何菁英是最貴的套組？
    (A) It includes a year of data storage. 　**(A) 包含一年份的資料庫。**
    (B) It offers a backup system. 　(B) 提供備份系統。
    (C) It provides high-tech surveillance. 　(C) 提供高科技監視器。
    (D) It is the newest product available. 　(D) 是最新的產品。

解說 商務演說類的「具體說明」，仔細聽和 Elite 相關的描述，判斷出正確答案：「雖然菁英套組有 365 天資料庫，但參觀過貴公司設施後，我認為這個套組可能會超過貴公司的需求」，上文推薦客戶三個月的套組即符合需求又划算，而 Elite 雖然有 365 天資料庫，但會超過需求，表示 Elite 貴在一年的資料存檔，所以答案是 (A)。

同義替換 365 days of archived data = a year of data storage

Questions 55 through 57 refer to the following telephone message and order form.

(美式男聲) Sylvia, ⑤⑤ this is Andrew calling from the ⓘ**head office**. I submitted an order for office supplies yesterday, but I hope you haven't started processing it yet. ⑤⑥ I just realized that we need to add another two PCs to our order. We have new employees arriving on January 15th, and we need to have all the necessary office equipment set up for them before that date. The rest of the order seems fine as it is. ⑤⑦ I've also sent you an e-mail regarding this change to the order. When you have a moment, please call me back to confirm that you can make this adjustment. Thanks.

Lawson Engineering
Office Supplies Order Form
Order Number: 903H2

Item		Units ordered
Office chairs		6
Drafting tables		3
Personal computers	⑤⑥	5
Adjustable lamps		8

問題 55 至 57 請參考以下電話留言和訂單。

席維亞，⑤⑤ 我是總部的安德魯。我昨天送出了辦公室用品的訂單，但我希望你還沒開始處理。⑤⑥ 我剛剛發現我們還要添購兩部個人電腦。1 月 15 日我們有新員工，在那天之前要準備好一切所需的辦公器材。訂單的其他部分應該沒問題。⑤⑦ 我也寄了一封關於修改訂單的電郵給你。等你有空時，請回電給我確認你能否修改訂單。謝謝。

羅森工程公司
辦公用品訂單
訂單號碼：903H2

項目		訂購數量
辦公椅		6
製圖桌		3
個人電腦	⑤⑥	5
可調式桌燈		8

單字 equipment (n.) 設備，器材 / adjustment (n.) 調整

55. Where is the man likely calling from? 男子是從什麼地方打來？

(A) A furniture store　　　　　　　　(A) 家具店

(B) A stationery store　　　　　　　 (B) 文具店

(C) An office supply store　　　　　 (C) 辦公用品店

(D) An office building　　　　　　 **(D) 辦公大樓**

解說 一般細節題，仔細聽可判斷「地點」的關鍵字：this is Andrew calling from the head office.「我是總部的安德魯」，透過 head office，可判斷是在總部，所以答案是 (D)。

單字 stationery store 文具店

同義替換 head office = office building

56. Which quantity will the listener probably adjust? 聽話者可能會調整哪個數量？

(A) 6　　　　　　　　　　　　　　　(A) 6

(B) 3　　　　　　　　　　　　　　　(B) 3

(C) 5　　　　　　　　　　　　　　**(C) 5**

(D) 8　　　　　　　　　　　　　　　(D) 8

解說 根據圖表題「秒殺三步驟」，步驟一：題目問聽話者可能會調整哪個數量，步驟二：找選項和圖表關聯處（四個數字），步驟三：音檔絕對不會唸到這四個數字，而是提到要訂購的品項名稱。原文中 speaker 提到「我剛剛發現我們還要添購兩部個人電腦」，當聽到還要加兩部「個人電腦」，表原本訂單內個人電腦的數量 5，會需要調整，所以答案是 (C)。

57. Why should the listener return the call? 聽留言者為何要回電？

(A) To confirm a delivery date　　　　(A) 確認送貨日

(B) To discuss sales numbers　　　　 (B) 討論銷售數字

(C) To verify the units ordered　　　**(C) 確認訂購數量**

(D) To explain survey results　　　　 (D) 解釋調查結果

解說 電話留言類的「建議」，要聽文章最後面，表「建議」的句型 please...：「我也寄了一封關於修改訂單的電郵給你。等你有空時，請回電給我確認你能否修改訂單」，題目問的是建議回電的原因，答案要綜合上文 I've also sent you an e-mail regarding this change to the order.「我也寄了一封關於修改訂單的電郵給你」，表示因訂單內的數字有更動，需要對方確認後回電，所以答案是 (C)。

單字 verify (v.) 確認

實戰模擬測驗　答案卡

聽力測驗（LISTENING Parts 1-4）

No.	ANSWER A B C D	No.	ANSWER A B C D	No.	ANSWER A B C D	No.	ANSWER A B C D	No.	ANSWER A B C D
Part1(Q1~6)		12	Ⓐ Ⓑ Ⓒ Ⓓ	Part3(Q25~42)		37	Ⓐ Ⓑ Ⓒ Ⓓ	49	Ⓐ Ⓑ Ⓒ Ⓓ
1	Ⓐ Ⓑ Ⓒ Ⓓ	13	Ⓐ Ⓑ Ⓒ Ⓓ	25	Ⓐ Ⓑ Ⓒ Ⓓ	38	Ⓐ Ⓑ Ⓒ Ⓓ	50	Ⓐ Ⓑ Ⓒ Ⓓ
2	Ⓐ Ⓑ Ⓒ Ⓓ	14	Ⓐ Ⓑ Ⓒ Ⓓ	26	Ⓐ Ⓑ Ⓒ Ⓓ	39	Ⓐ Ⓑ Ⓒ Ⓓ	51	Ⓐ Ⓑ Ⓒ Ⓓ
3	Ⓐ Ⓑ Ⓒ Ⓓ	15	Ⓐ Ⓑ Ⓒ Ⓓ	27	Ⓐ Ⓑ Ⓒ Ⓓ	40	Ⓐ Ⓑ Ⓒ Ⓓ	52	Ⓐ Ⓑ Ⓒ Ⓓ
4	Ⓐ Ⓑ Ⓒ Ⓓ	16	Ⓐ Ⓑ Ⓒ Ⓓ	28	Ⓐ Ⓑ Ⓒ Ⓓ	41	Ⓐ Ⓑ Ⓒ Ⓓ	53	Ⓐ Ⓑ Ⓒ Ⓓ
5	Ⓐ Ⓑ Ⓒ Ⓓ	17	Ⓐ Ⓑ Ⓒ Ⓓ	29	Ⓐ Ⓑ Ⓒ Ⓓ	42	Ⓐ Ⓑ Ⓒ Ⓓ	54	Ⓐ Ⓑ Ⓒ Ⓓ
6	Ⓐ Ⓑ Ⓒ Ⓓ	18	Ⓐ Ⓑ Ⓒ Ⓓ	30	Ⓐ Ⓑ Ⓒ Ⓓ	Part4(Q43~57)		55	Ⓐ Ⓑ Ⓒ Ⓓ
Part2(Q7~24)		19	Ⓐ Ⓑ Ⓒ Ⓓ	31	Ⓐ Ⓑ Ⓒ Ⓓ	43	Ⓐ Ⓑ Ⓒ Ⓓ	56	Ⓐ Ⓑ Ⓒ Ⓓ
7	Ⓐ Ⓑ Ⓒ Ⓓ	20	Ⓐ Ⓑ Ⓒ Ⓓ	32	Ⓐ Ⓑ Ⓒ Ⓓ	44	Ⓐ Ⓑ Ⓒ Ⓓ	57	Ⓐ Ⓑ Ⓒ Ⓓ
8	Ⓐ Ⓑ Ⓒ Ⓓ	21	Ⓐ Ⓑ Ⓒ Ⓓ	33	Ⓐ Ⓑ Ⓒ Ⓓ	45	Ⓐ Ⓑ Ⓒ Ⓓ		
9	Ⓐ Ⓑ Ⓒ Ⓓ	22	Ⓐ Ⓑ Ⓒ Ⓓ	34	Ⓐ Ⓑ Ⓒ Ⓓ	46	Ⓐ Ⓑ Ⓒ Ⓓ		
10	Ⓐ Ⓑ Ⓒ Ⓓ	23	Ⓐ Ⓑ Ⓒ Ⓓ	35	Ⓐ Ⓑ Ⓒ Ⓓ	47	Ⓐ Ⓑ Ⓒ Ⓓ		
11	Ⓐ Ⓑ Ⓒ Ⓓ	24	Ⓐ Ⓑ Ⓒ Ⓓ	36	Ⓐ Ⓑ Ⓒ Ⓓ	48	Ⓐ Ⓑ Ⓒ Ⓓ		

NOTE

NOTE

國家圖書館出版品預行編目資料

新制多益聽力滿分攻略 / 洪欣作 . -- 初版 . -- 臺北市：
日月文化 , 2019.09

　　面；　　公分

ISBN 978-986-248-829-4(平裝)

1. 多益測驗

805.1895　　　　　　　　　　　　　108012040

EZ TALK

新制多益聽力滿分攻略

作　　　者：洪欣 Olivia
總 審 訂：Judd Piggott
企劃責編：潘亭軒
校　　　對：洪欣、潘亭軒
封面設計：謝捲子
版型設計：蕭彥伶
內頁排版：蕭彥伶
圖片出處：https://www.shutterstock.com
錄音後製：純粹錄音後製有限公司
錄 音 員：Steven Barton、Leah Zimmermann、James Robert Baron、Elaine Salt、Michael Tennant

發 行 人：洪祺祥
副總經理：洪偉傑
副總編輯：曹仲堯
法律顧問：建大法律事務所
財務顧問：高威會計師事務所

出　　　版：日月文化出版股份有限公司
製　　　作：EZ 叢書館
地　　　址：臺北市信義路三段 151 號 8 樓
電　　　話：(02) 2708-5509
傳　　　真：(02) 2708-6157
網　　　址：www.heliopolis.com.tw
郵撥帳號：19716071 日月文化出版股份有限公司

總 經 銷：聯合發行股份有限公司
電　　　話：(02) 2917-8022
傳　　　真：(02) 2915-7212
印　　　刷：中原造像股份有限公司
初　　　版：2019 年 9 月
初版 4 刷：2024 年 7 月
定　　　價：380 元
I S B N：978-986-248-829-4

全書音檔與教學影片，可於以下連結下載：
http://bit.ly/2KtFSES

隨身音檔